𝔽ℂ

MW01134911

Blue

Alexandria Nolan

ISBN:1548305847
ISBN-13: 978-1548305840

Much madness is divinest sense
To a discerning eye;
Much sense the starkest madness.
'Tis the majority
In this, as all, prevails.
Assent, and you are sane;
Demur -- you're straightway dangerous,
And handled with a chain. ——Emily Dickinson

Men will always be mad, and those who think they can
cure them are the maddest of all—Voltaire

There is always some madness in love, but there is always
some reason in madness. —Friedrich Nietzsche

for TJN, who finds me when I am lost, and gets lost with me when required.

and for ADHN who is presently hibernating.

Prologue
Marjoram: Illusion
1887 Detroit

He is so very changed. At least, I think that is true. He was charm and warmth with the glow of the sun itself upon our first acquaintance, so many years ago. But over our time together he has grown hard and cold. He is seeing someone else too. Probably more than one someone. I'd found the gold-brown hairs on his jacket. He'd slapped my face when I held one out to him from the bed. I hadn't said anything, let the hairs speak for themselves. I didn't even mind, I suppose. Not anymore. Had I ever? Perhaps once I had loved him, yes. But instead now with my face still stinging from his hand—I was sure there was a cut from his ring—he sneered at me. "It's your hair, you mad woman". He said the words carelessly though, as if he were remarking on the weather.

It might be the same color, but I know that the hair is not mine. It can't be. My hair hasn't been that lustrous with health in ages. It falls brittle down my back and breaks when the maid tries to braid it. Doesn't it? I think I am right. He calls me mad, and mayhap I am, but I think I am right in this. But Simon's cruelty is his power. He wields it like an axe. He could convince anyone of anything. I wish I could ask Mama, but the accident happened years ago now. My first thought this morning was to write to her, but then I recalled, abstractly, that she was dead. Perhaps it wasn't her I wanted to write to at all, but the idea of a mother. Someone to confide in and confess my troubles to. But that is all my life is now. Troubles. The babies die in my womb, as if my body itself is a barren field where the growing fruit can take no nutrient from the soil of my blood and bone. Simon would say that these were maudlin thoughts. That I was killing the babies myself with my melancholy. He would find a doctor to tell me the same, and I might even believe it. Simon is right, I *am* going mad. More every day.

My last letter from Mr. Montague was confusing. I had hoped to change the terms of my will, hoped to make it airtight, so that Simon could have no more of my money. I wished to create a will that made my death an undesirable event to Simon. But Mr. Montague wrote as if he had seen me already, and lately. At first, I didn't believe it! I hadn't seen him since I was a child, since before Mama and Papa died. I don't think I've seen much of anyone except the servants and that odd cousin of Simon's mother that comes here sometimes. Always frowning at me, as though she'd spilled milk in the kitchen and didn't want anyone to know. But other than that, I do not leave the grounds of this house. The woods are large and deep, and the house itself has to be the largest in Detroit. What need do I have for going out, when I can make others come to me? And then I realized perhaps that is what I had done. I had ordered Montague here and changed the will. I was less anxious after this, but it still rankled. I could not remember, you see. Could not remember his face, or any details of the discussion.

Simon speaks of a spa treatment. Some man named Kellogg who has an institute in Battle Creek. I gather he has strange ideas about grains and diet that I don't much care for. It sounds like the place to send invalid soldiers, not heartbroken women with cruel husbands. I told him flatly, no. He seethed, and struck me, but I was not troubled much. He cannot ever get into my soul. It is already filled to the brim with my lost children, and if he can be believed, my own madness has consumed the rest.

I do not think it will be long now. I wailed and cried and cursed the world for some days. I spit in his horrible mother's face and scratched at the doctor. If one is going to be deemed insane, it is better to play it up the more, I have found.

No, it will not be long now. The little maid has told me that I have not stopped bleeding, and that my pulse is as light as a butterfly's wing. I like the little maid. I forget her name, but she is kind. Simon says there is no maid, just the doctor, but surely he is wrong. Or, perhaps not. Mayhap I invented her.

That odd relative of his came in with his mother some time ago. She looked at me and then the door, and bit her lip as though she would cry. I haven't any idea what she has to be aggrieved about, she knows me not at all, and Meredith Green, Simon's mother, is the devil's hand. She spoke to me about my will, tried to hand me a slip of paper to sign, but I turned away. I cannot bear to look at her face, she appears more repulsive every time I look upon her.

Simon has gone out. I think perhaps he has brought one of his someones with him. Behind my eyelids I glimpse a sea of faces, heart shaped, or oval, with cupid's bow lips and pretty blushes for his charms. Those cheeks and lips were mine once. But, now…it won't be long now. I can feel it coming.

Iris: I Have A Message For You
2011 Traverse City

Sometimes Eve thought that to love reading was a kind of curse. It was a gift too, of course, a simple love of pages to turn and words to consume. But also a kind of black spell, an addiction. There is never satisfaction in reading, instead a bottomless beast that takes in letter after letter, word after word, page and chapter and leather covers. There is never enough. One book finished leads only to the search and consuming of another. Never enough stories or time to read them. A hunger that is never sated, but grows hungrier somehow.

She'd lived in Traverse City with her parents for five years. At first, it was temporary. Time for her to get back on her feet, to re-find her place among her peers, and create a new life. But temporary has a sneaky way of drawing itself out until it's stretched so far that you're lost. She came after her divorce

5

when she was 26—and the trouble that followed after it. The divorce wasn't a nasty one, or even very painful. It was almost friendly. Two people who woke up one day and realized they didn't love each other, weren't suited, and decided to end it sooner than later. That's probably oversimplified—perhaps it was only Eve who saw it that way, and his heart had been shattered. She didn't know. But now she lived in the attic bedroom of her parent's house, and somehow she'd read her way into running this bookshop in the old asylum. She didn't own the bookshop—some rich down-stater bought the space inside Building 50 of the old mental hospital and decided an antiquarian bookstore would be a lark, though he was too busy to man it himself. Eve had found herself running the bookstore, though if asked how she'd even met Mr. Scott, the owner, or how he came to offer the position, Eve would only shake her head and shrug. It had just sort of... happened.

She'd been halfway through a master's in journalism when the divorce came. She had arrived at her parents house eight months after that, with an English degree, half a masters and basically good for nothing but reading in her room, taking the three dogs out for rambling walks in the forest, burying herself from the world, and worrying her parents senseless.

Even if divorce is your idea, it feels like a kind of failure. It had filled her with an odd, unshakeable shame, like accidentally dropping a glass on the kitchen floor, and wincing to know everyone will have to watch for shards for weeks.

Eve had been a shard herself when she arrived. Broken and jagged and not sure if she was fit to be put together or tossed out in the bin. She still didn't know, come to that.

Then she'd found the bookshop. It called to her, as books always did, and she followed that summons to Mr. Scott and had been behind the counter or straightening the shelves ever since.

Of course, she could have moved out of her parent's house, she had enough money. But even when she was in high school her parents were more like friends, the three of them fond roommates who enjoyed one another's company. Even if they wanted their adult daughter to move out, they wouldn't say it. They knew she was fragile. Embarrassingly so. Always had been, and more lately. Prone to crying jags and laughing fits and doldrum melancholy that manifested itself with a lot of sitting in the dark and weeping into a towel. But, there is comfort in ritual, and that's what Eve had found in reading.

But satisfaction was elusive. It was never found in books, she fervently believed, only the desire for more pages, more stories, more escape.

Eve thought about all of this. Her past, her parents, and the books, as she sat behind the counter in the antiquarian bookshop. 'Folded Corners' was the name, though any real bibliophile would never do such a thing to a book they cherished—bookmarks are encouraged at Folded Corners, despite the name. There hadn't been much business lately, never was, truth be told. It's a certain type of person that aches for a signed second edition of *Winnie the Pooh* or a first printing of the *Mayor of Casterbridge*. Eve wasn't one of them. Give her a secondhand paperback any day, something she could spill tea on or smudge with jam-covered fingers.

Still, Folded Corners had regulars, and did a lot of sales online. Buyers in Aberdeen and Cheshire, San Francisco, Savannah, Montauk and Yorkshire. But there are a few local faces, like Mr. Janson who is always looking for Mark Twain or Mrs. Pobocik who fancies herself an Agatha Christie expert, or Eve's Dad, who brings her a sandwich every Tuesday and sometimes on Fridays. So, despite a few smiling tourists, looking for books on the history of the asylum or a latest bestseller (most of whom take down a title from the shelves, see the price on the flyleaf, cringe and back away slowly) Eve was mostly alone all day.

It was Monday, and she was feeling a little sorry for herself, and gathered her long brown—dishwater blonde her mother says, though what a nasty term for a color—hair into her hands and remembers for the hundredth time that day that she'd forgotten to bring an elastic to tie it back. Sighing, she released it, and looked around the store. Everything was organized, e-mails have been answered, stock checked, new business cards ordered last week. Nothing at all to do.

She reached for the paperback she'd brought, an old mystery her mother had recommended, and felt a few tears sitting patiently behind her eyelids. Eve blinked them away, angry that they had come at all. It was days like today that she felt that *she* might be crazy, and if she had been there 50 years earlier, they might have been wise to lock her up in the asylum.

It wasn't as though she hadn't been locked up before.

Folded Corners is on the basement floor of the renovated asylum, and almost underground, but not quite. It's surrounded by other shops: trinkets and soaps, a Christmas ornament shop, an organic dog treat shop, a bakery, a deli and a lovely wine tasting room, among others.

Monday is as good a day as any for a quick glass of wine, and a tourist bumbled into Folded Corners, about two tastings too many for normal behavior.

She blinked her eyes rapidly to scatter any sign of the threatened tears and welcomed him to the shop. Friendliness came easily to her, even if she was not, in fact, really that friendly. The man was obviously a tourist, and she thought a foreign one. He had the look of a Central European businessman, the kind one generally sees in Frankfurt. Impeccably dressed, but in a fashion that would have made a statement perhaps ten years ago. He looked at her, fairly squinting, and smiled thinly, as if flattening his lips on purpose in an effort to look less drunk. He stumbled masterfully into the back of the shop, and she rolled her eyes. This was not the first someone who had wandered over from the tasting room, but she hoped fervently it would not result in a puddle of vomit and embarrassed faces for the both of them.

Some minutes later, after hearing an odd scraping sound, she had become sufficiently alarmed, and she jumped up to find him in the back of the shop, near the stone wall. The tenants of the renovated asylum were made to keep the spaces used for their shops as raw and close to the original as possible. Eve tended to admire the stone and brick, the mix of industrial and 19th century Italianate design, but it could result in some strange happenings. This tourist had evidently dropped a book—thank heaven not one of much importance —and when she found him, crouched down in the back of the shop, head against the wall, book at his side, she did worry he'd injured himself. It looked as though perhaps he'd dropped the book and hit his head picking it up again.

Eve stepped toward him, concerned but also annoyed.

"Sir...can I help you? Are you hurt?"

He froze at the sound of her voice and remained in the same attitude for some moments, as if he did not move she might think him invisible. She opened her mouth then to speak again, and crouched down next to him, thinking he was dazed from drink and a knock on the head. Instead, his face was red as a summer strawberry and he pulled his arm out from what appeared to be a hole in the stone wall. He apologized in halting English, and muttered something about kicking a loose stone and motioned to the book, as though that was all the explanation necessary. He shrugged, lifted glazed eyes and stood up, dashing out of the store. She looked from the book stacks surrounding her to the hole at the bottom of the wall, a few crumbling pieces of stone beside it. It didn't appear that he had stolen anything, so she chalked up his odd behavior to the alcohol and being caught doing something weird.

Looking down, Eve saw a palm-sized faded book lying on the floor, and beneath it a few letters, the ink so old it had washed out to a pale beige on the vanilla butterfly wing paper they were written on. She stuck her hand in the hole, tentatively, testing the space as the tourist had done, fingers searching for more buried treasure. Scrambling fingers around in the small hole, she felt something on her fingertips and drew it out on shaky hands.

A ring. It looked like a tiny emerald on a band of honey-thin gold. A wedding ring? She wondered, and decided she was correct, for no other reason than her gut said so. She could picture a lady slipping it off her finger and tucking it away. Looking around, making certain no one else had shuffled quietly into the store, she pulled it onto her finger and carefully picked up the book and letters, before securing the rock back into place in the wall.

Eve could picture the whole scene perfectly. Anticipation, excitement, just the barest hint of fear in the air. She shook her head. She was as bad as the lady who ran the natural soap and lotion shop down the hall. Always talking about communing with and seeing ghosts and fairies or some other bullshit to sell more cherry essential oil and pine bark scented shave lather.

Standing up, Eve exhaled, holding the book and letters to her chest. She briefly considered calling Mr. Scott, but chose not to. It felt like such a silly thing to call about, and she wanted more time with the treasure. It was probably a bunch of rubbish, besides the ring, but it felt important to Eve. A secret. She rolled her eyes at her own odd enthusiasm.

She sat back onto the tall French Empire style chair that was strangely comfortable. Mr. Scott had bought it and shipped it up, making her a gift of it when she said the stool he had behind the counter was a crime against humanity.

Eve spread the letters out onto the counter. There were only two of them, and she took the ring off and set it next to them. The gold of the ring was unreasonably shiny and the tiny emerald sparkled. It was no more than a quarter of a carat, but it seemed incredibly elegant. Eve touched the cover of the small book, running a hand over the linen and feeling a jolt of pleasure she couldn't help. Books, whatever they were, always greeted her like a friend. For a moment she wondered if she should put on cotton gloves before opening it, but decided the book couldn't be old enough to require them.

Holding her breath, though hardly knowing she did so, she opened the cover and stared into the past. Inside was a drawing of a garden, and woods beyond. It was executed simply, without much skill, but sweetly rendered nonetheless. Eve herself couldn't draw half so well.

She flipped the page and saw the forget-me-nots which still grew all over the asylum grounds and in the forest glades where she walked the dogs. These had been depicted with more skill, and had been painted in lightly with watercolor. There was something mournful about the small painting, something private. It seemed to Eve that the artist had been wondering if she had been forgotten as she painted.

At the bottom of the picture were initials:
C.T.

Eve furrowed her brow and looked closer, sure somehow it had been a woman who'd owned this book, and knowing instinctively that it had been a long ago patient. She turned the page, hoping to find more clues, and she gasped to find that it was, if not a diary, a confessional of sorts.

Her eyes consumed the first entry, detailing seeing ghosts and about the woman's madness, and Eve felt...disappointed. A real loon, then. It bothered her, that this woman had ben crazy and was now haunting Eve with her scribbled ravings.

She set the book down for a moment, and then cracked her knuckles and picked it back up. Eve wouldn't dismiss C.T. so quickly. It wouldn't be fair to simply bury her away and decide she wasn't worth anything because she had been locked up.

Would it?

Opening the book back up, she turned to the next page and read on:

...I find that I am afraid that wherever I go will be a kind of prison from now on. I cannot stay here, not anymore. It has become clear to me that he will leave me here forever, and even if he did not, I cannot return to him. I cannot go back, it is not the way—it never was, though I was too foolish to see it. I must get out. I might be here in this place of madness and sorrow, but I am not mad. Or, perhaps I am, but only in the way that we all are—or maybe this belief is what my madness is made of...

Eve read the next page hungrily, and then flipped to find...nothing. Three pages of writing, two pictures, and two letters. She felt unmoored suddenly. Like when she let the kayak drift too long on the lake before realizing how far she'd gone. She wanted to know more. If the last entry in the little book was true, then she felt for C.T., whomever she was. There was a frightening similarity between them, and Eve too knew what it was to be caged.

She looked over the letters. The first seemed to be from a lawyer in Detroit. Her eyes scanned the small crabbed handwriting and she read, eyes squinted,

My Dear Celia,

I've received your letter and I must say that I am heartily bewildered. I would question this decision, and it is in my power to do so, as you are a patient at an asylum, but even if I did not already think that if your mind was in truth diseased, it would be still more formidable than many of so-called sound mind, your enclosed note from Dr. Munson is proof. My dear, I know not what brings you to this pass, and I confess I did find you much changed the last time I saw you, though I had not seen you since you were young. But on our last meeting I thought you fit and well, as I could have ever hoped, and I shall do as you requested, for your sake.

Please send all further instructions to my offices through whatever trusted courier that you have found, and I will endeavor to return all replies through him as well. I shall await your reply.

The funds will be sent to the entity indicated, but only upon proof of your death. Please, my dear, be careful.

I am ever at your service.

Yours &c,

Mr. Harold Montague, esq.

Detroit, Michigan

July 30th, 1888

The other letter was a short personal note from an A. Barnsley that seemed to signify a depth of sadness and meaning that Eve couldn't properly ponder in her excitement. She needed help. She looked at the clock and saw that she still had an hour before close.

Pulling down a leather sleeve she sometimes used for shipping rare books to new owners, she slipped the book and letters within and then placed it all in her tote bag, and pulled the ring onto her finger.

A quick Google search told her that the original building plans, records and papers related to the history of the asylum had been moved from the historical center to the county clerk's office, and finally to the Traverse City Public Library.

She decided to close up a little early. Eve had work to do.

Hellebore: Scandal, Calumny.
1888 Village Of Traverse City

Celia was quite mad. She must be if she had been committed to this place. Insanity dwells here, after all. He wouldn't have put her here, if she wasn't, at least, a little mad, would he? Of course not. Simon was many things, a monster among them, but truly she must belong there. How could she doubt it? Perhaps it was further proof of her lack of sanity that she wondered at all.

But what if she wasn't?

She reached up and ran her fingers through her long, dull, ashy blonde hair. Sleep mussed and tangled, it was more brown than gold now, for she needed more sunlight to bring out the lights in it. She stretched and thought of getting out of bed, and then thought better of it and pulled the blankets over her head. The sheets were very white

17

and smelled of chemicals, which she liked, as it meant they were clean. Celia looked around inside the sheets, and breathed heavily in and out until she thought she would suffocate from not enough fresh air. She almost laughed, but checked herself. It didn't do to laugh here. Especially when you were alone. Only the very mad are giddy for no reason. At least, that's what Dr. Norbert said, though her father would have disagreed. Daddy had laughed all the time, and in her memory he was never without a smile on his face. Despite Dr. Norbert, it *was* humorous, to think of the air outside her sheets as fresh. It was filled with a miasma of madness, was it not?

She blinked her eyes a few times and then exhaled, drawing the blankets back. Celia was fortunate to have her own private double room, as most patients had only a small room, furnished with bed and window. But it was Celia's money paying for it, no matter what Simon or his parent's said, and she was grateful of it. She couldn't bear facing other patient's madness upon waking every morning. But private room or not, the nurses would barge in at any minute and set her to some useful task. They hadn't yet found one that she was good at, but Dr. Munson declared, "Beauty is therapy. Work is Therapy". The patients were meant to find purpose and sanity by fruit canning or furniture building, farming or sewing. Celia groaned at the thought and swung her legs around and onto the floor. She didn't mind canning, or gardening, but wasn't allowed out of doors without a trailing escort, if at all. The Greens told her she was lucky to live in such a beautiful place, away from the smoke and mess of Detroit. A "brand new institution," Meredith Green would sniff, actually sticking her patrician nose into the air, trying to make up for her lack of chin or social niceties. "Just finished construction a few short years ago. Lucky indeed to have Simon and the Greens who cared for her so." As though she had not been tricked into this asylum. As if they had done her a great loving favor.

Whenever Meredith spoke of care or affection it looked green and hard in Celia's mind. As hard and green as the small emerald ring on her wedding finger. A prickly cactus like she'd seen in a book about Arizona. When Daddy said love it had been blue and clear like the water in a quiet lake. Love was blue, Celia thought, and then shook her head for conjuring nonsense.

She shook her head again, clearing the thoughts away as she heard footsteps hurrying from the end of the hall. She quickly jumped up and poured a little cold water into a bowl and dipped a sponge, cleaning her face, under her arms, her stomach and anywhere she felt unclean. She dragged a brush through her hair, the curls bouncing back up from each stroke defiantly. And then, she skittered over to the small wardrobe. A knock sounded on the door, and she called out that she'd only be a minute, before diving into a simple but pretty grey dress. She opened the door carefully, eyes down, and Nurse Dockert bustled in, red-faced and huffing.

"Good Morning, Mrs. Green" she said, in a way that sounded as if she barely dignified eight o'clock as morning and that in any case, she didn't think there was much good about it. Her hair was red, but the orangey-carrot variety of the color and it had been pulled into a frizzy bun that looked likely to burst at any minute under her white cap. Nurse Dockert wasn't unkind, there were only a few at the asylum that could be judged so, but she was brusque and seemed perpetually surprised that everyone around her wasn't as busy as she thought they should be.

She clucked at Celia and sat her down on the edge of her bed, grabbing a handful of pins in the same motion from the dressing table.

"Your hair is lazy today, Mrs. Green. It wants pinning."

Nurse Dockert pinned it quickly and with efficiency, as she completed most tasks, Celia was sure.

"Please call me Celia" she said softly, but the nurse either hadn't heard or had chosen not to reply. When she finished, Celia was escorted to the breakfast room. She would eat two slices of buttered toast and two cups of very milky tea from one of the hospital's fine china cups, as she did every morning. The doctor on duty would look on approvingly. They liked routine.

There were only around 250 residents at the quarter-mile long Northern Michigan asylum, if Celia understood correctly, but many more eagerly awaiting the completion of the construction of other wards. New buildings, men and women's dormitories needing to be filled and families gladly lining up to deposit a relative or two within. Not all of the current residents were in the dining hall now of course. Some partook earlier, or some in their rooms, as they would not (or could not) face the assembled group.

That had been Celia until a month ago. Hidden away, for her own good, Simon had said. So she wouldn't be shouting mad tales at everyone who would listen, he had told her. Until they decided what was best.

They'd committed her after the third baby had miscarried in Celia's womb. Overly emotional they said. Her reaction to their decision after she awoke in the asylum and realized what had been done to her?—overly sensitive. Alarmingly distraught. Surely she was a depressive too.

They said these things, even told the doctors of screaming fits, sobbing, banging on the walls. All of it was true, certainly. Celia had done those things. She remembered it just as they did. Just two nights after the death, they had drugged her. Well, she imagined so anyway, because they had mentioned only that she should perhaps leave town for a while, wait until whispers died down and questions weren't being asked. Simon had suggested a retreat or a spa. But then she was here, and she remembered not a single detail of the journey up, or by what conveyance, or even if Simon had deigned to accompany her. But she woke up here, in her room at the hospital, and it had all been canning or sewing and buttered toast ever since.

And though straitjackets weren't used here, the staff was professional and usually not unkind, she felt as locked up and broken as a prisoner in a dungeon. She was mad, wasn't she? Which meant her own mind could not be trusted, that there was nowhere truly safe for her.

The dining hall was oddly quiet, as though every patient was engaged in his or her own private reverie. The whole asylum resembled a somewhat cluttered mansion, with chairs up and down the wards and art of varying quality gracing the walls, and the dining room was no different. Celia looked about, up and down over those assembled and thought of *Alice in Wonderland.* Her mother had read it to her when she was very small, before her parents's accident. She had thought that madness was more like the hatter and his tea party. Quick words and frantic pace, nonsense sentences and frivolity. But looking down the table, she nodded at a few of the patients she'd seen in the day room or in passing, her neighbors really, and thought madness looked different now. It was quieter and sad, and unbelievably lonely.

She scooped up her own plate and cup and handed it to one of the girls who worked at clearing up. She wondered briefly if the young woman was a patient assigned this useful task, or simply a girl from the nearby village, happy for the work.

At the end of the tables, she thought she saw…a woman. A woman she knew, but did not know. Her eyes were blue—like the lake in the distance. The woman smiled at her, in recognition. People always smiled at Celia because she was small, almost doll-like, her face was soft and pretty, and they generally couldn't seem to help it. The smile on the woman's face wasn't familiar for all that her face was. Celia knew her…felt it. Like her own shadow.

But Celia did not smile back. Instead she walked faster, out the corridor, past the nurses, and into the gardens which were the only place she felt safe. Celia was tempted to look back at the woman that was now well behind her. Sorely tempted to go back and smile and say hello. But there were no ghosts being treated at the asylum, and saying hello to an invisible specter would be very mad indeed.

Celia passed out into the forget-me-not gardens of late spring. The whole asylum was covered in the blue flowers. She wondered if it was a strange joke. To decorate every corner of the buff brick with a flower called "Forget-Me-Not". As if anyone remembered her, or anyone here in this faraway northern place.

She came to sit on a bench and studied the three story building, its towers, bracketed eaves, and dormers. It was new, but it looked ancient somehow, as though the woods around the asylum had formed the bricks and towers from the rocks beneath their roots.

The morning was still chilly, and she shivered. Celia had many ghosts. Some that were living, like

Simon. He hovered just out of sight at odd times. She heard his drunken snore beside her in bed, jolting her awake. The crush of his body on hers in the night, the sound of his cough in the hallway sent fear racing up her spine. And there were other ghosts too. Friendly memory ghosts of her mother and of Daddy. Tinted pastel memories of moments and stories and adventures that were gone forever except in her mind. Then, there were the other ghosts. Smoky shadow figures that crept out of the gloom and caught the corner of her eye. Cold fingers that grabbed her arm and whispered in her ear. She had seen them since she was a child, and even when they were a little frightening, she had only felt sorry for them. They were not haunting her always, but every so often a shade would fall across her path, or a whistle would linger in her ear, and she knew one of the dead was with her, even just for a moment before it found its haunting place, or crossed to the other side.

Celia shook her head, but couldn't unsee all the ghosts. Then, a voice from behind her spoke, and dispelled the memories of the visiting revenants immediately.

A pleasant voice that seemingly tugged her ears toward it and lifted the corners of her mouth to hear it. She turned slowly on the bench, making herself wait. He wasn't speaking to her, wasn't speaking words at all, but singing. She'd only seen him from her window before, from above, and once at a distance as she crossed the lawn. He had been tending the flowers then, lovingly, as though each bud was a child's curls. It was his voice that first captured her, always singing as it was, and it seemed to her that perhaps he didn't speak at all, but only sang.

The second part of him that caught her attention was his hair. It was like polished copper or a newly lit flame. She'd stare at that beacon of fire out her window, and follow it with her eyes like a firefly in the night.

Now he was behind her, and she turned slowly, deliberately delaying the pleasure of seeing him close for the first time. But, when she turned her head, the lazy baritone ceased, and she realized he was much closer than she had expected.

He, too, was staring at her, his eyes wide and sort of blue-grey like a stone in the bottom of the lake, or the morning fog. He was a large, burly man, broad-shouldered and tall, but his voice was gentle and she saw now that his face was for smiling.

Celia fidgeted, she knew she should look away or say 'good morning', but she found she could not. The gardener and his songs had been the bright spot in her days these past two months, and now she could not look away. Madness, it must be, she thought. Only a madwoman would stare at a stranger so brazenly with no words to speak.

But then, he did. His smile, as she had anticipated, was broad and glowing and took over his face.

"For a moment, I thought you might be a wee ghost. Your skin wants sun, I think, if you don't mind me saying so, and it's a fine day for sun."

He put a hand to his forehead and looked up, as though checking to be sure that the weather was going to keep its end of a bargain they'd struck in advance.

He stepped closer and held out his hand. She took it, gingerly, and shook.

"Owen Flynn, if you please. Gardener and groundskeeper here at the asylum. Though, my mother would say I belong in here myself." He smiled wider and Celia returned his expression.

Suddenly, he hit the heel of his hand against the side of his head, lightly, as a mother would do to a rude child, "Ach! But that's a fine thing to say to you. You've probably kin that's whats in here, eh? I'm forever speaking out of turn, no offense meant, Miss…?"

"Thorne. Celia Thorne." She nodded her head down and smiled into her lap. He didn't know she was a patient. It was freeing somehow, to be a visitor, treated as though she were an ordinary lady, here to visit a relative or an old friend. She could barely remember the last time she'd been treated as such. Maybe when Mama and Papa were still alive, or when she had first met Simon. Before she'd been faced with the truth of him, when the illusion of Simon was intact. The Greens had treated her as Simon's property, a means to the fruition of their plans.

But now, she smiled and motioned Mr. Flynn to join her on the bench. For a moment, she thought he would, taking one eager step toward her, before turning his head and looking at the unruly forget-me-nots and the riot of dandelions that had cropped up on the lawn.

"Another time, perhaps, Miss Thorne. I've…well, I've no business shirking work to talk to visitors, even lovely ones like yourself. Especially as breakfast is just over for the patients and whomever you've come for will be ready to receive you in the common room shortly, I'm sure."

He shook his head and smiled again, a little sadly this time, and backed away. "Pleasure to meet you, Miss Thorne."

She nodded at his retreating figure, "The pleasure was mine entirely, Mr. Flynn. Your flowers are lovely, by the by."

He paused a moment, and acknowledged the compliment with a dip of his chin. She continued:

"And your singing as well."

He smiled larger, and dropped his chin again.

"Many thanks, Miss Thorne."

"Please, it's Celia." She replied, surprising herself further, wondering why she dared to be so familiar.

"Celia," he said, nodding slowly, and he bit his lip before turning around and walking toward the gardening shed on the far side of the property. The builders were come now from town. They were waiting near the specially built rail-line for more of the local Markham Bricks to arrive. She wondered how many more dormitories would be built, what other patients that would come. She was still watching the figure of Mr. Flynn and daydreaming about the asylum when Nurse Brattle came scurrying out to collect her, and from the distance, Celia could see the admonishments already on her lips. Many patients could walk the grounds freely. After all, way up north here, where would they go? But Celia was not awarded this privilege. She rather thought it had something to do with Simon, but she was supposed to be supervised at all times, to prevent "self harm". This was the third morning she'd slipped away after breakfast, and the third time she'd gone out to the gardens unsupervised.

She sighed and stood up. In the distance she could hear Owen singing again, and she remembered his large grey eyes and his ready open smile. She brought the image of the sunlight setting his bronze hair aflame and the ease and comfort of his manner. He hadn't thought she was mad. It made the scolding she saw coming worth it.

Sure enough when Brattle arrived she grabbed Celia forcefully, and held her arm tightly as if Celia was a mad dog pulling at her leash, and led her back to the asylum.

"...and Dr. Nobert will not be pleased, Mrs. Green, not at all. Perhaps he should write to your family in Detroit and tell them you're not fit to be seen this month, that perhaps we believe it's best that you are shut up in your room again..."

Celia hadn't heard the beginning of the tirade,

but had let these last words roll into her like a wave, and like standing in the tide, they had knocked her a bit off balance.

"They're not my family."

"They most certainly are." Nurse Brattle said, speaking to her with authority and no little disappointment, as one would a child who'd forgotten their lessons.

"That's your husband and mother and father, Mrs. Green. What a thing to say!"

Celia frowned and felt her arm go rigid clasped in Nurse Brattle's thick, capable hands.

"Mr. Green may call himself my husband, but he's a brute and a liar. Meredith Green is *his* mother, not mine. My parents are dead, and thankfully so, for it would kill them where they stood to see me now."

Celia could sense rather than see Nurse Brattle's face turn red, and her teeth were set in gritted fury. Celia didn't care.

"That's enough of you, Mrs. Green. I think perhaps an hour or two of quiet reflection and then a visit with Dr. Norbert might change your mind."

Celia sighed, and as they made to step into the Main Central building, something caught her eye. The approaching form of Mr. Flynn from the left side of the lawn, wide-eyed and mouth agape, as if in shock, and then the terrible almost physical blow to her chest the moment his face registered his earlier mistake. Like a cloud over the sun, his features grew less bright, and his eyes went smaller, pruning shears dropping to the carpet of green grass and sunshine colored dandelions at his feet.

Disappointment filled her to the top, and she felt like crying, although she didn't know why. She didn't know Owen Flynn, had only met him today, but he had thought her ordinary. He had treated her as such, had even flirted with her a little. And now, she was mad Celia once again, being shut into her room like a recalcitrant child.

She turned away from his gaze and was pulled bodily back into the bright corridors and sunshine filled asylum, though Celia saw only the shadows now.

Just as they reached the stair that led to the women's ward, peeking around the corner was the woman from breakfast. Celia blinked, thought to wave or call out, but then, the ghost woman was gone.

A few moments later, Celia was pushed into her room, and the door clicked in the lock, the metallic sound of the key thundered in her ears, and then silence.

She walked to her window, crestfallen and confused about the phantom woman and the ghosts of her own madness. Then, she heard Owen Flynn singing softly outside somewhere. She couldn't hold back her small smile.

Meadow Saffron:
My Happiest Days Are Past

The doctor would come to fetch her soon, and not the administrator, Dr. Munson, who believed in kindness, pleasure, beauty. The one who had told her to spend time on the grounds and to sketch nature. He was busy of late, with the dormitories under construction. No, it would be the odd doctor. Dr. Norbert— whose eyes seemed under her clothes when he looked at her. Who seemed overly concerned with her thoughts and about Simon, and whose hands were always on her arm, or on her shoulder. There was something about him—a wrongness that she found troubling, but doubtless that would be called madness too, if she were to say it aloud to anyone.

She picked up a pencil and a small leather bound book of unlined paper. It was of middling quality and had been a gift from Dr. Munson, when she had been judged fit for the outdoors—though, not unattended of course. It was meant for sketching the pine trees around the asylum and drawing the gardens, or the asylum itself in its Italianate beauty. This, she had attempted on a few of the pages, but she was no artist. She did not draw or paint, nor sew nor embroider. Her father had not taught her these things. Only books, and writing, study, and of course music. But the only piano was in the common room, and playing in there was somehow dreary, and she was locked in her room at the moment in any case. So she sat down on her bed and drew the writing desk up from beneath the springs. She had been allowed one, as Simon had requested letters from her and the doctor to keep apprised of her 'health'. It felt odd to have something from home, something from before Simon, in her lap. It had been a gift from her father, and she opened the lid and felt around for the hidden compartment in the back, relief flooding her to find it there. She had many secrets, but only this one gave her any power. A place to hide her truth.

She closed the lid again and opened the little sketch book, feeling a little nostalgic for the days of study she had spent in this attitude, or in memory of the different places she had used this portable desk to write from.

Everything in this asylum was miles away from her old life. Both in terms of distance and otherwise. She smoothed her skirts and tucked a loose curl behind her ear, and began to write, realizing immediately she would have to make use of the secret compartment in the desk to hide all the words escaping her pen.

If anyone had seen all that I have, perhaps they too would be judged mad.

I try not to think of such things, but it is like forgetting to breathe. One doesn't have to remember, but one keeps on inhaling and exhaling anyway. That is how the memories are with me. Always there. Like the ridges on my spine, always there, though I cannot see them. And like those knobby bones on my back—they follow me. A tingling sensation, a quick, almost imperceptible kiss of cold. I spin around and there is nothing. There is nothing to see, because that tingle, that touch, that coldness—it is inside of me.

I do not know if it was truly 'for my own good', as Simon said. I suspect not. Simon does only what is for him, and ninny that I am, I did not see it until I was buried too deep. I thought at the first that it was the talk of ghosts that sent me here, but Simon never listened to a word about my gift until it suited him to use it against me. The way he looks upon me, as if I am a faulty, broken thing. Like one of his watches that couldn't keep time. He looks at me as though he'd like to take me apart, fiddle with the pieces of me that were deficient. But also, he looks at me as though he knows he won't find something to fix, but instead smoke and rain and blackness so thick it would stick to him, sullying him somehow. Is it insanity to think he saw this in me all along? That it was one of the reasons he chose me? Because darkness is easier to smother than light?

He would have me be alone, but I am never alone. The ghosts, they follow me. They follow me because I know them, or at least, I have come to know them. It is madness, I know, but ofttimes it seems to me more a lunacy to deny my eyes, the rapid beating of my heart, the cold that starts in my back and fingertips and crawls in on icy feet to my core...

She slammed the book closed and secreted it into the hollow of the writing desk, grateful for its convenient size. Celia placed the desk under the bed and stepped to the window to hear a few last words of Owen's song before the door opened, suddenly, and Dr. Norbert walked in, eyes too bright, smile unsettling.

Balm Of Gilead: Relief

Dr. Norbert stepped into the room, eyes darting all around, and Celia was put in mind of a large reptile. The eyes looked at everything in the room, but somehow never left her. She felt a cold crawling sensation down her spine that had nothing to do with ghosts or memories.

She was oddly relieved when the odious Nurse Brattle entered the room, though she could not say why the woman's presence would introduce such a feeling.

Dr. Norbert stepped closer to her, thinning hair and thin lips on a tall body, as though everything about him had been stretched to sparse. He put one clammy hand on the bottom of her chin, and tilted her head up, smiling slightly, though it did not bring any warmth to his features.

"Mrs. Green, what is this I hear about you wandering the grounds unsupervised, yet again? Perhaps we should return you to your former restrictions? This room may be a safer sanctuary to confine your roaming, yes?"

He removed his hand, and she felt her shoulders relax slightly, though she had not felt them tense. She looked from doctor to nurse, and then away at the window, drawing strength from the blue sky outside. She had to tread carefully with Dr. Norbert. He was known somehow to Simon, and thus had eased the process of her admittance. The asylum was supposed to only have opened to the overflow from Pontiac and Kalamazoo, but Simon had slipped her right in, with this man's help. She kept her gaze on the clouds outside, and kept her face neutral and finally, spoke softly.

"Dr. Munson, he, ah, advised time on the grounds. And I was not…wandering, sir. But, simply…sitting. Within easy sight of the asylum. Perhaps if we asked Dr. Munson? He might…"

She let the question and unfinished thought hang in the air, and Nurse Brattle had gone red, her whole body stiffened as though preparing a strike.

"Ask me what?" A voice spoke from the hallway. The voice was as soft as the one she had adopted to speak to Dr. Norbert, and had an air of distraction about it.

Dr. Munson, carefully attired and kind-eyed, stepped into the doorway. He was still a fairly young man, no more than a few years older than 35, but he seemed older, or perhaps, had the look and confidence of one who is suited to his place in life that only those who have seen many years can usually muster. Celia thought she heard Nurse

Brattle inhale sharply, and when she looked at Dr. Norbert's hands they were clasped so tightly together that the knuckles had gone white. If she wasn't a madwoman, she supposed she would declare that Dr. Norbert was frightened of Dr. Munson. But, there was nothing at all frightful about the hospital superintendent in the least, so that conclusion didn't make a jot of sense.

No one had moved or spoken, so Dr. Munson took another step into the room and looked from one person to another, his smile never faltering. "Ask me what?" he said again, and stepped forward, once more, to Celia, and reached to grasp her hand.

"What would you like to ask me, Celia?" He asked, and she smiled in return to see that he had remembered to call her by her given name, as she preferred. His manner made her bold, and so as she saw Dr. Norbert lick his lips and start to respond, she spoke out, seizing her chance.

"Dr. Munson, sir, I seem to have gotten myself in some trouble. I…well, I know that I am restricted to walking about only when supervised, but, I have walked the grounds a number of times now without a chaperone of any kind. But, I promise I have always been within sight of the asylum and never more than three minutes slow walk away. I know it was wrong, sir, but the gardens are so beautiful and tranquil."

She ended her speech intentionally, and didn't feel at all guilty, as it was true. Mostly. It wasn't only the beauty of the grounds and gardens, but also the freedom from too close walls, occasional wails of the more disturbed patients in the furthest wards. The air that came in from Lake Michigan soothed her, and outside she was able to listen. To the ghosts, whose presence was familiar and somehow calming, and to Owen Flynn's singing, and to her own memories. She didn't say any of that though, as she could tell there was no need.

"Well, there's nothing much to ask, is there Celia? The grounds were created with exploring in mind, and they are tended carefully for the pleasure of the patients here. The flowers are grown for admiring, the trees for inspiration. It is part of your therapy to spend your time thus."

He smiled benignly as his eyes went to the window, and to the green outside. The soft moment was broken by Dr. Norbert clearing his throat.

"But, sir, there is the matter of supervision. Mrs. Green is a special case. She is more than welcome to partake of *meaningful* activity within the asylum rather than idly wandering the garden."

Nurse Brattle nodded, almost violently, in agreement, and Dr. Munson twisted his mouth in thought, and squinted his eyes, as though filtering ideas through heavy lids.

The room was silent, and Celia desperately tried to think of something intelligent to say that would keep her freedom, and his goodwill.

"Hmm, yes." He finally said, a slow smile creeping over his mustachioed face, like a cloud moving across the sun. "A valid point, but perhaps...yes." He turned toward Celia again, and gazed at her, searchingly. "Do you like gardening, Celia? Horticulture? Botany? Herbs?"

She nodded, uncertainly. "My parents, rest their souls, had a great interest in exotic plants, sir."

He nodded, as though convinced. "Splendid! Then you shall assist our gardener in his work. Only safe activities, you understand. Planting and weeding and such. He has so much to do with the new buildings and keeping the institution tended, and I hadn't thought to hire new grounds staff yet —Mr. Gringler still out with a broken leg for some weeks. What say you, Celia?"

Celia smiled, involuntarily. The idea of spending more time with Owen Flynn made her head buzz, unaccountably, even if it should prove awkward as he now knew she was a patient. Nevertheless, before she could think on it too much, she was nodding her head eagerly.

Dr. Norbert cleared his throat again, a grating hacking sound that startled Celia. She spun around to see him licking his thin lips preparing words she knew would not be to her benefit. His long, tapered index fingers pressed together as though making a point that he would shoot like an arrow through Dr. Munson's idea.

"Dr. Munson, you are the head of this asylum, of course, but I must protest. Mrs. Green is a patient, and Mr. Flynn though...affable, I suppose, it is not a trained medical man. What if she has a fit, or needs to be...subdued? He is not equipped for such an eventuality. Not to mention the impropriety; there is a reason we separate the sexes, Doctor."

He spread his hands apart at the end of his statement as if letting his words loose on the room.

Celia's shoulders had slumped. Powerless. She felt the anger begin to simmer within her, and grow afraid. Afraid of her own mind and feelings. But this was what an asylum was. What her relationship with Simon had been. What every day of her life had been since Mama and Papa had died. A total loss of herself, Simon had made sure of that. He remade her into his own creature until she had only the memories of herself to cling to. Watching her own life, decisions, discussed in front of her as if she was a scrap of paper everyone would prefer to toss in the bin and be rid of. She felt herself begin to crumple, the gloom of that powerless uselessness settling over her like night fall.

And then.

Dr. Munson stepped forward and clapped Dr. Norbert on the shoulder. "Protest duly noted, Doctor. But Mr. Flynn *was* an orderly at the institution in Pontiac before I brought him up here and appointed him head groundskeeper. So, he does indeed have some medical training. Miss Celia has hereby been cleared for gardening, and if something does arise, Mr. Flynn is more than capable to deal with the situation adequately. And as for your questions about propriety, Dr. Norbert, I hope you are not insinuating that Mr. Flynn is less of a professional than you or myself. He understands his duties."

The air seemed to go out of the room to be replaced by a whooshing breeze of a thousand arrows flying and Celia could almost picture them landing on Dr. Norbert's chest, revealing the black soul he hid underneath.

Black soul? What a thought. She chewed her lip a moment, but then smiled. A victory! And not a small one.

"And now, Miss Celia, I will escort you to the other patients and perhaps you can aid Miss Hattie with her sewing project for the schoolchildren in the village."

Celia doubted it, as she had no skill with a needle, but gracefully accepted the good doctor's arm as they stepped past Dr. Norbert and Nurse Brattle and toward the hall.

She turned around to see a look of fury, embarrassment and something like...fear on Dr. Norbert's face.

She'd made an enemy. Or, perhaps he'd been her enemy already, and she just now was seeing it?

Pink Rose: Friendship

Dr. Munson had deposited her in the common room on her floor some time ago, telling her to be ready for her first day of gardening tomorrow morning. His voice had been friendly, but professional. At the same time, she hadn't missed the gleam in his eye. He was one of those people that genuinely wanted to make the world better. He desired that the people around him be made well, and happier. It was a noble trait, something she hadn't encountered too much in the world before.

Celia had instinctively sat down at the piano, but only played a few minutes before her fingers began tripping over memories, every key contained a hundreds of her father, and the tears had blurred the black and the white until she had to quit. She willed herself to be happy today, for she was to go outside tomorrow and she could not let the tears

42

come. She found herself vaguely drifting over into a rattan chair, the woven wood shifting and muttering loudly as she sank into it. Some of the other patients had looked up at her entrance, but most had turned back to what they had been doing previously almost immediately, and she doubted if anyone had listened to her playing. Some gazed outside, and the other women seemed to look at nothing, or perhaps they were gazing at horrors or fantasies that were hidden within.

Celia understood that perfectly.

A few women sewed in the corner and one large woman grinned idiotically, a rope of saliva falling from one side of her mouth, her eyes glassy and blank. Celia felt herself shrink away from her, even though she was far across the bright room and had made no move toward her, and seemed oblivious to her presence. A shadow, next to the woman seemed to turn, and Celia recognized the ghost. Her ghost. The ghost that had followed her here...

"Don't mind Agatha. She's harmless, and actually tells very funny stories on a good day."

The ghost had winked back into shadow, and Celia realized that the voice was speaking to her. She heard the sound of someone settling into the chair beside her, and shifting her eyes away from the older woman, she felt her face flush at being caught scrutinizing the piteous sight of the woman's madness.

"Oh, I hadn't meant to stare…" Celia muttered, softly and with no little shame.

"How could you not!" The woman replied. "She's a strange looking one. Almost frightening really, puts one in mind of a witch in a fairytale, almost. It's not that she's insane, you understand, it's that she's been pickled most of her life. She's been here a few years to dry out after she accidentally poisoned herself for the third time."

Celia's eyes crinkled in confusion and the woman sputtered a laugh. "I'm sorry. I forgot that you're new." Seeing Celia about to protest, she amended, "Not new to the facility, I know you've probably been sequestered some time. But Agatha was a drunk, and her sobering up has only made her, well, less functional. Strange, eh?"

She stuck her hand right out, boldly. "Annie Barnsley. I'm here for tuberculosis."

Celia's eyes went wide, and Annie laughed again. "I'm on the mend, don't worry. My family ought to have fetched me by now, but has probably forgotten about me. Well, all except Andrew. But, my family, they're Chicago folk. My father is in meats, you know. But there's eight of us in the Barnsley litter— and it's probably a relief to have one less underfoot."

Celia nodded, though she couldn't quite understand, being an only child herself. But it had been some time since she'd had a woman around her own age to speak to, and she rather liked the idea of having a friend. She wondered if now was when she was supposed to reveal why she was in the asylum, and felt her face pale at the very thought.

Annie just kept on talking.

"I'm almost certain you're not *quite* mad. Perhaps only a little, which is fine by me. People who have a little less sanity are more interesting anyway, don't you find? Like Nelly Gromer, over there by the window? The one holding an umbrella? She's only a little mad as well. The girl was in a rainstorm, poor dear, and then she fell ill. She's been a little bats ever since. Laughs hysterically at anything even mildly funny, which makes me feel very droll indeed. But she cries absolute rivers when you tell her you owned a cat as a child and then reveal it has since died. Makes one feel as if one's small tribulations are vastly important."

Annie shook her head as if satisfied at Nelly's level of emotions being higher than they ought.

"Anyway, you're Celia Green, then?"

Celia was stunned. How did this woman know her? She sat back in her rattan chair, emitting further groans and creaks from the protesting twisted palm. She took in Annie from this vantage. Dull, wheaten hair, with a pale complexion more faded whitewash than alabaster. She had hollow cheeks and a decidedly crumpled way of holding herself that made her look like a used paper bag. Celia herself was small but cherubic with round apple cheeks, and though not fat, she was decidedly not angular. Annie was. She looked like Nelly Gromer's umbrella turned inside out by a storm.

Consumption—that's what she looked like. But her eyes were bright and strange, and she laughed easily, which she did now again to see Celia's expression.

"I help out in the records office. I'm technically *not supposed* to look at other patient's files, but when you came in I was curious. You looked somewhat familiar. So I took a peek before I sent the file along to Dr. Norbert's office."

Celia stiffened.

"But, it turned out I was mistaken. There'd been an article some time back in one of the papers, I don't remember which— about some society lady meeting with a grisly death or illness? Or she'd run away? I don't remember. Or maybe I am making it up." She shrugged, uncaring.

Celia relaxed, for a moment she had thought maybe that this woman knew Simon, but Annie clearly did not. She had already changed the subject and suddenly grabbed Celia's hand and had visibly brightened. "Well, I suppose I ought to introduce you around!"

Her voice had gone merry, and she pulled Celia to standing with more strength than Celia could have imagined an ailing woman to possess. She gestured toward the group of ladies in the corner who smiled kindly, if not bizarrely, in Celia's direction.

"This is Myrtle and Sarah" she said, indicating two silver-haired ladies whose mouths never seemed to fully close. One, Celia supposed it was Sarah, had eyes that had gone milky white and brown spots like

46

dripped paint up and down her gnarled hands. Both the women nodded in Celia's general direction and their grins grew somehow wider than before, which produced an effect of friendly terror in Celia. She wondered if the blind woman had created her own world now that she didn't have to see the reality of the one that surrounded her.

Without any regard for shame or privacy, Annie blurted out, "Sarah has been in asylums ever since her husband decided she was better out of the way, and Myrtle here was committed by her son, who owed her money. Apparently locking her away was much simpler than paying back the debt, eh, Myrl?" Annie chuckled as if this were humorous, and Myrtle nodded, smiling. Celia could find nothing to laugh about at all, and was indeed, horrified. She looked again to Sarah, and bit her lip to keep back a spontaneous sob that threatened. Husband shut her away? Was this then her future? Because she had blindly trusted a lover that needed her out of the way, too?

Then Annie gestured to the third woman, who was sitting near Myrtle and Sarah, but not quite with them. It was as if the few inches that she had put between her knees and theirs declared her wholly separate. "This fairy queen here is Caroline. But I call her Queen Caro."

Caroline nodded regally in their direction, an expression that was somehow dreamy yet imperious was fastened to her features.

"How *do* you *do?*" Caroline asked, nodding slightly at them again, her eyes shifting over for just the smallest of moments before settling back into seeing things that weren't there, or were, or had been at one time.

Caroline was tall, or would be when she stood. She had long brown hair the color of cherry wood that hung in lazy curls down her back and shoulders. Her eyes were overly large and eerily green, like a mixed potion in a fairytale. Her skin was fresh cream and her lips were pink and slightly parted. She was lovely, but child-like, more so than Celia even. Celia had features most often seen on porcelain dolls, though her skin was a bit darker. But Caroline was something else entirely, a beautiful goddess of a woman with the mind of a child. Though there was nothing about her to cause such a reaction, Celia decided she was a little afraid of Caroline.

Annie watched Celia's reaction, and chatted on with her Queen.

"How do *you* do, your highness?"

"Well enough, I suppose, though the kitchen seems to have run out of cherry tarts," Caroline narrowed her eyes and twisted her lip petulantly.

"Oh no!" Annie tutted, "A great shame! But I must take leave of you now, Queen Caro."

Caroline nodded in their direction and Celia watched as Annie performed a curtsey before looking at her sharply, indicating she was expected to do the same.

Bewildered, Celia executed a passable curtsey

and was pulled away roughly by Annie.

"Poor thing. Kicked in the head by a horse when she was a child. Though, I suppose there are worse things to be deluded about than believing yourself royalty." She paused a moment and then looked at Celia.

"Don't approach her alone, mind you. She might look sweet and child-like, but she's a holy terror when she's wound. Madder than a bag of ferrets, that one." She arched her brows meaningfully and whispered, "Violent".

Celia shivered.

"I shan't introduce you round to the more disturbed ladies over there until either an extra orderly comes in or Nurse Davis over there leaves. You either need extra support or to be left alone entirely, you know?"

Celia nodded as it was clear that was the only acceptable response.

They came to sit upon a wicker bench near a window, and Celia glanced outside, furtively searching for a flash of red hair, and finding none, turned back to Annie, who was still watching her.

"I hope we shall be friends!" Annie gasped out, grabbing onto Celia's hand and squeezing. "This asylum is ever so much nicer than the one I was in downstate, and of course, now that the tuberculosis is cured, I have so much more freedom. It's absolutely gloriously beautiful here in the summer, don't you think? But, the winter, well, that's…well,

I'll let you find out on your own—no sense in scaring you!"

She smiled and Celia couldn't help but return the expression.

"Aren't you just a doll! A china doll! You must have broken a lot of hearts, Celia."

Celia felt heat rush to her cheeks and her heartbeat galloped in her chest. She was always embarrassed by such compliments. Everyone always imagined that it was such a treat to be beautiful, but Celia found that it was the source of most of her problems. Beautiful women stuck out, and when a man saw one, it only was a matter of time before he found a way to twist her around and make her his own. Like an enchanted rosebush in a palace garden, he connived a way to steal it, uproot it, and make it his own. And then somehow was surprised when it no longer bloomed in his own dark garden. Better to be plain, Celia thought. Better to be useful and plain and attract no notice above what labors one could perform with your hands or mind.

Annie sighed, a sad sound that held unshed tears of regret or some other strong emotion. "Anyway, where do they have you 'working as therapy'?"

Celia tore herself away from her dreary thoughts, and had to fight the glow that filled her from toe to top. "In the gardens...with Mr. Flynn."

"Lucky you!" Annie said smacking Celia lightly on the shoulder. "He's not the handsomest man I've ever seen, but he's handsome enough. And, Big!

Like a giant bear. I wonder sometimes he doesn't crush every petal he touches. Me, I'm mostly in the records office, and sometimes I help out in the kitchens. Not much, because I'm not actually a very good hand with cooking, but I can peel a potato, same as anyone, and the cooks are the best for stories and gossip. In fact, just this morning, I heard…."

But her thought was left unfinished, as Nurse Dockert appeared, out of breath and hurried, as usual.

Open Rose (Placed Over Two Buds): Secrecy

2011, Traverse City

There were two people working behind the desk at the public library, other than that it was empty. Something about that made Eve shiver. Like the first moment you see that your parents have gone grey, are getting older. That shudder of impending loss. The scholar in Eve mourned the thought of libraries run by machines, or the total digitization of records, ready and available to anyone, anywhere. She frowned, having to admit to herself that if this *was* the case, she never would have made the trip over to this lovely newish building on Windemere Street. In fact, it bothered her that the building wasn't a dusty, crumbling repurposed church or old schoolhouse turned into a library. But instead bright and shiny, humming with computers and Young

Adult novels. Strange to want your library to be a certain way, but never want to go there yourself.

Eve stood a little straighter and affixed a smile to herself like lipstick, tucked her hair behind her ear and inwardly vowed to do her part and visit the library more often.

Of the two people working, neither paid any attention to Eve. An older woman was scanning books and then placing them on a trolley to be re-shelved. A man around her age whose spectacled eyes were trained on a computer, seemed oblivious to the books around him.

Her smile strained at the corners. It was one of those practiced ones her mother had cultivated for good school pictures, and she stepped to the counter in front of the older woman. Eve cleared her throat loudly, and smiled wider. The combination of her presence and her guttural throat clearing finally captured the woman's attention.

"Excuse me, I'm looking for the Historical Society's collection, specifically..."

The older woman's index finger came up and hovered in front of Eve's face. "Oop! Let me stop your right there" she then pointed to the man at the other end of the counter, "Eric is the man you want."

And with a closer look at him, Eve wondered if the woman had deliberately used the double entendre. Even with the odd round glasses, Eric looked a bit like the kind of guy she'd have angled to sit next to in college. She nodded thanks to the woman and scooted down the counter, using his sustained obliviousness to steal a further assessment. When he stood, he'd be average height, maybe an inch or two taller than her own 5'8" frame. He had walnut brown hair that looked as though it was perpetually mussed, and hazel eyes behind the glasses. Slim, but athletic and seemingly radiating restless energy, as if his own skin were a cage he was trying to escape.

She was staring.

"Can I help you?" He asked, eyes glancing briefly away from the computer screen, lines in his forehead deepening, which told Eve he'd asked the question more than once.

"Y-yes. Sorry, brain short-circuiting after a day at work, I guess." He replied with the smallest upturn of the corners of his mouth, and then he took his eyes from the screen and cocked an eyebrow, waiting for her to finish.

"Yes, you can help me…" Eve blurted, suddenly even more awkward. Why was she being so strange? "At least, I hope you can." She started to fish the letters and the little book out of her bag, but then stopped, and inhaled. She didn't want to lay all her cards out on the table. Not just yet. What if he made her return the items? Called the police and said she stole them? (Which was mostly true) or what if he tried to claim them on behalf of the historical society?

She exhaled, and moved her hand from her purse slowly. Eve looked up to see him still waiting, both eyebrows up, fingers hovering over the keyboard.

Eve began again. "I...I work in a bookstore, in the old asylum—*Folded Corners*—and I was hoping to learn a little more about the original building. Old architectural plans, some kind of site directory, patient information—any of that."

Eric nodded and tapped his fingers on the counter, biting his lip a moment, as though processing.

He looked at her again and smiled.
"Why?"

His hazel eyes met hers and she felt a little jealous for a split second because his were more green than hers, and it really wasn't fair that men could have eyes so pretty. His question unsettled her, but so did his gaze and she couldn't help feel that it was intentional. She was at once too young and too old for men like this, her throat was suddenly very dry and she swallowed.

"I have to find something...someone, maybe both." Surprised at her own honesty, she shrugged as if it didn't matter as much as her face surely said it did, and he smiled. The smile transformed his face.

"Ok, I can help."

He stood up, all in one fluid moment as though he'd never been seated at all, and Eve was hit again by the impression of perpetual motion emanating from him.

He turned and spoke to the older woman.

"I'm taking this young lady to the basement, Miriam." Her head moved a fraction, and she made a noncommittal sound in their direction, and then winked, before returning to her scanning.

He stepped out from behind the counter and began striding toward the back of the library. Eve nearly tripped trying to catch up to him.

"Thank you!" She said, a little breathlessly as she matched his pace. "I know it's strange but…" He cut her off, waving a hand. "This is the library, only weirdos, elementary school kids or octogenarians come in here to research anymore."

Eve wondered if she should be offended as she wouldn't categorize herself as any of those, but the expression on his face was not even vaguely insulting, so she simply nodded.

"Eve" she said, as they walked.

"I beg your pardon?" He said, turning his head to look at her.

"My name is Eve Parish." He nodded and then laughed.

She paused, confused. "What is it?" She asked, suddenly self conscious.

He shook his head. "Nothing really, it's stupid." He offered her another smile and chuckled. "I'm Eric Chapel."

She shook her head and laughed a little too. "Small towns, huh?" She said, not knowing what exactly to say, and he shrugged, smiling back.

They approached the door Eve supposed led to the basement, and he took out a key, and turned it in the lock. They descended and he led her to a stack of folders and drawers, with numbers and letters that reminded Eve why she usually avoided libraries and the Dewey Decimal system.

"The map will be easy. I've got a few different ones from different years, and as far as plans and architectural drawings of the asylum, I've got quite a few of those bumping around as well. What period of the asylum's history are we after?"

Eve filled with a foolish lightness that she knew was hope. Maybe…maybe this was going to be easy.

"Around 1885-1890"

"Ah, early days then?"

"Yes…just after it was built. 1888, specifically."

He cocked an interested eyebrow, but she ignored the implied question and scanned the table wondering which stack, which paper, which document held the answers she was searching for.

"Then you're only going to need the plans for Building 50. The rest of the wards weren't finished being built until a little while later."

He rifled through a few folders opened a drawer or two, drawing out what appeared to be the plans he had spoken of, and a map or two of the area.

She was staring at these upside down, as she was standing on the opposite side of the worktable, when he spoke, startling her out of her concentration.

"Folded Corners, eh? Speciality rare books and all that, right?"

She shrugged. "Yeah, it's all very elitist and museum feeling. But literature is my degree and my passion. I guess it feels like an honor just to touch some of the first editions, or signed copies." She then leaned across the table and whispered, "but between us, I prefer paperbacks."

He grinned. "Good girl."

He pulled an ancient looking large piece of paper close to his face and inspected it for a moment. "Yup, I think this is what you are looking for. Is this it?"

She started to nod, and then shook her head. "Not, not completely, sorry. Patient information records?"

He nodded slowly, his eyes far away, an odd expression on his face.

"Right. Well, shit. Bad news. That kind of thing is much harder to find, and sometimes, depending on the kind of information is not really...public."

She frowned and felt disappointment start to pool in her stomach.

"Good news..." He smiled, eyes glittering, "This is exactly the kind of thing I like to search for."

Eve matched his smile. "When do you close, and where do we start?"

Chickweed: Rendezvous

Traverse City, 1888

The evening was a routine of useful tasks and nourishing but slightly bland supper that made Celia fondly long for and remember sitting in the sunshine licking honey off of her sticky fingers and fresh whipped cream so thick it was difficult to swallow. But the asylum used good, local Michigan fruits and fish from the lake, and the vegetable garden that she was to assist with was growing heavier with squashes, herbs, courgettes and cucumbers.

She'd slept in fits and starts, nightmares of events that never happened and more horrifyingly—some that had. A bed full of blood announcing the loss of yet another of the babies. Animals found in the forest, dying, blood on their little hooves and paws, blood-covered muzzles and scared, dying eyes. *Her* eyes, growing faint, the light behind them dimming, dimming until only shadows remained behind those eyelids. Dead in a room of death. The death room, but her body covered, hidden, left to decay alone in the dark, unmourned, unnoticed. Death haunted her dreams, dreams so tangled she couldn't know which were real or which had really happened to her, or which were phantoms of her own troubled mind. Celia woke up over-hot and felt as though an unseen child or imp had been clinging to her tightly, binding her arms and legs.

She'd thought to cry a little, but could not muster any more tears. She'd cried so many—before. She'd read in novels about dramatic heroines who cried so much they had no tears left, but did not agree. She may have been out of tears for now, but like springtime, the rain would return. Sorrow, like so many gathering pools behind her eyelids would replenish the dams, and they would break, leaving a fresh deluge down her cheeks and onto her pillow.

Celia had awoken earlier than usual, the nightmares felt distant after a few hours of unbroken sleep. She knew a nurse checked on her every so often, and that her door was kept locked. the nurse entered she would spin around and re-lock the door she had just come though, the suddenness of her movements and the finality of the tumbled lock always gave Celia a moment of panic.

She rose now and drew out an older green dress she had used for long rambles through the forest back before she had met Simon, when Mama and

Papa were alive. It was a faded green and several years past fashionable, though that didn't matter here—not in the asylum or in Northern Michigan. She hadn't known why it was packed for her at all, it was probably thrown in a bag in haste, but she was glad of it. It was hers in a place where nothing felt her own. Not her time or her freedom often even her own thoughts were strange to her.

Quickly pouring a little tepid water into a hip bath, she hastily washed, not wanting to wait for a nurse to come and lead her to the washroom. She then dressed and began pinning back her unruly waves. She gave her cheeks a light pinch, more from habit than any other reason, and then waited.

Within a quarter of an hour, and just at the moment she had begun to be anxious, Nurse Dockert peeked her head in, and for the first time, Celia thought she saw her smile.

"What's this then? Already up, Mrs. Green? Perhaps on account of your new task in the gardens? If I'd known it'd get you out of bed at sunrise I would have suggested it to Dr. Munson myself." Her mouth almost quivered up again, but then she shook her head and clapped, "All right then, Miss, let's get you outside."

Celia followed Nurse Dockert out the door, which the nurse quickly locked behind them, as though Celia had been roomed with a serpent or a winged monster that might escape if she did not lock fast the door at that exact moment. Despite this, Celia felt as if she floated, though the idea seemed silly enough the moment it entered her mind. But she *did* feel lighter this morning and the old dress was familiar and had happy memories of a life long past within its stitches. Really, it had been less than five years, but it felt as though it had happened to someone else, mayhap someone she'd read about in a novel with a title she barely remembered. But, no, it was her life, her memories, and her dress, and she was something like happy. The gardens would be hers to care for, and Mr. Flynn's voice would mix with birdsong and wind and though perhaps she might, in truth, be mad and locked away, today promised to have something sweet contained within.

Her steps slowed, her smile faltered, and the shadows that gathered near the corners of the too-sunny asylum seemed to grab her elbows as she walked. Behind her, she heard something and she spun around, seeing only the black lace of a dress disappearing behind a corner. The woman's dress. Somehow she knew it immediately and without question. It was familiar to her, after all, wasn't it? She turned back around deliberately and set her mouth in a firm line. Only a ghost. It was only a ghost. Though why this particular ghost was still following her caused her some worry.

The ghosts hadn't visited her much of late. Dr. Munson would say it was a good sign, but she'd never told him of the ghosts at all. She had felt them about her, of course. Plaiting her hair as she slept, or whispering into her ear as she dreamed, only to disappear within moments of waking. Seeing the woman twice—yesterday and now—were her first sightings in as many weeks.

Celia and Nurse Dockert emerged out the front doors of the asylum into the early sunshine. The sun had risen but was still waking up and Celia could see dew drops shining in the grass, and the blushing rose pink lights of dawn illuminating the sky.

The nurse began speaking, but Celia heard not a word. Her fingers itched for earth beneath them, and the damned ring from Simon was suddenly too tight. Her fingers wanted freedom from that too, wanted to be pulling and planting and folding roots into dirt. She'd never been much of a gardener. Her father had kept orchids for a time, and then had tried his hand at lemons, though it was much too frigid for them, but somehow, he had coaxed them into growing, before they had all left again, on some adventure. It wasn't that her parents hadn't put down roots anywhere, but instead that they put down roots everywhere they lived, every place they traveled. And since they had died, she'd been rooted to nothing at all. Except to Simon, who was more like an anchor, holding her down to an existence where she could not grow, or thrive and barely lived.

Now, the urge was upon her to ground herself in something alive. Perhaps that had been the force that had been pulling her from the asylum and out into the fresh air these past days. The need to flee into vibrant *life*. The asylum seemed a kind of dead place, for all its newness, beauty, and for the most part, kind staff. It was filled with forgotten souls. Like plants that no one remembered to water, they shriveled inward, forgotten by their family, their neighbors, and sometimes, by themselves. Or was wrong? Perhaps this was only how it seemed to Celia, and all those within the walls of the asylum were heartily glad to be safely ensconced inside the Markham brick walls, away from those who cared not for them.

But though the paint was still bright, and the conditions she was kept in were favorable, she felt that she could not truly believe the asylum would help her until the sun was her cap and the wind was in her hair.

Nurse Docket was finishing up whatever speech she had been making.

"…not to overtax or overtire yourself nor are you to pester Mr. Flynn with personal questions. He is trained, of course, in both the tasks for which he is now director, and in those of any orderly and had some basic knowledge of nursing, though, we trust that will not be required. Every morning, at exactly 7, sharp, mind you, I will fetch you and you will begin work out of doors under direction of Mr. Flynn. You will be fetched for breakfast at your regular time…" she opened up a log book and ran a finger down the page to find Celia's name. The nurse spoke for a few more moments in the same vein and then her voice fell away from Celia's ears.

She saw him.

Briefly, she felt panic rise in her chest, remembering their last encounter. He would, no doubt, chock her behavior up to her madness, and she was certain this was for the best. It was futile to explain—and much too intimate—that his mistaking her for a visitor had brightened her mood.

But, he did not look back at her with pity, or concern. Instead, he smiled lazily, and nodded a thank you at the nurse before motioning toward a table where large leather gloves, trowels and spades lay, ready to be picked up and wielded.

"I would introduce myself, but we've already met." he said, his voice kind. He looked at her askance and bit his lip. Celia stifled an awkward schoolgirl giggle, feeling exceedingly foolish.

"Right" he continued, "Dr. Munson informed me yesterday evening that you were to become my assistant in the gardens and grounds."

She nodded.

"You aren't afraid to get your hands dirty, then?"

Celia shrugged. "It's not as if anyone here minds dirt under my nails, I think my days of playing the lady are over. And, besides, it looks as though you've a fair number of gloves."

Owen shook his head, a crease forming in his forehead. "Gloves, I have. And as for being a lady, I'll have you know my mam always worked the garden. So I think it takes a special type of *lady*, indeed, to make things grow."

He gestured toward the table, and Celia picked through the thick leather gloves, searching fruitlessly for a pair that half-fitted her small hands.

Pulling on a well-worn pair, she wiggled her fingers about, marveling at how strange they looked in the large gloves—almost like a long extinct primordial animal. She smiled at her own fancy and looked up to find Owen looking at her, eyes soft.

"I reckon those are a mite too big for you."

She waggled the over-large gloves in front of him, and he laughed. He made no other response but to gesture over to a plant bed over to the left, close to the main drive. There were flowers in flats scattered around the bed, the dirt was dark brown and recently tilled. Celia realized she didn't know anything about this. All that she'd ever planted had been in the earth outside one of their houses, and that had been as a child, with no thought if the flower would live or die. It hadn't dawned on her that certain plants might need special food or care, that some flowers could not thrive without the proper soil.

They had walked over to the bed he had indicated, and Owen Flynn knelt down next to the bed, and gestured for her to do the same. It was odd how intimate it was, putting one's hands in the earth, surrounded by soil near a strange young man she barely knew. Almost indecent. She was past indecent now, though, she well knew. In fact, she realized she could barely remember when she had been someone decent. Celia brought her gloved hand over her face, pulling the thoughts away, and attempted to focus on what Owen was saying.

"Take hold of it here, where my hand is, close to the bottom and pull—gently!—gently! Yes, just like that. You've done a marvel. Now, we're to place each of these purple ones, *Tradescantia ohiensis*, or Spiderwort, which is a far cry easier to say—and place them about three inches apart along the edge. See, now place yours just there...perfect!"

His hands were so large and they looked rough, as though they'd scratch your skin as soon as touch you. Owen Flynn didn't need gloves, she could tell he wanted nothing between his hands and the earth. The sky above seemed to pull more freckles from his skin by the minute and his hair was alight with the sun.

He was dazzling to look at, she thought. Not so much because he was handsome, though he had a pleasant face and even enough features. But instead because his presence glowed, and was startling—it would have been almost frightening if his voice wasn't so low and gentle and almost like a slow song she used to know but at sometime, long ago, had forgotten the words.

Once he felt she had the hang of the task, he stood up and wiped the excess dirt from his hands onto his dungarees. He then reached for some pale pink geraniums, scented fuchsia, primrose and periwinkle, teasing them out gently from the flats. It seemed he plucked them at random, and quickly tucked them into the soil like tired children into bed. For every one heliotrope or spiderwort she planted, he seemed to plant five blossoming flowers of varying colors. The effect was dizzying to her senses, long dulled by the inside of the asylum. White sheets, white walls, white china and black and white marble tiled floor. White nurse's uniforms and the plain buff brick of the buildings.

The rainbow before her seemed almost sinful, but she delighted in it nonetheless. What had happened to her? The fearless and clever young thing she had used to be. Wasn't she? She was almost certain someone had called her thus at one time. What had happened that flowers could bring her such joy? She leaned her head to the side a moment, considering, but then gave up and continued working, leaving off only when the nurse appeared to take her to breakfast.

She'd gobbled it down quickly, two pieces of toast, as usual, with a boiled egg, which was not. The nurses smiled approvingly, but also seemed to squint as they recorded it in their neat scrawl into their little notebooks. What did it mean? She was sure they were wondering. It had to be a positive sign? Perhaps progress? Even if it was outside routine, Celia was not especially hungry but had taken the egg only because if she was working out of doors her mama—rest her—would have wanted her to take it.

When Nurse Dockert delivered her back to Mr. Flynn, she was unreasonably glad to see he'd paused for his breakfast as well, and so had not finished planting the bed without her.

They both resumed their labor, working in companionable silence. Or, it would have been if Celia wasn't bubbling with unasked questions.

About the plants, about Mr. Flynn himself, about a hundred things she would have liked to discuss with any person that was not patient, nurse or doctor. But she bit her tongue, literally, so hard that she tasted blood in her mouth and knew herself to be as insane as others believed.

About an hour later, Celia looked up. A discordant shift in the attitude of their morning, though she could not identify what it was that she heard—if she had indeed heard anything at all. She glanced back to the entrance of the asylum, and she saw a line of women, obediently following Nurse Dockert and a nurse she recognized from another floor. Celia watched the procession as the women began their trek close to where Celia was toiling, but thankfully, not too near.

Owen mistook Celia's confusion and curiosity. "Would you like to be joining them?" He asked in that low sing-song voice. Celia looked from him to the women, and then back to his face again. She shook her head resolutely.

"Absolutely not, Mr. Flynn. I'm perfectly occupied here, thank you. It's just…" she heard her voice begin to relent even before she made her mind up, "…well, I don't know what they're about, you see."

Owen looked down at his hands in the dirt, and she noticed again that he was not wearing gloves. The sight oddly thrilled her, and she could not remove her gaze from his hands. To see all that he grew with them, there must be a kind of magic contained there in those hands. If his voice was the first thing that seemed like magic in a world that had gone shadows and hopeless for her, then Owen Flynn's hands were the second enchantment. She was shaken from her reverie by his response, and his words seemed heavy, as though he had trouble pushing them out of his mouth for the weight of them.

"It's the women's daily walk, Miss Thorne. On the woman's walking trail, through the woods. It's glorious lovely. Haven't you...haven't you seen it?"

She wondered if his hesitation was due to her being a patient. She realized he must feel strange around her, unsure how to treat her. Not as a friend or visitor, fellow worker, or even assistant, for all that they called her so. And in the back of his mind, she knew, he must still wonder why she was there. What had she done or suffered to have been shut away in an asylum? But searching his face, she saw neither pity nor fear.

No, she could not put a name to it. For no one had ever looked at her the way he did. She looked away, needing a break from those dove grey eyes, and in so doing, caught a glance from Annie Barnsley as she walked with the other women. A glance that was hard and angry, and confused Celia even further. Angry with her? Distressed in general? She could not tell, but something in that look alarmed her.

Celia turned quickly away, plunging her hands back into the coolness of the soil, and then she heard the screaming.

More than startled, she was scared. For a moment she wasn't completely certain it wasn't coming from her own mouth. She'd heard that scream before, had felt it reverberate through ravaged lungs in a scraping, hollowing note that would leave the mouth raw. Her fingers came up, unbidden, unthought, to her chest, but she felt no vibration other than the rapid tattoo of her own heart.

She looked up then, finally trusting herself to do so, but she could not see any one. She started to stand up. The screams had stopped, but she could not help but seek out the cause and maker of those screams.

They had been screams of fear.

Celia knew what it was to fear. Simon. Her life since she had met him. Her own mind. The truth of herself. All of these had become demons to her, terrors she could not trust.

She stood fully and took a step, but found a hand on her elbow. It wasn't a rough restraint, nor was it overly gentle.

"Leave it be, Miss Thorne. I'm certain the nurses have it well in hand." His words were soft, but she heard the strength behind them too.

"I was only wondering…if I could help…" she said lamely, pulling a gloved hand over her forehead to tame some flyaway strands of hair. She felt the soil from the gloves on her forehead, and she felt foolish, but not enough to try and brush it away.

She put her head down and stepped back to her

work, kneeling upon an old dirtied cotton cushion, gloves finding a home within the earth.

"There is nothing wrong with wanting to aid another, nor in being curious of strong emotion. But here....here, curiosity can be upsetting..."

"For patients." Celia finished quietly, fighting tears she did not understand, but thinking perhaps they were made of shame.

"For anyone." He replied, bending down to his own work. He began humming then, and the sound of it calmed her, until she saw a nurse emerging from the trees, and Annie—no longer the bouncing, enthusiastic girl of yesterday, nor the angry woman she'd seen a moment ago, but now leaning on the nurse, seeing nothing, eyes glazed like ice over a winter window.

It was heartbreaking and somehow...expected. They were at an asylum, after all, one should expect to see the horror of madness.

But Annie wasn't insane. She'd been ill.

The nurse walked Annie in, and Celia went on listening to Owen's soothing song, her mind tumbling over what had upset Annie so, and shame that she had done nothing, could do nothing for her at all.

His song ended, and silence fell between them, and even her thoughts and worries had silenced.

"Thank you" she said quietly, patting the dirt around heliotrope, making a little wish it would grow as she did so.

"For what?" He asked, distractedly.

She swallowed and reached for another purple flower, though she didn't know for sure what type this one was.

"For...for calling me Miss Thorne, even though I'd really rather you called me Celia. Everyone here besides Dr. Munson calls me Mrs. Green."

He nodded, but didn't look at her. "That's the name they gave me too. But, I figure you've a right to call yourself what you like. And if a woman doesn't like her husband's name, she doesn't have to use it. Besides, I like thorns."

She chuckled. "A gardener that likes thorns?"

He smiled back at her, "All the smartest blooms have them, you know. Best way for something beautiful to take care of itself."

She could feel her face redden, but couldn't bring herself to meet his eyes. He began humming again then, and she let the sound wash over her hands in the earth, the flowers around them, and let the upsetting thoughts fall behind in the shadows.

Dog Rose: Pleasure & Pain

A few days passed and summer arrived in earnest. Celia worked outside daily, until her pale skin turned olive and her hair took on the sheen of dark gold. Mr. Flynn spoke little, but he seemed to see everything. Two days after they began their work, she found a canvas apron with pockets for tools, and small gloves, just the fit for her.

She'd turned to thank him, but he hadn't been looking at her. Instead he was singing quietly, in a language she did not know, but thought must be Gaelic. They'd worked side by side this way, him singing low and rhythmically, digging, planting, pruning, and it seemed the days flew by in a contented haze. As though his songs were magic that made time pass more quickly and sweetly.

Maybe they were.

She found she did not want to know what the words meant. That the mystery of them was part of that magic and she wanted it to remain so.

All this time she had not again seen Annie. Not at breakfast, nor walking with the others on their way to the women's trail, nor did she appear in the evenings when all but Celia seemed to sew socks or embroider handkerchiefs. Mr. Flynn had assured the nurses that Celia would be too exhausted from her work out of doors to take part in the evening handiwork. She flushed at the thought of this small thoughtfulness from him, then scowled. How little she expected kindness now.

What had her life become?

She was tired at night from working all day, and the muscles of her arms and back were sore. It was a kind of pleasure, that pain. Born of purpose and hard work, and she had rainbow colored beds of flowers like gems in a jewel box to show for those tired hands and beleaguered shoulders.

Sleep came so easily at night that she did not feel the ghosts if they did come, nor did she hear Simon's voice in her dreams or see the phantom woman for some days. The doctors and nurses approved of the new outdoor routine and how dedicated she was to it. As much time as she spent outside, she hadn't occasion to see Dr. Norbert or Nurse Brattle. Her life was, for now, if not happy, then, bearable.

They had moved on from the first flower bed and were working on weeding and replanting one he'd created in the spring. It had been over two weeks since they had begun working together, and yet they had spoken very little, conversing mostly by glances or nods of the head, gestures, and moments spent mopping brows. The quiet and hum of the near forest and the sound of his voice was healing, in that it allowed her thoughts to gain wings in ways they had not been allowed for some time. Memories surfaced. The near solitude was a balm.

Until she heard a scrap of song on his lips, and without thinking, lent her own voice to the words he sang.

Celia did not know how long she sang along, for the song first began in her mind, and she couldn't be sure when the melody escaped her lips. She only knew it had grown quieter suddenly, and she did not know the reason until she looked up and found his eyes upon her as though seeing her for the first time. As if he hadn't really known she was alive and near him until he heard her voice.

It was an oddly vulnerable kind of feeling. An experience of being laid bare and of having a ray of sunlight sweep all over her briefly, showing pieces of herself that she usually left in the dark.

Neither of them spoke for a moment, and Celia began to grow angry as the silence stretched. As if he'd taken something from her, though nothing was taken and there was no cause at all for any emotion. She had sung, what of it?

"Your voice is lovely, Miss Thorne, I'd not expected to hear it. Seems you've been hiding it from me."

She nodded slightly, just the smallest inclination of the head. "Thank you, Mr. Flynn, you already know I admire your singing." He colored a little, but continued working.

A moment later, he spoke again, casually, without looking up. "I...I thought perhaps we should call one another by our first names, as you had once suggested. As we work side by side every day, it doesn't seem too forward, does it?"

Celia shook her head. "Not at all. I'd like that." She pulled a weed, with more precision than normal, her whole body seemingly focused on the action. But then, before she could stop herself, she asked one of the thousand questions she'd wanted to ask him since the first day, questions she hadn't allowed herself to give voice to before.

"Tell me, Owen, about the forget-me-nots."

"What about them?" He asked, still intent on the flower bed.

She sat back, and stretched a little, considering how to phrase the question.

"When I first saw them, they seemed a kind of cruel joke, or at least an incredibly maudlin flower choice for an asylum. Forget-Me-Nots planted all over a place where people are expressly sent to be forgotten."

He sat up then, and looked at her. She meant to avoid his eyes, but the sudden intensity of his gaze pulled her face to his like flowers to the sun. He bit his lip a minute, and she saw how his impossibly broad shoulders had straightened, and a shadow had fallen over his brow. He smiled then, and it was edged with tragedy and it made her sad even before he spoke.

"Celia…the forget me nots have always grown here. You could not stop their growing if you tried, nor could you pull them all out if you wanted to. They won't be forgotten, just as you, yourself, are surely unforgettable."

He stood up then and walked back to his tools. She was shocked at his words, but pleased, and confused all in one. It wasn't just a kindness, the words were more, or could be, she could feel it. She didn't delude herself into thinking he was declaring himself or anything of the kind, but he thought she was unforgettable. He saw her as someone…worth missing. She held the realization close for a moment, and then let it go. She couldn't dwell in fairytales, not anymore.

But, even for the minutes he was away, gathering tools and materials in the gardening shed, she found that she missed his voice. She'd grown so accustomed to its rhythm as she worked, the way it seemed to guide her hands to the right tasks, and keep her mind from the dark places it tried to venture to.

He returned, and bent back down to the flowers, and she again wanted to give voice to one of the questions that had been bubbling in her mind. Not so that he might compliment her again, as gratifying as that was, but because she needed that voice, and she was bold enough now, or drunk enough on the vibrance of the flowers to speak.

"How'd you come to be a gardener, Owen?" she asked, hating how breathy her voice became when speaking his name.

He looked at her and brought a soil-covered hand up to scratch his glowing copper hair. He offered a kind of crooked half-smile, not really to her, but to the question itself. He rocked back to his shins and looked at the clouds before he answered, grey eyes never leaving the sky.

"It's an odd story that. I trained to be a doctor, did you know?"

She shook her head. "No."

"Of course not. None but Dr. Munson does, so how could you've? Well, I should say I started training, but never finished. Didn't even come close, truth be told." The crooked smile pulled a little wider and he looked behind him a moment, as though he wanted to be certain he wasn't being overheard.

"My Mam and my Da were farmers in Ireland, before I was born, mind you. When we came here, my Da got a job on the boats, and my Mam started growing frivolous things. That's what she called the flowers. She got a hold of some book about the meanings of all the different blooms..."

"The Language of Flowers" Celia interrupted, and then colored when he smiled at her interjection.

"That's the one. I was just a lad then, of course, more interested in swimming in the lake or stealing a kiss behind the schoolhouse from Katie Conroy. But Mam always had me digging this or that and she would tell me what each of them meant and what the message was when you put the flowers together. How a posey could speak all your deepest longings without a single sound."

"I bet that made you popular with the village girls," Celia teased quietly, but he didn't seem to hear her.

He was quiet a moment, and Celia realized she had let her gloved hands falls by her sides and that her lips had parted in anticipation of his words. It was odd to hear this giant brawny man talking of the sentiments of flowers, but odd in a way that felt lovely. He continued on, and the lovely feeling melted with his words.

"I never thought much of the flowers again until I began my training as a doctor." He swallowed and his face went rigid.

"I was home from school, here, actually. This was my home as a boy, did you know? No, of course not. But I was home, and there was fighting at the docks. One man was stabbed and the one who'd done the stabbing had been beaten nearly to death by the rest of the crew afterward. I was called in to help—there was no asylum then, of course, and no other real medical facility of any kind besides the village doctor. There was only the barest of surgeries, and there'd been illness in the town, so the doctor was stretched thin as it was. So, I was called in, being a medical student."

He paused again and those midnight blue and storm grey eyes went back to the clouds above. Clouds that seemed to be gathering, congregating, turning the day dark.

"What I did not know was that the man stabbed, the man dying on the table was my Da. And the man they'd have me save was his murderer. Not that they realized what they asked, nor did they realize who I was in the chaos of the moment."

She felt the first drop then, but she did not move, could not. It was as though the sky itself wept for Owen, but she said nothing, barely breathed as she waited for him to continue.

"I did what little I could, but every nerve of me strained toward my own blood—my father, lying on the table nearby. I applied the right amount of pressure to the man's wounds, no more than necessary though I ached to give him pain, I stitched him straight and true, and tested bones gently. But, I prayed he would die. In my heart, I wished it."

Owen swallowed hard and exhaled.

"And he did, the bastard. And so did my Da."

He stood up and walked back to the little rickety table that held his tools, and then reached for a flat of flowers, stowing them beneath the table so they would not drown in the rain that was beginning to fall with more and more force. Celia had a hundred questions, and realized he still had not answered her first one.

Owen walked over and offered her a hand up from the dirt as the rain tumbled down off the brim of her hat.

"We'll have to go in, then."

She helped him scoop up the rest of the trowels and spades, and walked with him to the shed, willing him to speak again.

"I'd gone home that night and found I had so much to say to my Mam, so many apologies, but she would not hear it, and I could not speak them. Instead, she took me to the garden, amongst all her frivolous flowers and there we planted and weeded, and still I could not speak. Our grief was silent, though I screamed inside. That I was training to be a doctor and could not save my father, that I thought I could pledge to heal and yet was glad when a man died beneath my hands. It was that day, I knew I was no doctor. A doctor heals, no matter what. For a week we toiled in that garden, even as the day of the funeral came and went and we stood silently together at the church. But when we arrived home that night, my mother offered me a strange posey."

They were walking back to the asylum now, and his arm was so close to her own she fancied she could feel the heat of him through his shirt. The rain fell steadily on her now, but not violently, leaving tracks through the dirt turned mud on her arms. She knew she must looked mussed and sodden, but she found she did not care. Celia cared only for the story on his lips, the gift he gave her of intimacy and honesty.

"What was it?" She asked, tasting rain on her tongue and thinking of the clouds it had lived in before it fell to earth.

"Coltsfoot. Justice shall be done. Daisies for innocence, and yellow roses, which ask the receiver to forgive and forget. And it was simple. The flowers spoke when we could not. Our time in the dirt and the weeds had healed me. I saw that hard work and soil yielded such beauty, and…I felt a calling, I suppose. There is so much that nature is trying to tell us, I think, if we would only listen. So, I went back downstate to sort out my affairs, and took a job at the other hospital with Dr. Munson,. I worked as an orderly and spent my spare time on the grounds, until the offer came to come up here and be the groundskeeper and gardener full time. It may not be prestigious, but it is good and true and it brings me joy."

He seemed embarrassed at the last, and his cheeks pinked a little.

"I suppose you had not bargained for such a long tale, nor to be drenched so thoroughly in the hearing of it. I apologize for both." He smiled, the same crooked smile and his freckles peeked out like stars.

"Oh no! Not at all!" She cried, "It is some time since I've heard a story worth the hearing. I think your chosen profession is wonderful, truly! Who could stand to be cooped up amongst the sick and dying—though noble as it is—when one could be out of doors, in the fresh air, surrounded by flowers and freedom?"

He seemed about to tease her, his mouth twisted up and his eyes merry. But, perhaps he thought better of it, and instead gave her a little nod.

"Indeed, I couldn't have said it better myself. Thank you, all the same. I thought you were entitled to the story since you are now my assistant."

He reached forward then and touched a raindrop on her nose, before stealing his hand back quickly, as if the water had scalded him.

"Beg your pardon, Celia, most…inappropriate… I…"

She waved him off and bit her lip, unsure what to say. They had just gotten to the door of the asylum, and she would need to walk in at any moment.

And then Nurse Dockert opened the door, and was upon them. "Thank you for bringing her in, Mr. Flynn! Just in time too!"

"Yes, the sky is fairly weeping." He said, his voice strange, and he took a step back, no longer looking at Celia.

Nurse Dockert peered outside, "Raining! Oh, well, yes, I suppose it is! Why, Mrs. Green you're drenched entirely! You must hurry to wash and change!"

Celia looked at the nurse confusedly. "Change? For what, pray? What am I just in time for, Nurse?"

The carrot-headed nurse smiled and stepped forward, taking Celia's arm. "Your husband is with Dr. Norbert now and will be visiting with you directly. Come, let's get you out of those wet clothes. Thank you, Mr. Flynn."

She added the last part of her statement to Owen, dismissively, and hurried Celia down the corridor, toward her ward, but not before Celia had turned to find Owen wide-eyed, crooked smile fled from his face.

Hydrangea: You Are Cold

1888

Simon sniffed at the air and made a face. He wrinkled his nose as though something putrid lingered. His eyes never looked at hers, and she wondered if it was because he could not look her in the eye after what he had done to her. But instead those reptilian eyes ran over her figure like so many grasping hands. Nurse Bell, whom Celia did not really know, sat in the far corner of the otherwise empty common room writing in a little book and seemed to pay them no mind at all.

She spent the intervening silence studying Simon. He was unbelievably handsome. The devil comes in many guises, her mother had always said. Even that of a Renaissance angel, apparently. His hair was golden and hung in spun curls, and his eyes flashed turquoise green. Full lips with sandy clipped mustachios and a strong jaw all sat on his tightly muscled form that seemed made for dancing or riding a horse. Though Celia knew that it wasn't restless energy that his body yearned for, but violence. His clothing was perfectly tailored, purchased with his wife's money, no doubt, as she knew he had none of his own.

But, for all that beauty there was something empty about Simon. Something so lacking that for all that she could see his obvious charms and attractions—she was repulsed by him. Not that she had always been, of course. It had taken time for her eyes to adjust to the kind of wicked, hollowness that he was comprised of. But now she felt that she might be actually physically ill, and she swallowed bile many times in those first silent minutes.

Finally, he quit his investigation of her person and stood up, walking to the window and his eyes slid back and forth through slitted eyelids across the rain falling hazily outside.

"Hello…Celia. They tell me that you are making yourself, well, if not useful, then better than useless."

She did not speak, she knew she was not expected to.

"No more crying and wailing though, which is, I should say, a great improvement."

Celia still did not speak, waiting for Simon to finish, as she knew she was supposed to do.

He stepped away from the window, quickly, like a cat pouncing on a beetle, and he was there, crouched down beside her, inches from her face. He looked at her, his eyes not hard as glass but, harder and green like emeralds, like the emerald she wore now on her finger, that she always felt was like one of his eyes watching her. But his eyes were sharper, not smoothed and polished like the stone.

She wondered briefly how many women had looked into those dangerous bottle green eyes? How many had drowned in them like a drunken man drowns in whiskey since he had shut her away here? There was too much green there, like a kind of poison, or a snake about to strike.

"Are you keeping your mouth closed, Cee?"

His voice was quiet, and that sent a jolt through her. Her heart pounded and she could feel the sweat under her arms, down her back, and between her breasts. She closed her eyes, but when she opened them he was still there.

"Yes, I mean, I don't...I don't know what you're talking about. You said...." She whispered, tightly, her face becoming taut and filled with fear.

He grabbed her hair in the back, pulling it so that she felt he might rip her scalp off. Still, she did not cry out, as he knew she wouldn't, even as tears gathered in her eyes from the pain, nor did the nurse look up from her book. It was not Mr. Green's behavior that they monitored, but Celia's.

Simon pulled her hair and stood a little so that his face was directly over hers, searching for something. She felt the tears in her eyes begin to stream down her cheeks, a river un-dammed, and she wanted to scream and scratch at his face, but she did not.

"Yes, remember what I told you. Good. There's a good girl now."

As if he had never grabbed her at all, he nodded his head and let go, stepping back to the window. He completed it so suddenly and with so little emotion that Celia wondered if somehow she had imagined it.

If maybe again, as Simon had told her, this was further proof of her madness.

"Good, good." He nodded to himself while looking out the window. He cleared his throat and rolled his eyes about the room, looking at the nurse and back at Celia's person and then around in his head as though the whole situation was ridiculous and he couldn't believe he found himself where he was.

"You've been playing at acting as Mother Nature, I hear."

She nodded, but he did not see her, was not looking at her at all.

"Under the direction of this ginger caveman?" He asked, gesturing lazily to a spot out the window that Celia could not see from her chair. She did not like Simon to speak of Owen that way, but it would earn her nothing to say so.

"I ought to have a few words with the man. Warn him about you and your tendency toward tales."

Celia made a little strangled sound with her throat and immediately looked down. Simon smiled to himself and tapped his nails on the window. "Yes, a capital idea. Poor man, doesn't know what kind of loon he's being forced to monitor."

She bit her lip, willing away tears that she knew would do her no service.

The look in his eyes just then caused bile to rise in her throat and she felt the retching begin in her stomach. She looked away from him and to the dark area of the room, wishing she could crawl into the shadows there, and hide until he left again.

Smiling again, his face still all innocence, he continued, "I'll need to have another chat with the doctor, I suppose."

He examined his nails for a moment, still smiling that horrible grin, and drew a sheaf of papers from his pocket. He came to sit across from Celia and spread them out cheerfully, as though he were an architect laying out some grand plan for a palace.

"Ceelie dearest, your lawyer is being a pest again. He says he feels uncomfortable performing any actions on your estate without you present, or at the very least without your signature. I should have known bringing you to his office that time was a premier mistake, but we didn't know how the wind would blow then, did we? We most certainly did not. So, we need *your* signature, Mrs. Green, or else the beastly man will not release any more funds to my account."

He cleared his throat as though the respectful, almost pleading tone he'd adopted hurt his throat.

"I need you to sign here, poppet." He pushed the papers toward her and pulled a pen from his waistcoat. Her eyes ran over the words on the document. She remembered the little old lawyer in his office, his kind smile and sent him out silent blessings for not handing over everything to Simon the moment he announced she was committed. He had retained for her a little power, in a place where she had none, and with a man who had never allowed her any. They had an agreement, or rather, he had told her they had an agreement, she knew, but that money was her last freedom.

She put the papers back down on the table and shook hr head, but did not meet his eyes.

"Sign the damn papers. What are you playing at, Celia?" The words were clipped, but spoken in a kindly undertone that made Celia's jaw clench. She shook her head again, and gathered her courage.

"You have arranged things nicely for yourself, Simon, and you have me gone. I will arrange for you to be given more funds, but this document I will not sign."

He looked at her and the little paper on the little wooden table and then snatched it up, crumpling it between his hands. He sat back into the wooden chair, which cracked and grumbled with the force of his shifting form.

"Fine." He said, in a tone that indicated it was not. His face kind and handsome, but still somehow so keenly missing something that she felt her stomach drop.

"If you will but give me some paper, I will write a letter…to Mr. Montague, authorizing some of the funds from the Estate to be released to you. But I will not give you unfettered access."

"Lovely", he said but did not look at her, she could see he was frowning, and this both pleased and worried her in equal measure.

He drew a small scrap of paper from his pocket, wrinkled and dog-eared, and handed it over to her. She scribbled the necessary note, handing it to Simon quickly, exactly how one would deliver dinner to a caged tiger.

He took it up rapidly too, as though she might dare to snatch it back, and tucked it into his pocket. Immediately after he completed this he talked of his mother and father, and the dinners he'd been to in the city, and the people he'd met.

And as was part of her particular madness, Celia listened. She felt the knots in her stomach loosen, and her face relaxed so that in a few moments she was smiling and almost fooled into thinking she enjoyed his company. She didn't even flinch as his hand stole across the table and lay over top of hers.

Somehow, he always did this to her. Like a warm blanket over frozen skin, he made her forget she'd ever been cold. He had a way of speaking and smiling that she didn't ever fully trust, but was so grateful for his light when it turned on her, shining into her eyes, warming her up, that she forgot his darkness, his coldness, at least for a few moments. So starved for that warmth and comfort was she that she couldn't help but soak it in when it was shone, however briefly and artificially on her.

It was the way he had first charmed her. When he put his mind to it, Simon Green could have almost talked her into anything. And he had.

He spoke for a few minutes more, praising young ladies of his recent acquaintance and spoke of investment opportunities she neither cared about nor understood. He patted her hand once more and then snatched his away, wiping it on his trousers as though madness was catching and her hands held the contagion.

He then looked at the clock and back outside. "Right then, if I'm to speak with this gardener fellow, I'd better do so now—I've a rail journey ahead of me in the morning, and the rain will only get worse if I tarry."

So taken aback was she that her own sharp intake of breath startled her.

"But...Simon...no. You can't...please, don't do this..." She reached out for his arm and he snatched it away again as though her touch was poisonous and he looked at her as he would look upon a misbehaving hound.

"Celia, you are in an asylum for the insane. I have to travel much too far and long in order to obtain access to money that is mine by right of marriage. Because you...you had your episode and have been...sent here, where you unfortunately continue to tell mad, unbelievable stories."

"Simon, I haven't said...." She began and then shrank back with one look.

"I'm disappointed in some of your decisions today, Celia." He replied after a moment, his voice so quiet she had to strain to hear it. He picked at an imaginary speck on his coat, his voice becoming louder, harder and more righteous as he went.

"And you do have a way of inspiring sympathy and fondness in others. I fell for it myself once upon a time, no, don't object and don't speak. People take your moods and pity you instead of seeing what you really are—all of your shocking, insidious unwomanliness! So those who are near you must be warned. You must be…brought to heel. And eventually, perhaps, with good behavior and obedience, you can be brought to *heal*, so to speak, and you can be welcomed back at home."

He grinned at his own tired quip, and stepped behind her, lowering his mouth to her ear.

There was once a time his lips this close would have sent shivers of desire down her spine. They still sent shivers, but now they were shivers of terror.

"You, darling Celia, sweet Ceelie, must learn to behave. No more of this defiance and refusal. I want what is mine. You will learn when to keep your mouth closed—the difference between real…" He reached down into her bodice and grasped hold of her breast eliciting a faint beginning of a sob. "…and what is in your mind." He quickly snatched his hand away and stepped back from behind her.

She felt the burn in her cheeks, the heat that rushed from chest to stomach, that special shooting heat she knew was shame.

"Goodbye, Celia" He called back as he stepped to the door.

She listened for his footsteps as they retreated down the hall, and when she could hear them no more, she wept. For the violation of his visit, for the ideas that he planted that made her believe he never hurt her, never scared her, that it was all a product of a diseased mind.

Her diseased mistaken mind. Once someone makes you doubt your own thoughts, memories, your very self, then you can never be sure of anything again.

She stood up and walked to the window, placing a hand on the glass to steady herself, to hold herself in place. The nurse was still in the room, sitting quietly in the corner, but had not been in position to have a vantage of Simon's unwanted touch. It was just as well, for Celia would have been twice shamed to have her violation witnessed.

Still, she stood and steadied herself on the glass, preventing herself from running to the door and into the hall. She thought perhaps of throwing his head against the brick walls until his brain became deficient and he too was locked into the asylum. She thought of chasing after him and throwing her arms around him, of acting precisely how she had when they had first met. Before she told him of the ghosts, before he'd hurt her...before she'd realized what kind of man he truly was, what he really wanted from her.

She shook her head and concentrated on the glass beneath her palm. The nurse was still in the room, but looking at her notebook, perhaps taking advantage of these moments with a pensive, maudlin patient to finish some work or notes.

In the corner of her eye, Celia saw his hair like a newly lit bonfire amidst the falling rain. His entire tall, broad frame crackled with life. He was standing near a patch of forget-me-nots, near the window in the subdued sunlit drizzle of rain. She thought perhaps if she rapped loudly enough he might hear her and look up with those blue summer storm eyes. But she did not rap, but simply watched him standing near what looked like a shimmering blue lake of blue flowers, a mirage pool in the middle of the green grass and buff beige asylum. As though he were an island in that forget-me-not blue.

Only a few more moments until Simon found him and told him about her. Horrible, shameful things, and she could not say if they were lies or no. Was she mad, or he? It must be she, for here she was watching out an asylum window, waiting for Owen Flynn to learn what a lost cause she was.

She watched as Simon approached, golden hair like a reflection of sunlight, the haughty, confident way he walked. The rain carried on drizzling, but the sun still shone through the mist of raindrops. It was strange how small he looked now, how insignificant he appeared from the window, or maybe it was how he looked when standing next to Owen Flynn. She watched as Owen turned away from the flowers his expression open and friendly, his hand extended.

They shook hands and then Owen's smile grew wider still, and he nodded.

And then, it happened, before her eyes. And though she could not hear the words, she felt them as they were spoken and saw the reaction on Mr. Flynn's face. His brow furrowed, and his face darkened as Simon gestured back toward the asylum. She felt herself shrinking as she wondered what precise words he would use to describe her, her fits, whether he rolled his eyes in his descriptions or if he would play it sympathetically. Celia knew only the glass stood between her and the truth, her and the words. And though she could not control them, she might, perhaps, hear them spoken herself. Celia's palm balled into a fist on the pane of the window and she saw her fist swinging back, shattering the glass like added drops of rain onto the garden, but she held fast, watching his face, her hand still.

Now Owen Flynn was shaking his head, and he looked…upset, no…angry. He put a hand in front of Simon as if to stop and silence him, and Celia thrilled to see that large hand in front of Simon as though that hand could obliterate his cruelty. Owen was speaking now, his face calm, but his body rigid, anticipating to be called to action. Simon backed away, both hands up, and then spun on his heel, shaking his head until he stepped beyond her line of sight.

Owen looked straight up into the sky and stood like that for some moments, as though he were a plant himself and the vague sun behind the rain clouds was his energy. Slowly, he turned his head to the asylum, his eyes coming to rest on the window Celia stood at. And though she knew he was blind to her presence there, the rain creating a hazy cover for her in the darkened room, she felt that he saw her all the same.

He drew his large hand through wet, red curls and crouched down to the forget-me-nots and Celia smiled.

Then a voice spoke from behind her.

Ranunculus: You Are Radiant

2011

Eve wished she could say that it remained an exciting treasure hunt for the rest of the evening, but as time drifted by, her enthusiasm dwindled. Eric's however, did not.

They began by searching through the archives quietly after he had given her a few promising-looking stacks to poke through, and clues and keywords to look out for that might prove helpful. After about forty-five minutes though, she couldn't stay silent any longer. She sat up straight and twisted her spine, releasing a startling amount of cracks, and flicked her gaze to his perpetually mussed brown head. He'd taken his glasses off, though she wasn't certain where he'd put them. Eve listened to the rustle of paper for another minute, and then she broke the lingering quiet that had stretched between them for far too long, well, in her opinion.

"So..." She began, trying to sound casual, even though there was nothing remotely casual in this entire strange encounter. "...how'd you end up in the library?"

Lame, she thought, at her own query. Asking someone about their job was second only to remarking on the weather for bland, pointless conversation. But, Eve admitted to herself, she was genuinely interested. For someone who loved books as she did, she thought it would either be a kind of heaven or an anxiety-ridden hell to work in a library. Trusting that the books would be returned, worrying that they would be defaced or ruined, wondering if a certain patron could be trusted with a precious volume...

His fingers stayed busy in a sheaf of papers for a moment, as these thoughts raced through her mind, and he nodded at the papers, seemingly not having heard her at all. He picked up a few of the documents and set them over to his left on a small pile he was creating. He pulled his hands through his short hair and raised his eyebrows as though pulling an invisible mask from his face, and then, to her surprise, answered her question.

"Not sure, really. It was never the plan. But my great-aunt—Miriam upstairs, or really, probably gone home by now, was the librarian here as long as I can remember. And somehow, I've wound up with a library science degree on top of a political science one. I toyed around with being a pilot for a while, but then had a bit of a freak out behind the controls and that came to nothing. I think I'm more surprised than anyone every morning when I wake up and realize that I'm a librarian. But, I like dusty research, and as a science it's much more technologically forward than people think. Ultimately, it feels like home here, so, I guess that's my long answer."

She smiled and looked down at the newspaper in front of her. Dated 1887, so she felt it was not quite what she was looking for. She took a moment to consider his words.

"Funny, isn't it?" She asked after a minute. "Best laid plans and all. Life never seems to stop throwing curveballs."

He nodded, distracted.

"What about you, Eve Parish? You didn't grow up here?"

It wasn't a question. He already knew she hadn't. Eve wasn't certain precisely what to tell him of herself. There was some shame, certainly, but she didn't like holding back her secrets. It made things muddier, messier, less honest. She peeked at his face, just briefly, and clenched her teeth. Not yet. She didn't want to ruin it just yet. Let him think she was just a normal, well, kind of normal eccentric lady who liked tracking down information on asylums. She inwardly winced, but convinced herself, to just hang on to the full truth a little longer.

"Well, no. I'm originally from downstate. My parents moved up here when they retired. I, well, after college I took a job in Louisiana, got married and moved to Texas, divorced, and uh, well, I came back home. I mean, I came back to my parents. I...I had kind of a rough time for a while."

He nodded, still not looking at her. "I can imagine, divorce can be tough."

Eve exhaled a steady stream of air from her lungs, as though the air was confessions she hadn't given voice to, and she needed to expel them from her chest before they weighed her down.

"Yeah, it's no picnic. But, I get to work with books, and my parents are...great. Very roommate like, I guess."

He looked up at her, finally. "You don't have to explain anything. I've moved Miriam in with me for goodness sakes. Doctor said she needed to be in a home, but, I figured, we spend all day together here anyway, and I inherited a big enough place for three great aunts, so now she's *my* roommate."

They both smiled then, and she went back to her search. She flicked through a few old deeds and a document that seemed to be a glorified grocery list, and then another newspaper. It was dated 1888 and it was a Detroit paper which surprised Eve. What would a Detroit paper be doing all the way up here? She started to put it down and move on to the next, saying "Eric, you really need to organize these..." and she stopped. Something caught her eye.

Celia Green

Something about it gave her pause. Celia was the name in the letter, though the initials were different from the sketch. But that could be a maiden name or a middle name, couldn't it?

"I think…I think I found something."

Eve pulled the newspaper closer to her face and read the headline and short article following it. She knew the moment he saw it there would be questions, and that she'd have to reveal the papers she'd found in the shop. She sighed as she read, and then felt her eyes go wide. *This* was definitely related.

"What? What is it?" He said, excitement sounding in every word. Eve didn't have to wonder why he'd agreed to help her search, nor why he'd stayed so late to do so. It was evident from those few words that he lived for the elation of discovery. She smiled and pulled the moment close before handing over the paper. It was healing to recall the kind of pleasure one could derive from pursuing a passion, she realized that at some point she had forgotten, and he was reminding her.

He snatched the paper, but gently, from her hands and pulled it to him. His glasses were back on his head, but as he read she could see his hand go to his pocket, then the other, then to the front of his polo shirt, fruitlessly searching for frames he was not using and clearly didn't need.

The article was short and it showed a grainy image of what appeared to be a petite woman, dressed fashionably for the period, if a little severely. She was pretty, or looked to be, but she looked sad. And not just in the way that most women in old photographs looked sad, but as though some hidden tragedy had attached itself to her. Or, perhaps not. It was a lot to assume from one grainy photo.

Eve watched Eric consider the picture a moment, and then he stood up and came to stand next to her so that she might read along as he read it aloud.

A Lady Missing

It has been reported that Mrs. Celia Green has disappeared from the facility in which she was convalescing after an extended illness. Mrs. Green is the wife of Mr. Simon Green, originally of New York City. Sources close to the family report that Mrs. Green was ailing for some months and was discovered missing early Tuesday morning. The family has denied repeated requests for information, saying only that the area where she had gone missing has been thoroughly searched. It is not the belief of the officers in charge that she has been abducted, as there has been no ransom note. Mrs. Green is an heiress of considerable wealth and great beauty. She was a popular fixture in society for the past two seasons, after having lived in relative isolation before then. The police say there is no evidence of foul play, but this paper must present the facts which are that Mrs. Green was present one day, and gone the next. The police claim that they are hopeful of her return. If you have seen Mrs. Celia Green, or have information regarding her whereabouts, please contact your local police station.

He read it, narrowed his eyes, and then looked to Eve. "What are you not telling me?"

She exhaled, and stared int his green-gold eyes for a moment, allowing herself to weaken.

"I...I haven't been completely honest with you..." She began.

"I deduced that much, thank you." He snipped.

She took a breath, felt the blood flood her cheeks. "Can you keep a secret?" Oh, God, what was she, eight years old?

He looked down at his brown loafers and pinched the bridge of his nose. He regarded her a moment, weighing her somehow, and nodded.

"I'm going to say absolutely."

She exhaled, relieved for one reason or another to have passed muster to whatever measure of scrutiny she'd been under.

Eve walked across the room and grabbed her purse where she'd left it on an old child's school chair. She unzipped the side pocket and fished out the book and letters and walked them over to Eric's waiting hands. He looked at her, brow creased.

"What is all this?" He asked, fingers already opening the cover of the little book. She saw his eyes take in the signature on the first sketch and his eyes sparkled with intensity.

"It's the same first name, but that doesn't mean anything. Where'd you get this?"

She could almost feel the electricity of his enthusiasm.

"It was…behind a stone in the wall of the shop. A customer bumped it and…this was what was inside." She drew her hand in front of his face, "and also this ring." She pointed then, to the photograph in the newspaper, where it looked as though, the woman was wearing the same one. It was a simple ring, certainly, and so small as to be unidentifiable in the photograph but there was something… unmistakeable about it, at least, to Eve. He took hold of her hand, and his skin on hers made her stomach leap. His hand was warm, and while he was holding onto hers to inspect the ring, she felt that he held it just a few beats longer than he needed to. He released her hand. Maybe she'd imagined it.

"Wow. Wow! Unbelievable!" He exclaimed, the full force of his smile upon her now, and she found she was grinning too. "Read the rest!" she urged, catching his excitement like a sickness. Almost reverently his hands pulled the book and letters into the light, and he was quiet for a few minutes. She watched his eyes travel across the pages, lingering here and there on a certain word or a turn of phrase. After a moment he walked a few steps to an old computer chair near where they had been searching and sank into it, and then swiveled around in circles for a bit. He really couldn't seem to keep still.

Finally, he met her eyes and held the letters up, the book still in his other palm. "We've got to get to the bottom of this."

Eve filled with a strange light kind of hope. Because of his enthusiasm, or the mystery itself, or the elation of having a project to be working on—she didn't know. But she grinned at him, wide and bright.

"You'll keep it a secret?"

He rolled his eyes and jumped up from the chair. "I said, 'absolutely'."

"Well, what do we do next?" She asked, his excitement now beyond contagious.

He frowned. "Well, right now, I've got to go home. It's past midnight and we've been searching for hours."

She felt her face pale. "It's that late? Shit! Why haven't my parents called? Oh God, something is wrong!" She paused in her panic to see him waving her emotions away.

"No, no—there's no service down here, that's all."

He picked up the leather envelope and placed the letters, the small sketchbook and the newspaper inside. He then added the plans for the asylum, the map, and a few other papers from the stack she'd seen him making.

"Ok, we can reconvene tomorrow? Yeah? Can you come here after work?"

"Yes." She answered immediately, not even allowing him to quite finish. "Good." He sighed, a pleased expression on his face. "I'll try to dig up what I can on the web, and we'll go from there. Though I wonder..."

"What?" She asked, honing in on his sudden strange expression.

"I wonder...well, the paper didn't say. But I wonder if Celia went missing from Detroit, and it was because her family placed her in the asylum and didn't want anyone to know...or, if she went missing from the asylum itself. Or if she went missing at all. Seems like that could have been a misprint, or a mistake."

Eve bit her thumb, an old habit that seemed to resurface when she was puzzled, or nervous, or didn't know what else to do.

He shrugged, "Perhaps we'll find out, I guess." And with that, handed her the large, sturdy envelope, meaningfully.

"Since you're trusting me with your secret of where some of these items came from, I'm trusting you with the archives I added."

She had the urge to bite her thumb again. She didn't know what to say. Trust was hard. She'd lost it from so many that it felt momentous to have it so freely given. She wanted, for the briefest of instances to tell him the truths about her she'd left out earlier, but she swallowed the impulse down. It was just a project they were working on that they had a mutual interest in. She was not required to bare her soul to everyone.

"Great, see you at 5." she said simply.

Eric led her up the stairs and walked her to the library doors, unlocking them so that she could leave. Her phone erupted in notifications of a few missed calls and texts, so distracted was she that she barely registered his hand shooting out to shake hers until it was upon her. Warm and steady and right. She shook her head. Stupid. It was late and she was conjuring love stories out of politeness.

"Tomorrow then, Eve Parish" He said, and she smiled, lamely. "Here's my card, it has the library number…and my personal number…just in case, you, uh, find anything else in the store or whatever" he added quickly.

Then the door closed and she was on the steps of

the library in the moonlight holding a sheaf of research treasure. She breathed the Northern Michigan air in, all lake water and summertime. For the first time in a long while, good things were coming for Eve. She could feel them.

Red Balsam: Touch Me Not

1888

"Mrs. Green, you've been in this dark room much too long. I think it high time for an examination to mark your progress."

The nurse who had been ignoring Celia, and had taken no notice of Simon, now sprang up from her chair, cheeks pinked at Dr. Norbert's entrance. Nurse Brattle walked in behind him and gave Nurse Bell a look that would rot cherries.

"Nurse Bell, please leave us. You are wanted in the dining hall."

The young nurse scurried out like a mouse from a cat's paw and Celia was left alone with Dr. Norbert and Nurse Brattle. "Come along Mrs. Green" He said, his voice brooking no arguments or hesitations and he waited for her to stand up before exiting the room, followed by Celia's timid steps, and Nurse Brattle bringing up the rear. She spun around to lock the door almost violently before following into Dr. Norbert's office.

The doctor turned once, and something about his face, a shadow of an expression she couldn't quite translate made her feel sick. And then she felt it. A sharp tug on her arm, and looking over, she saw the ghost woman was pulling her back and away from the doctor. It felt so real that it caused Celia to step back into Nurse Brattle, who stumbled at the contact.

"Mrs. Green! What are you about?!" The thin, ax-like face of the nurse fairly cut into Celia and she gasped, feeling the tug on her arm begin anew.

Dr. Norbert turned around again, his face a mixture of confusion and annoyance, and he grabbed for Celia, but she moved her shoulder and twisted her body, running toward her own ward and room. She wanted nothing but to be away from the doctor, Nurse Brattle and the insistent ghost woman whom Celia suspected she had wronged.

She ran to her room and tried the door, but found it locked as expected. Celia twisted the knob in her hands, this way and that, hoping it would somehow unlatch and click open. She felt the frustration gathering in her breast, expecting Dr. Norbert and Nurse Brattle to appear at any moment. Fear came in cold, icy breaths, fear of the doctor, and of Simon, and of herself. She inhaled, a ragged sigh escaped her lips, and felt a sob rise in her throat. She put her back to the wall and slid down, and just as she gave up her will to hold in the emotions any longer, thunder shook the asylum and all was chaos.

Screams—coming from the dining hall, starting as maybe two or three scared voices, then multiplied and became six, then twelve, and then so many voices that Celia could not be certain that all the shrieks she heard were real at all. The voices seemed to come from everywhere, echoing through walls and blowing from the dining hall and out from under locked doors. Like a sickness, the fear was contagious. Perhaps it was not only fear, but the excuse to let out a wail of anguish, one's specific voice going unremarked among the multitude.

Celia fought the urge to cover her ears, she wondered if holding her hands like muffs over her head would appear insane, or if not placing them over her ears would appear more so. She curled her body up against the wall, hugging her knees, wondering if Dr. Norbert would come for her— when she saw the ghost again.

Her hair hung softly down her back, and her gaze seemed to go through Celia. She had expected the ghost to be hostile, or at least…angry for all of the time it had spent haunting her. But instead she seemed only sad, though Celia was not sure if it was for herself or for Celia. She put a finger to vague pink lips as she pushed open Celia's locked door. The ghost motioned for her to enter. Celia stood up shakily, and looked beyond at the room that had been revealed, when she turned back, the ghost was gone.

Nurses bustled around the halls as though they were being clocked for an upcoming race, and Celia walked backward into her room, hearing the keening of the other patients slowly cease until the near silence of shuffling feet and lingering sorrow became a dull hum. She dropped into the uncomfortable wicker chair in her room, but she left the door open. Watching the space in which she'd last seen the ghost, wondering why she haunted her.

There was something familiar there, more than familiar. But, like fireflies in a jar, every time she thought she had captured what it was, she found her ideas empty, or the recognition flitting off into the darkness.

Nurse Dockert entered the room, redder than usual and seemingly bewildered by the open, unlocked door. She stepped to Celia tentatively as though Celia was a stray dog she was uncertain of.

"What's this then, Miss Green? How...how've you come to be in here then?"

Celia offered a lazy shrug, unsure how to answer, looking over the frizzy hair sticking out all over every which way from the woman's head. Her chest was heaving and a sheen of sweat shone on her upper lip and forehead.

"My goodness, Nurse! You look thoroughly bushed!" She felt strangely guilty and not a little sorry for the frazzled woman before her, who couldn't be too many years older than herself. A woman who lived and worked with mad and sick patients all day and was still, unbelievably, kind.

The nurse's hands, which had been assertively set on her hips, now dropped to her sides as if she had surrendered something, though neither woman could say what. She sighed deeply.

"I am well and truly knackered, Mrs. G, and make no mistake," she admitted, her voice a little softer than usual. "But please tell me how you got in here. I checked the door myself earlier this evening."

The expression on the nurse's face was difficult to look at, exhaustion and bafflement written there and for that she had somehow failed because Celia was back in the room she was to have locked.

Celia straightened. "Ah, a nurse happened by and unlocked it for me during the confusion. She didn't lock it back up, and I wouldn't want her in trouble, so I'm afraid I shouldn't like to tell you which nurse it was."

Nurse Dockert sighed deeply again and Celia met her eyes. "Good enough, Mrs. G," she said, and with another word about the storm being now too brisk for further gardening, she promised to retrieve her for dinner. She left then, locking the door behind her, and Celia was left alone.

Alone with memories of ghosts, and Simon's shadow which was a phantom that he left with her always, and the memory of the tall broad shoulders and piercing blue-grey eyes of Owen Flynn as he'd sent Simon off, obviously unsatisfied. It was that memory she gathered close to her now, to combat the merciless pouring of the rain outside, battering the windows, washing the traces of Simon Green cleanly away.

Pennyroyal: Flee Away

1888

Celia dreamed of fire.

But not the warm flame of Owen Flynn's red hair. This fire was smoky and stifling, the flames licking and devouring paint and wood and linens. A fire made of screams and fear. In the dream, she stood in the midst of it, felt the sweat between her breasts and the drip of it down her back. A heat so hot that her skin felt painful and heavy, and she wished she could remove it like a chemise. Her vision was blurred, but she saw the ghost woman, and now she had a companion. An old woman who looked to be blind, milky hollows for eyes that saw nothing, even in death. But they sat calmly, the pair of them, on a brass hospital bed, those same blank eyes that saw nothing, feared nothing. The woman idly twisted a strand of hair around her phantom finger. Celia wanted to scream or run or fall into the flames and burn—anything to flee the eerie sight of the calm of the ghosts, but she was held in place, transfixed, paralyzed. The ghost woman twisted the hair around her finger until a few strands snapped, and then looking at Celia, whispered, "Awake."

Celia woke up, a sob lodged in her throat and her nightdress soaked with sweat. She was breathing hard and heavy and her eyes scanned the room, but found nothing except darkness, and out her window, only moonlight and soft summer rain.

Footsteps outside her door, and she heard a key turned hurriedly in the lock. The silhouette of a woman approached her bedside, and Celia instinctively shrank into the bedclothes, her disturbing dream still fresh. The woman leaned in closer and Celia saw that it was a nurse, though not one that she recognized. "I'm awake" she whispered, as the woman had begun to reach out, warily, to wake her. "What's happened?"

The nurse stiffened for half a moment, startled, and then spoke. "There has been a fire. Please put on your dressing gown and follow me outside, we are evacuating the women's ward. The men from town are already here to put out the flames, but it was near your room and it will have to be examined for safety."

Celia's room in the women's ward was close to the administrative offices and the staff living quarters. Since she was judged "not disturbed," she and those who were only "mildly disturbed" were kept toward the middle of the quarter mile long building, and those who were more deeply disturbed were kept farther out in the wings, away from the general population of patients. Which surprised Celia. She would have thought if a fire was begun, it would have been amongst those who were more thoroughly insane. She rolled her eyes at herself as she followed the nurse out of the door of her own room. Why had she assumed the fire was deliberately set? Too many novels, she thought, wrapping the flannel dressing gown more securely about herself. The nurse motioned for her to pause as she stopped at two other rooms, hurriedly, and brought out other tired and bewildered patients. Soon, they were out in the cool night of a Michigan summer, with only a quarter moon's winking light.

The rain was soft as a moth's wing, and for Celia, even as she huddled into her wrap, the cool was a relief after the heat of her fevered dream. The fire had only affected her floor of the women's wing, and two offices. She looked about the slivered moonlight darkness searching for a familiar face. She found Nurse Brattle, which was not a welcome sight, and Nurse Dockert, hovering over a gangly form that Celia knew well. Without hesitation, she turned and moved in their direction.

"Annie!" Celia cried, relieved to finally see her friend again. Though they'd only met the once, she couldn't help but think of her with affection and had missed a friendly face in the evenings since her 'illness'. She realized now, seeing her, that she'd been more concerned for her friend than she had thought.

"Annie!" She exclaimed again, bending down over her. Her wheat hair was listless and stringy in the moonlight, and her eyes were glassy, almost liquid.

"Annie, are you all right?" The woman who'd been so animated and chatty before, now moved her head toward Celia's face and shuddered, opening and closing her mouth like a fish on a riverbank. Celia looked at Nurse Dockert in confusion, and the nurse petted Annie's hair gently.

"Miss Barnsley hasn't been well, Mrs. G. And I think tonight's excitement hasn't helped." Celia had a dozen questions on her lips, but she turned away at the sound of Doctor Munson's voice. His thick mustache and short light hair looked perfectly in place, as if he slept standing up, or never slept at all. He was all that was comfort and composure, even in the dead of night with smoke pouring out of the windows of his hospital like steam from a boiling kettle. His voice was steady and calm, as always, and he extended his arms out as he began, like a preacher with his flock.

"All right, then. We've had a small fire, confined to an office, though the smoke seems to have snuck in under some doorways and through the wards to give us all a good scare. But none of us has been hurt, except by time spent out of doors on a cool night, and some files and patient notes that were burned and singed. I'm sorry you've been rousted out of bed in this weather and taken from sleep, but the county fire brigade has come and assured us all the nearby rooms are safe."

He smiled, she could see the expression clearly, even in the darkness, and brought his hands together in a way that signaled the end of the whole debacle. Celia looked up at the stars and drew the gown a little tighter near her neck. The moisture on her skin cooled her in the night air, and she shivered as she said goodnight to the stars and re-entered the asylum.

A shiver that continued when she felt the woman's chilly hand slip into hers, though she dared not look over as the ghost walked alongside her all the way back to her room. Cold breath of wind fingers slipping from her own the moment they reached her doorway.

She dreamed of fire for the next two nights, and all the dreams were the same. The old woman, the familiar woman, and Celia's inability to move forward or back, to speak, to engage at all beyond staring at the two phantoms. She'd seen ghosts since she was a girl, old men, young men, girls no older than three, and women her own age, all drifting by, stuck in this world, or on their way to the next. Women in bonnets and children in their Sunday best burying clothes and men with a pince-nez and confused expressions. As though they knew they were dead but couldn't quite remember why. Those ghosts had been the passing by kind. That's what her Papa had told her. He hadn't been able to see them, but believed that Celia saw them. He convinced his daughter that they were naught to be afraid of, just whispers and shadows of those that had lived, passing by the living, glad to be seen once more by anyone. Sometimes they moved about as they had in life, a circle of unending routine. A wife sitting next to her husband in a chair, keeping him ghostly company. Other times the ghosts would haunt one place—the place they died, or a place they were most happy in life, or just a place they were used to. Some ghosts, her Papa warned her, (though how he knew she never asked) were the message bringing kind. Spirits with something to impart, a mission they had to carry out that involved a member of the living. Her Papa would laugh then, and wink at her, his eyes finding something else to settle on. "Though the dead won't have anything much to discuss with one as alive as you." And she had been that lively girl then. When her parents were alive there was no such thing as a cloudy sky or a grey day, and tears were often just a heartbeat before a fit of giggles. Even when her cousin Algernon had drowned when they were children, and his tiny spirit had waved goodbye, or when her parents train accident came to pass, she had mourned but then looked forward. She had smiled through her tears, because she knew her parents would want her to, and death was not frightening to her. Not as frightening as life would become.

Because then, there was Simon.

Now, she dreamed of fire and of ghosts and felt the tug on her elbow, the delicate ghostly fingers twined through hers throughout those next two days, but she could not divine the meaning.

And it rained. Celia was surprised to awaken from crackling flames to the music of rain at dawn. A symphony of raindrops that was to Celia a funeral dirge, as there was no gardening in the rain. Instead, she was sent to help in rag folding, and then to the kitchens, though there wasn't much for her to do.

She spent the days sitting in an out of the way wooden chair in the bustling kitchen. Celia wondered about Annie and the fire that had been set. What office? Why? There were some whispers about it, but none loud enough to be caught in Celia's ears.

Sitting in her lonely part of the beautiful kitchen, she studied her shoes and the black and white marble tiled floor. She constantly reached back to fidget with her pinned hair that had grown longer and wild in the asylum. Her mother would have said it was the northern air, or that it was what came from smiling at a man you loved.

Loved.

Celia paused in the midst of her thoughts, eyes darting around the kitchen as if someone had overheard her mad imaginings. But she was nearly invisible in a pale grey dress that was neither pretty nor plain, but somehow designed for blending in. She chewed her lip, half hoping to draw blood, considering her inappropriate feelings for Mr. Flynn, it was a small punishment for herself, but she was too cowardly of the pain. Was it not punishment enough, that she was somehow brought to being ignored in a kitchen in a faraway asylum—though far away from what, she couldn't say. Home? She hadn't one. Home wasn't a place where one stayed, or one slept. It was a place of love and belonging and welcome, and she hadn't had one of those since before Simon.

Her mind drifted, and someone placed a colander on her lap and bowl at her feet. The colander was full of peas to shell, and she almost laughed. It was as mindless a task as she could have imagined. And then, she almost cried, for she knew that with the rain outside and the peas on her lap, there'd be no reprieve from her thoughts now. She had nothing else to hold her attention. So Owen Flynn rose again to her mind, to torment her no doubt, and she felt the clench of her stomach and the sparrow wing flutter of her chest, and then the past came, as it did, to break her heart.

The green of the peas bothered her, breaking into her thoughts of Owen. They were like the green of Simon's eyes. So her mind cast out to happier things, like wild strawberries that grew near the creek at her parent's house when she was small. They had lived in lots of houses, always moving around. Her papa said they were restless folk, and that there were a lot of places worth living in, so how could he bear to stay in just one? And so they moved and moved, and traveled and explored, and home was something that they brought with them, from one place to another. But those strawberries tugged her memory, and made her sadder somehow. She wondered if another child was picking them now, or what family lived in that white and blue house with a creek. Celia was an orphan now, though it seemed strange to call herself so as a grown woman. But if she traveled far enough into a specific memory, she could almost touch her parents again.

Her hands were touching the cold sterility of the colander, but they were also pushing sticky blackberries into her mouth as she and Papa picked them for jam, putting a finger to his lips as he did, so that mama wouldn't know. They were on a train next, and the smell of the burning coal makes Celia wiggle her nostrils. The train is loud, like a stampeding herd, but the only sound in their carriage is mama turning pages of a book and papa sketching the scenery as it passes. But no, she looks at the creamy page and smiles, he has been drawing her.

Celia smiled wider, and then it faltered. They'd met the Greens on that trip to Europe. Her parents had been tickled to find people from a nearby city. Celia felt the tears start to collect as she remembered her parents initial pleasure which had turned to wariness. She'd been so young, so flattered by the Greens, so taken with Simon. He was everything a young man was supposed to be, but her parents had seen it, somehow. And then, after they died, she'd betrayed them. She bit her lip in earnest now, and tasted blood, her tears falling amongst the peas.

Her betrayal to them. The words she said—the promises made and then broken—they struck like a knife in the heart that's been turned in the wound. It would never close, nor heal, only remain, gaping and bloody and unforgivable. The pain sharpened so that she thought she might collapse from it. The memories laid on her chest like stones, piling, one by one, until she was gasping.

Someone took the peas from her then, and she thought she saw some of the other patients Annie had introduced her to through the haze of tears. She never made a sound as the nurse led her into her room, unpinned her hair and helped her into a nightdress. She bade her lay in bed and tucked her in as though she were a child, and then put something on her tongue, and Celia knew no more.

Flowering Almond: Hope

2011

The next afternoon after their meeting, she looked up from the computer at Folded Corners to see Eric entering the shop. He was holding a large envelope, and he kept it close to his chest as if it were a baby bird or an infant. He didn't seem to notice her for a moment, his eyes hungrily sweeping shelves and stacks. He then seemed to physically re-focus himself, and he looked to her, seated at the back of the shop to the left, tucked away as to "not be distracting", as Mr. Scott, the owner, had said. He used his index finger to push his glasses up on his nose and walked toward Eve, though his every movement looks to be a struggle not to burst into sprints until he reached her desk.

Eve wondered what it would be like to contain so much energy all of the time. Like a lit sparkler or a slingshot pulled all the way back.

"Hi" she offered lamely, eyes wide and unsure. She was surprised and a little taken aback. The book shop was one of her 'safe places', where she felt in control and in charge of her surroundings. But now, he was there and she felt oddly as though she was a little more uncertain than she'd been a moment ago, emailing a Signor Grimaldi about a rare copy of Italian Folktales she'd finally located.

"Hi" he replied back, and then turned around to look about the small book shop in a way that made Eve think he was searching for someone. He turned back and raised his eyebrows. "Alone then?" He asked, his voice quiet. She nodded, and narrowed her eyes, feeling the lines form unattractively in her forehead.

He darted one more glance around and then, seemingly satisfied, brought the large envelope on to the desk and leaned in so close she could see the golden lights of his eyes. Without meaning to, she leaned in closer as well, elbows on the desk, wondering what secret information he'd come to her with.

"Sorry for showing up like this," he began, not looking sorry at all, "…but I took an early lunch and left Miriam…" She gestured for him to get on with it, and he swallowed, his face breaking into unrestrained excitement. "…right, well, I did some digging in the archives and I found a couple of leads I still need to follow up on. But what I *did* find is the record of an 'Annie Barnsley', being treated at the Northern Michigan Asylum. She was one of the earliest patients. She was admitted in 1885 and then apparently, cured, or moved to another facility, because she was checked out in 1888.

Eve had a tingling sensation roll up her spine like static electricity, and she shivered. She hoped that the woman had been sent home cured, or at least back to a loving family who wanted to care for her. But what if…she shook her head. Morbid thoughts would do no good.

She nodded to him instead, and brightened her expression, shooing dark wonderings away.

"But, that's marvelous! However did you find that? The surname and initial are a perfect match."

He smiled, wide and warm and reddened a little.

"Oh, it was simple enough. Her family was apparently a big deal in meat packing in Chicago, sent her up to the asylum, real hush-hush. But because she was important, or at least, her father was, the hospital obviously took great care to keep good records of her. Though… her record is a little, mysterious. Looks as though whatever she was suffering from was also kept pretty quiet, which must have meant it was something…somewhat shameful."

Eve rolled her eyes. "Everything was shameful in the 1800s. Tying your shoe and showing your ankle or getting mud on your hem was inherently sinful. Women were put in asylums for reading novels and being too enthusiastic about religion. Men are frequently needlessly ashamed of women."

He laughed, but hollowly. "True, you're right. But, nevertheless, we are talking about the 1880s.

So, I suppose I should have said her family thought something about her was shameful, and as a result, used their clout to keep the records frustratingly vague."

Still simmering in a little righteous indignation, Eve cleared her throat, and returned to the matter of A. Barnsley and any other clues. "Are most of the records lost then? If the patient was not 'important'?" She asked, tucking a lock of unruly hair behind her ear.

"Not, it's not as if they were shoddy record keepers, but the name of the asylum changed through the years, different doctors were more meticulous and precise in filing and maintaining records—and expectations for paperwork changed as well. There seems to have been a small, contained fire in 1888, strangely enough, and some water damage in other years. Some files and patients are easier to find than others, and, luckily for us, Ms. A. Barnsley was one of them."

She couldn't help but allow herself a small smile in return for him using 'us', though she felt extremely silly. He was looking at her now, waiting for questions, or ideas, and she thought a moment, a nagging idea from earlier resurfacing. Meeting his eyes, she said.

"Let's have a look at that letter from A. Barnsley one more time."

She stood up and retrieved the leather envelope from her book bag, unfolding it carefully.

Dear Celia,

I hope I am not presumptuous in using your first name, but you did me the courtesy of introducing yourself when we first met, and somehow it seems more correct to be writing to a friend. Even if we are not acquainted enough to be called such, I know that you were a friend to my sister.

I have used the past tense, Celia, for she is no more. She has ended her own life in the Cook County Asylum. She spoke of you fondly, admiringly even. I wish you could have known her before. Before her illness, of course, but especially before… well, I'm sure you understand what I am referring to.

She was sunnier than a clear noon day sky. But now she sleeps, though I much doubt it is with the angels, for they would be too tame of companions for her. Thank you for befriending our dear girl, and I pray that your trouble, whatever it is, may soon be put right so that you may live yourself, and for her.

In friendship,
A. Barnsley

"It is a strange letter," Eve said, after reading it aloud. "And I do not know how we did not see it before, probably we were wrapped up in our mystery that we weren't paying attention, but this A. Barnsley is definitely a man, and he is writing to Celia about the death of his sister, Annie."

Eric sat back in his chair and brought one hand to cover his mouth. "Holy shit, you're absolutely right. I…I didn't even think of it, I guess because the style of writing back then is always so flowery and lovely it…seems…feminine? Is that all right to say?"

She laughed, and handed over the letter to his outstretched hand. He squinted as though he were seeing through the paper it was written on into the past itself.

"Yes, a strange letter and a sad one. It strikes me as unusual how blunt he would be to send such a letter to a patient in an asylum."

Eve leaned in closer and peered over the letter in his hands again. "It seems pretty obvious that they had met though, at the asylum, and if he didn't know Celia, then he felt as if he did in some way. Notice, he says 'trouble' and 'put right', and not 'affliction' or 'healed' or any of the medical words one would expect..."

Eric suddenly had an odd look in his eye. "Unless..."

Eve looked at him, one eyebrow raised speculatively.

"Unless he *knew* she wasn't crazy."

The truth hit Eve like a mighty gust of wind, leaving her off-balance. Eric warmed to his idea, pushing the glasses up on the bridge of his nose, and began ticking a list with his fingers.

"As you mentioned earlier, people, especially women, were shut away in asylums for all kinds of incredible reasons. Depression, tuberculosis, imaginary female body trouble, over-action of the mind, jealousy, tobacco usage, masturbation, hysteria....Hell, I read about a woman up here at the asylum who was put away because her parents were cousins."

"That's ridiculous!" Eve cried, and put a hand to her chest.

"What's ridiculous?" a voice from the door asked.

Eve looked up to see her father. Salt and pepper hair with a trim little mustache, he looked worried, and immediately stepped forward to assess the situation.

Eric looked from Eve to the newcomer and back again, and must have found the resemblance, because he exhaled, relaxed. Eve wondered for a moment why he could have been unsettled at all, and then colored. Gross. He had probably thought her father was her boyfriend. Ugh.

But why would he care?

Her dad was already introducing himself. He was a charming guy. Her mom always said he "couldn't help but flirt with the world." He smiled expansively at Eric after a moment. "Shopping for old books?" he asked, his voice suggesting he knew Eric was not. "Eve's got the oldest books in town—save the library. But they don't let you buy those, unless they're roughed up and discarded for the book sale. Barely let you look at the ones worth looking at though."

Eve bit her cheek so as not to laugh out loud. Eric smiled at her father and surprisingly, agreed. "You're right about that, sir. We do have a bad habit of hoarding the delicate ones. We'll get them all online someday soon, I hope."

Her dad looked at Eve, questions written clearly on his expression, and she explained.

"Eric works at the library, Dad. We're…we're working on a project together."

Her Dad nodded, and from the look on his face, Eve thought if he could spin his mustache, he would. He extended an eager hand.

"Sal Parish, I'm Eve's father."

"Eric Chapel, I'm…I'm the head of Library Technology for Grand Traverse County and…I'm Eve's friend."

Sal Parish waggled his eyebrows at the both of them and pulled a paper bag out of his pocket.

"A sandwich for you, my dear one. I'm going to get some cider from that place your mother likes out in Suttons Bay and then I'm for home. Are you… having dinner with us tonight, darling dear?

He was asking Eve, but his eyes were on Eric, who, like an actor in a poorly acted play took his cue and cleared his throat.

"If it's all right, Mr. Parish, I was going to ask Eve if she'd have dinner with me on Front St. tonight so we could discuss our project."

Eve's dad shrugged and turned to leave. "Well, go ahead and ask her then, it's nothing to do with me." He winked at Eve and left.

She couldn't stop herself from laughing at Eric's expression. "Yes, I'd love to. Don't mind Dad. He's refreshingly progressive about women. Doesn't go in for any of the 'ask the father' nonsense."

Eric nodded and then they were both quiet, unsure what to say. The ghost of her father's presence hovering about them still.

"He…he worries about me," she said reluctantly, and a little pathetically.

"Fathers generally do that," he said, shrugging.

"No, not like that, I've…I've given my parents cause for worry. Not…not always, you understand. But, I had a rough patch."

The moment was quiet, and the shop suddenly seemed too small, the books oppressive, the stone walls heavy and closing in around her. She was inside again, trapped, broken…

She felt a hand on her arm.

"It doesn't matter. We all…make mistakes, and it never gets less lame to say that out loud, but it's true. Miriam has some stories about me that would probably make you lose my number in a second."

He smiled and adjusted his glasses again, his blue eyes peeking expectantly from behind the lenses.

Eve exhaled, feeling awkward, but also…slightly better. "Thanks, seriously, and now, about dinner…?"

"Great, yeah. Say 7? I'll meet you outside the State Theatre on Front Street." He smiled then, again, one she hadn't seen before. A boy's smile that was hopeful and unrestrained.

"I'll bring some files and…we'll talk."

As he turned and headed out, stopping once at the door and waving once more, some tourists wandered in, hand in hand. Eve greeted them, saw immediately they weren't the buying kind, and then relaxed back into her comfortable seat thinking about how quickly the air had changed. The store was no longer oppressive, she was no longer panicked. Her secret was still hers—though she knew it would have to come out if there was... another date. Was that what it was tonight?

Scared and hopeful, she bit her lip, eyes moving to the back of the shop, searching for a distraction from her thoughts. Celia. Where had she gone? Where was she from? And why had she hidden traces of herself away?

If Eve believed in ghosts, she might think that Celia's spirit wanted to be found. *If* she believed.

Tuberose: Dangerous Pleasures
1888

When Celia awoke the next morning, the sun was shining and she felt a bubble of joy gather within.

She jumped from the bed, washed and dressed and was ready the moment Nurse Dockert unlocked the door. The nurse offered a faint smile, or at the very least, a look of approval, and pinned a few pieces of Celia's hair a little tighter. She led her outdoors to Mr. Flynn and Celia thought perhaps there was a difference in the nurse, as though she'd melted a little toward her.

"Take care to stay out of the mud, Mrs. G" she called back to her. She gave Mr. Flynn a wide-eyed look that contained a message Celia couldn't read.

"I'm so glad to be back at work" Celia said earnestly the moment Nurse had walked out of earshot. Owen nodded, but didn't meet her eyes as they headed for the shed to collect their tools.

Normally Owen was singing by now, and Celia could feel the creeping of something amiss. She pulled the leather work apron over her old green dress and drew her gloves on quickly, before blurting out.

"Is something the matter?"

She looked at Owen's eyes, willing him to look back. It appeared he was going to deny it, but then shook his head and met her gaze.

"There is Miss...Celia." His voice sounded sad and his eyes had dark circles beneath as though he hadn't slept since she'd last seen him.

"What is it?" She asked, her voice quiet but steady. The morning was still cold and the grey dawn matched his eyes. It felt like the gardens had not forgiven the sky for so much rain, and the sun was hiding, ashamed of itself.

He sunk the shovel he'd been holding into the soil, so that it stood mostly upright, and turned to face her.

"Celia, *why* are you here?" He asked, his eyes fixed to her face, as though he might glean the answer there before she could speak.

She bent down at the edge of the herb garden, wishing it was flowers they were working with, but also aware that the bright colors could not improve her mood. She sighed, loud and long, pushing the sorrow that sat on her heart out, out, past her lips, if only for a few moments before it gathered again. He didn't move, but instead waited, patiently, knowing that she would tell him.

And she would. Truthfully, she was glad to be rid of the secret of it. Unspoken it hung on her like a wet dress, weighing her spirit down. She wanted the truth out, more than anything, wanted him to know even if in the telling of it, he believed her mad.

But she could not tell *all*, not today, not even to him. She sighed again at this knowledge, and called what she could safely disclose to mind.

Celia motioned for him to kneel down near the thyme, and swallowing her hesitations and biting back half the truth, she spoke.

"I am here," she began, voice low but clear, "because I am an unhappy creature. And I have stumbled into a trouble that is too big for me, and I was too wrapped up in my own fear to see what was happening until it was done."

It looked as though Owen might speak, his bottom lip separating from the top, but she rocked back onto her shins, shoulders back, and narrowed her eyes in a way her mother had used to do that signaled quiet.

"I have not always been a melancholy thing, though my life, now that I think of it, has always held some tragedy. My cousin died—drowned—before me when we were children, in the lake outside our home. But at least then I still had Mama and Papa and we loved one another completely."

She paused, realizing she'd answered none of his question, and then reddened. He looked up at her face, willing her to continue, and she sighed inwardly and licked her lips. Owen removed some brown leaves on a creeping piece of sage and Celia spoke on.

"I met Simon on one of my family's trips. He was charming and handsome and made me feel as if I was important..." She saw Owen's jaw clench, but he said nothing. "...and I was young and naïve. My parents didn't take to him. And then they died, quite suddenly, in a train accident."

She felt the tears then, but did not brush them away. Celia was glad to shed them, for inside each teardrop was a liquid memory of her beloved parents.

He reached out toward her, but did not move closer, nor did she move toward him. She did not want comfort for their deaths, nor did she deserve any. Her sorrow was its own kind of comfort.

"I'm...I'm so very sorry, Celia..." he began, but she shook her head and swallowed her grief like stones down her throat.

"No, no. You've asked why I'm here, and I've still not yet told you."

He pulled his hand away, slowly, and returned awkwardly to his task, but she could see his fingers were not as nimble as they usually were, and his hands seemed to fumble at the leaves.

"After the accident...I was not myself. I was mourning, certainly, but still...optimistic about my future. But something was missing, and one day, Simon reappeared, and he, well, he convinced me that I belonged with him. He can be so very charming, so…convincing. He made it easy to go along with whatever he wanted, I fairly forgot myself, I daresay. I had really nowhere else to go, you see. No other family. I…I did not know what else to do. The Simon I'd met abroad was affable and gentle and beautiful. I knew him to be only that. Even if his suggestions and words sometimes seemed…peculiar or, sometimes even amoral, he always had an answer for everything. Do you know the type? The kind that convinces you black is white, and you go away wondering how you ever thought it was other than how he said."

Celia faltered, she looked at her gloved hands but her vision was hazy behind her tears. Owen said nothing but she could feel him watching, waiting for her to finish. She took a deep gulp of air and exhaled a ragged breath out, determined.

"Owen, he was not the gentleman he pretended. He is…a monster. He was and is unkind to me in every way and in ways I cannot fully describe the horror of." She shuddered as memories flew into her mind like flies, buzzing and swarming. "The things he did to me…the way he treated and spoke to me…I would not do the same to a mangy, rabid dog. He…he…he used me worse than a whore." Her words were so quiet that she wondered if she'd had the courage to say them out loud. One glance at Owen confirmed she had. His stone eyes were hard and intense, they blazed like iron at the forge, and his knuckles were white around the spade they held, so white it appeared he'd squeezed the skin off completely and what she saw now was bone.

"All of this, I could have borne, I swear it. I did bear it. But I saw what a brute he was to…to others as well. He beat me down into believing I was nothing, that I was too damaged and unworthy to be a wife, or a mother, or even alive or loved—by anyone. I was a little insane even before this though. I've always seen ghosts, heard them. This too, he taunted me with, used as proof that I was defective, broken, worthless. But I was never haunted until he came into my life. I began to speak of the ghosts freely and wailed, sobbing all night, until I could cry no more, and I became a ghost myself. Floating through the rooms, silent, trembling, empty.

She met Owen's eye, unflinching. "I am here because I am mad, but it is because he has made me so."

They did not speak for some time, both mindlessly poking at the dirt. Some minutes later, when she could bear it no longer, she looked up to catch his expression, hoping to divine his thoughts. But the more she looked, the more confused she became.

"Owen," she said finally, "what are you thinking? Perhaps I ought not to have told you."

Panic seized her like a grip around the waist, a panic that pounded in her chest and made her want to run, but she was held fast to the spot, just as she was when she was amidst the fire of her dreams. This felt like that same moment, surrounded by panic and nowhere to go, nowhere to hide. She had said too much after all, she had not held back enough. Now, there was nothing to do but face the moment head on, facing the flames of her own confession. She let out a breath she hadn't known she held and waited.

"What am I thinking?" He stood up, stretching his broad shoulders and cracking his neck back and forth. He met her eyes. "I am thinking that there is some madness in all grief. That tragedy and the evil of others has never followed logic. I think to react any differently to your treatment by this...this villain...would be true insanity." He paused, and she felt he looked straight into her heart, "I am thinking you are very brave, and very beautiful, and that you do not belong here at all."

"You would send me home?" She asked, eyes wide and voice afraid.

"No, I would keep you with me always. And it is my own madness to admit such a thing."

She smiled a small smile that filled her with light, she thought she might be so happy that she might stop breathing, or that she would wake up and find that he had never uttered such lovely, powerful words to her at all. "You believe me, then?" she asked, "Even with my ghosts?"

It seemed incredible, and she waited, wondering if like Simon he would now laugh, telling her what an enormous idiot she was. But instead, he cocked an eyebrow up and tilted his head to the side as he stepped over for a watering can.

"Ghosts? Don't we all have them? If they're a sign of madness then all of Ireland should be locked up, I'd reckon."

She smiled wide then, and felt the ripple of laughter rise in her throat and float out her lips. Then she looked down, and poked her trowel into the herbs ineffectually.

"I would stay with you, if I could. You and your flowers and your singing," she admitted quietly, shocked at her own boldness.

"Then we shall aim to make it so," he said, cryptically, and then winked at her, as if sealing a promise.

They planted and weeded and picked herbs for the kitchens for the rest of the afternoon. They spoke of Western Ireland and of the wide ocean and memories recalled that had been long forgotten. The feeling settled over Celia that it seemed unbelievable that she had not known Owen Flynn her whole life. Perhaps her soul knew his, she thought. For their spirits seemed familiar to one another in that unexplainable way that feels true and right from the moment two people meet. A spark, a recognition, and then the comfort of a feeling that should have taken more time to grow, but like a dandelion in a field, sprouts overnight and grows hardy. She ached to ask him what he had meant by his strange comment, but did not. Some moments are so fragile they must be held loosely in an open hand, lest they be crushed by trying to seize onto them too tightly.

As the late afternoon came, Owen walked over and held out a dirt-covered, freckled hand to help her up. Her small gloved hand practically disappeared into his large paw, and the touch gave her such a thrill that she could almost pretend she was still a silly young girl, about to be led out to dance. She wished, suddenly, that she did not have the gloves on. She stood up and tilted her head to see into his face. Those inscrutable grey eyes, that she could not read though they hid nothing. She noticed too, the hints of blue like pebbles in a stream, the same forget-me-not-blue of the gardens was contained in those eyes. It was unbelievable how much warmth could be inside those water and stone eyes, as if they'd been soaked in all the sunlight of the day and held the heat there in his gaze.

She opened her mouth to speak, but Nurse Dockert appeared to take her in to supper.

That night, she did not dream of fire or ghosts.

Cypress: Death

1888

Annie was at breakfast the next morning. Celia had been brought in at her appointed time from the grounds, only to find Annie Barnsley sitting down to a bowl of porridge with fresh cherries on top, looking for all the world as though there was nothing strange at all in her sudden reappearance in the dining hall.

Celia was elated. She caught her friend's eye and Annie smiled just as she had the first time they had met. Celia brought her plate, with jammy toast and a hard boiled egg and sat across from Annie, mouth never completely closing from the shock.

Annie looked drawn and exhausted, as though she'd been wrestling demons for days on end, but her eyes were bright, her smile broad and this comforted Celia.

"Hello, dear! Where on Earth have you been?" Annie exclaimed, sticking a heaping spoonful of porridge into her mouth and then continuing to speak. "It's all been dull without you! One evening you were there, meeting the whole gang, as it were, and then, POOF! Disappeared like a puff of smoke!"

Celia felt her forehead crease and her eyes squint together in confusion. She dropped the slice of toast she had been bringing to her mouth back onto her plate. What in the world could she mean? She had been exactly where she ought to have been. *Annie* had disappeared. Annie had been the one brought out the night of the fire, eyes blank, tongue lolling and moaning as if she were terribly ill.

For the briefest of moments, because of the certainty in Annie's voice, Celia worried. Perhaps... she was mad. Perhaps, it *was* she who had disappeared...

No. It is folly to begin down that path of doubt. Annie had been ill. Annie was the one who had been missing, despite whatever she now claimed.

She was tempted to speak all of this aloud, but something in the paleness of Annie's skin, the hollows in her already thin, angular face stopped her.

"Well, I've been busy, Annie. I have missed you, though."

Annie smiled and nodded, taking another hearty bite. "Will we see you for embroidery this evening in the common room?" She asked, and the look on her face was bored, but beneath it Celia glimpsed a straining hope that confused her more than ever. Annie Barnsley was certainly a strange girl, but Celia could not help but like her and be glad of their sudden friendship. She treated the asylum like a soiree or a spa. Someplace to gossip and form cliques. There was something refreshing in that outlook that gave Celia a little of her old self back, and so she readily agreed that she'd be there in the common room that evening.

They both finished their breakfasts, amidst meaningless prattle that made Celia forget for a few moments together that this wasn't simply a morning visit with a friend. Annie spoke of an absurd orange bombazine dress her mother had worn to a dinner party, the way her sister's husband's nose seemed to be ceaselessly running, and a little black terrier who'd she'd trained to bite heels on command.

"I'd say, 'Rags! Bite!' and he would trot right over to whomever I was pointing at and nip their heel. Drew blood sometimes. It *was* rather wicked, but he always seemed so *pleased* with himself. You can hardly fault me for not wanting to steal a dog's greatest happiness, can you?"

Celia had giggled and shook her head, assuring Annie that she had been completely in the right. And then a nurse came and fetched Annie, who rolled her eyes dramatically, as children do when their mother calls them in from play.

"All right, Celia dear, until later."

As Annie walked away, Celia noted again how thin and fragile she looked, and wondered what had really happened. Had the consumption returned? Surely not, she would be quarantined if it had. She looked down at her empty plate and sighed. Annie's hearty voice and cheerful conversation belied the truth of her illness, whatever it was. Annie was a puzzle, and perhaps it was not meant for Celia to solve.

As she stood up, lost in thought, Nurse Bell came toward her, ready to walk her back to the grounds. Just before she left the dining room, her eyes fell on Myrtle and Caroline, the women Annie had introduced her to that night. Celia paused a moment and said hello, bowing her head slightly, deferentially, to Queen Caro. She and Caroline exchanged good mornings, but Myrtle was silent and distracted, hardly even seeming to realize that Celia was there at all. She said goodbye to the ladies, and walked toward the door, more confused than ever. She paused, bringing both feet firmly together, as though knowing she had to stand her ground against the answer to a question she had to ask.

"Nurse Bell" she said, turning toward the same nurse who'd shared the uncomfortable room with her and Simon, "what is the matter with Myrtle?"

She tightened her lips in response. "That's none of your concern Mrs. Green." Her voice was not unkind, but rather the reply seemed a refrain.

"I know, but can you tell me, has something happened?" She made her voice small and her look guileless. Nurse Bell pressed lightly on her back, prompting her to continue walking forward.

She was quiet for a moment and Celia had given up on finding out anything, when she answered, her voice just above a whisper.

"Mrs. Green, I suppose it wouldn't hurt to tell you that Miss Sarah Childs has died."

When Celia looked back at the nurse, confused, Nurse Bell leaned in a touch closer and whispered, "She that was blind?"

And Celia nodded, thinking. She felt a sharp pang of sadness, though not because she mourned the woman, she had only met her the once, after all. Instead, the sadness was from the realization that people died in the asylum. Could die there. Locked up instead of free.

And some of those at the Northern Michigan asylum would prefer this, she knew. The asylum was their home. But not hers, please God, not hers.

"When?" she asked, suddenly, Owen only a few yards away. Nurse Bell frowned and looked away. "The night of the fire, it was."

And smiling at Mr. Flynn, for no one could possibly look at him and not do so, the nurse walked away without another word.

Celia closed the gap between her and Owen, and reached out for the leather apron that he held out to her.

She let it slip through her fingers and gave a tiny shriek, just loud enough to twist Owen's face into worry, and he reached for her as she began to swoon. Quickly, she revived herself, shaking off the fuzzy edges of her vision and stood back up, his hand still on the small of her back.

"What is it? What's wrong Celia?" He asked, his voice full of sudden fear.

But she couldn't say. Not even to him. Blind, milk-eyed Sarah Childs had died the night of the fire. The same night she'd seen her with the ghost woman, in her room, surrounded by leaping flames.

Marigold: Despair

1888

The summer days could have blended together. The sun's heat producing an unladylike sheen on her forehead, arms, and the back of her neck as she toiled. The breeze off the bay would then take its turn, cooling her as the winds turned. They could have blurred together, but they did not.

For one, Celia learned something new of Owen each day. The way he bit his lip a moment before he answered a question, or how he tilted his head a fraction when setting a plant in its place in the soil. Or the way he threw his head back and laughed with abandon at his own stories, right in the middle of the telling, and his whole face would light up as Celia told something of her life, as if he was committing it to memory. As though what she said was important to him, her voice as essential as the sun to the flowers they planted. And his connection to the soil and the things he grew in it seemed to hold a kind of magic. He would look up at the sky and seemed to almost speak with the sun and clouds above, instructing them to shine brightly on certain plants, and cover others so they wouldn't burn.

She also learned about his mother, who'd since moved over to the east side of Michigan, on Lake Huron with three cats and four basset hounds in tow. "She says she prefers sunrises to sunsets," he told her, and then he'd grinned, probably picturing his mother and her animal brood. He claimed the sunrise over Lake Huron was magic, but for himself, he liked to see the day crash to an end in a blaze of orange, pink and bright red glory over the horizon. Celia told him she wished she was a fast runner, or had a team of speedy horses for she would like to see the sunrise over Huron and then race across the state to see it set over Lake Michigan.

He smiled at her then, and gave her one of his looks. The expression on his face saying all the same things that whispered in her heart.

Why hadn't she met Owen Flynn when she was young? Would she have seen his worth then? A burly, red-haired gardener at an asylum in Northern Michigan? But, no, back then he would have been a bright eyed medical student, as untouched by sorrow as she herself had been. Would she have loved him then, before it all? And every time she puzzled this, the answer was inescapably the same. Yes. She couldn't imagine a world where the goodness of his soul didn't shine through to even the blindest eye.

Her wonderings, doubts and fears stayed mercifully away when she was near to Owen, in his company alone, she could pretend there were no ghosts or asylum or madness in the world. But she had to remember that to all the world she was mad. She had Simon and all the wrong he had done her weighing her down—and all the wrong he'd made her do.

For all of this that pressed upon her, she did not allow the heaviness to consume her whole. No, there were lovely days, beautiful moments. But even when she was happily weeding or picking herbs or planting flowers at Owen's side, there were many other reasons the days of summer did not blur together.

She'd long since added Dr. Norbert to her puzzles. There was something about him that wasn't quite what it ought to be. Something nefarious and inordinately cruel. Everything from his looks to his character was in strong contrast to Dr. Munson, and whenever she'd catch sight of him in the ward or walking past the common room, she felt her entire body tense, and she scarcely breathed until he passed by. Though he was the doctor in charge of her, she had lately met with Dr. Munson, who spent most of their time together speaking of his family, or something interesting he'd read recently. Sometimes Celia would find that they'd done nothing but discuss *Huckleberry Finn* for forty minutes together. Whether it was part of her convalescence or simply one of the doctor's quirks, she didn't know, but she certainly felt much happier and more sane after discussing something interesting with the kind doctor.

Inside the walls of the asylum itself, outside of her time with Owen, or her scattered meetings with the doctor, Celia began to see that there was more happening than she had originally thought.

The ladies were gathered in the evenings, after the suppertime meal into the common room. There was normally a nurse or two, and a few orderlies wandering in and out as needed. To Celia they appeared to be more like furniture than staff. Functional, staid, solid, without much interaction with patients. They flanked the walls like side chairs, but she never saw them speak, and seldom caught them moving, only noticing they had left when they had already gone. Unless there was a problem patient—but those poor souls weren't fit company for the common room, and had their own room at the end of the asylum. Although, once in a while one of the more disturbed patients would be allowed in and generally sat silently, wide-eyed and listened as Celia played the piano or someone sang.

To an outside observer Celia supposed it would appear civilized, dignified, proper. But to Celia, some of the patient's brave attitudes did not seem altogether genuine. Those that were seen most often in Dr. Norbert's care were...odd. Even more so than she had originally considered for patients of the asylum.

She was particularly concerned for Annie. Something was terribly amiss. There were moments where she was the young woman Celia had first met, and others where she seemed like a foreign creature entirely. One day they'd share sparkling conversation over breakfast, but by supper time Annie was distracted and muttering into her soup. She'd make clever, pointed jabs at someone's expense, displaying an intelligence and wit that Celia admired, and then the next morning she'd barely speak, staring into the distance, or make quick, curt responses to Celia that punctured like barbs.

She would disappear for a few evenings together, and then re-appear, bleary-eyed and grey, her bones jutting out grotesquely. The next night she'd be sharp wit, talking animatedly with the other ladies. One night Celia found her trying her darndest to comfort poor Nelly Gromer, whose umbrella had been taken away quite ruthlessly, the loss of which seemed to have crushed her spirit completely.

Another night, Celia entered the common room to find that Annie was bowing to Queen Caro and asking her pressing questions about the state of her kingdom. "Your highness, how is the gooseberry crop this year? Bumper, I most fervently hope! And have you considered the suit of Prince Redmund of Aslingar? The way you described his proposal was quite romantic."

Celia looked on, nodding and smiling awkwardly, unsure how much of what Annie said she believed, or simply said to humor those around her. Myrtle had been crushed since the death of Sarah—a death that no one spoke about or accounted for. The nurses would shake their heads and change the subject, either looking away or smiling too broadly afterward.

One evening, a few weeks later, Celia found herself sitting next to an animated Annie, while she herself felt she must fight off the day's exhaustion like an underdog pugilist. It had been one of those sticky late July days where the breeze is too lethargic to blow, the air thickens in the golden sun, one's vision goes almost sepia and all around it feels like life has been dipped in honey.

She felt slow, tired and weighted down by her heavy clothes. Celia could feel the sweat still gathering everywhere under the suddenly too tight, too thick dress, even though she'd had a bath before supper. She couldn't wait for night to fully fall on these overlong days so that the cool of darkness would sweep over the oppressive heat like a broom and rush through the wards and corridors clearing the way for a cold night of sleep.

She intentionally widened her eyes once again and leaned a bit closer to Annie, hoping the proximity would aid her efforts to remain awake.

"...then there's my oldest brother, Clyde, he's to be a lawyer, and Edward, he's going into the church, though for what religion I'm sure I cannot say. And then I've told you about Alice before, she's the baby and an absolute brat, though of course she has all the looks in the family. Just like in the fairytales, you know? Where the youngest daughter is the fairest and all that? But the brother I wanted to tell you about is Andrew. He's just one year older than I am. Andy and Annie—it's so sweet I might be sick, isn't it though? Well, he's coming to fetch me..."

Celia straightened up.

"Coming to fetch you...from here? To take you...away?" She was legitimately horrified. Annie was not well. It was clear that despite what she had claimed, she did not have tuberculosis. Or, if she had at one time been sent here for that reason, it was not the malady that had kept her here at the Northern Michigan asylum.

"Yes, of course to take me away, you goose! I wrote to him and told him all about Dr. Norbert and his funny ideas and what he was trying to do to me..." Her voice grew very quiet, and her eyes flickered around the room, searching, as though the walls were listening and she cushions beneath them were spying.

"But, Annie...are you perfectly well?" Celia asked, eyes wide.

"'Am I well'?" Celia! What a question! Not all of us are as mad as a march hare! I'm here for treatment, as I told you, and my illness is cured."

She looked angry and her cheeks were red, her eyes wild. Celia nodded and leaned forward grasping her hand before Annie could yank it away, and squeezed it, suddenly afraid of the look in the girl's eye and the violence of her reaction. "Yes, of course, Annie. I'm....I'm glad for you, truly. Truly, I am. Only, you see, I'll miss you." She smiled, and hoped that it was convincing. "Promise me you'll write."

Annie nodded, rolling her eyes back into her head, communicating that she thought Celia was absurd. "Of course, Celia, of course." She patted her hand, patronizingly, and Celia swallowed, wondering if her fears were unfounded. Perhaps she wasn't leaving at all, and it was part of a delusion that her brother was coming. She certainly didn't seem like someone who was healthy enough to go back to the smoky streets of industrial Chicago.

But she pushed the thoughts aside, and they spoke the rest of the evening in hushed tones about books they'd read and loved, ("There was never a better story than "The Moonstone"!) and places they'd hoped to visit one day, (Celia waxed rhapsodic about visiting the pyramids and visiting the jewels of India, which seemed to bore Annie. For her, it was San Francisco, and Celia was given to understand she had a female relation there who chewed tobacco and wore dungarees and rode a horse bareback.) But the longer they spoke, the wilder Annie's eyes became, the paler her expression.

At some point, and Celia could not say precisely when, as she had been fixed on Annie's words as they ran from carefully chosen and clever to rambling, Dr. Norbert had entered the room. He wore a grim expression by the time his presence caught Celia's eye. He approached Annie, and motioned for a nurse to assist her to standing and bring her forward. When Celia stood to say goodnight to her friend, Annie's eyes were wilder and her skin appeared slick as if she were sweating.

As Annie was led away, like a convict to the hangman's noose, Celia felt the familiar tug on her elbow, and turning her head ever so slightly, she beheld the familiar ghostly woman. She motioned for her, unspeaking but almost imperiously, and without a thought, Celia followed the phantom, a tingling sensation at the back of her neck telling her that the spirit led her down a path she would not be able to retreat from. She was at the precipice, and inevitably, this decision would change her forever.

Stepping past the nurses, as if she herself were invisible, Celia followed the ghost out and into the emptiness of a remarkably unguarded and empty ward.

The spirit stepped silently and looked back from time to time to see that Celia was following her, as if concerned that Celia would not be able to keep up with her phantom feet. They walked down the corridor, past the dining hall, up the stair and over to a row of doors that Celia knew to be Dr. Munson, Dr. Norbert, Dr. Bixles and the other medical staff offices. The ghost paused at Dr. Norbert's office and disappeared through the door. Celia paused, looking around. She felt very vulnerable, and realized how unbelievably insane it would look—did look—to follow a ghost anywhere. Much less to trespass on a trained doctor's personal medical office. She envisioned the lock outside her own room clicking in place, closing her in, the hollow clank echoing in her ears. She felt cold all over, like she was being dipped in ice and fear like freezing fingers clutched the back of her arms, her neck, her palms.

The woman poked her ghostly head out the door and a thin, urgent hand beckoned. Celia exhaled and stepped forward. If she *was* mad, it was certainly too late to get well now. And if this was real, then who was she not to follow the directions of the dead? She brought her hand tentatively to the door and somehow saw it for the first time. Scorch. It had blackened around the edges, and as she turned the handle, it shuddered wearily open, the action painful for the marred wooden door. Stepping through the threshold, she was instantly hit by the smell of smoke, still strong in the room. Looking around, she noted the ghost was gone, at least for the moment. She coughed only a little, and as quietly as she could manage, the smoke still lingering about the space, the ghost of the fire that had been.

Celia brought the fabric of her sleeve to her mouth and took a deep breath, and then began to survey the small room, getting her bearings. The office was cramped, and patient files seemed to be everywhere, covering every surface. Some of the files were badly burned, some only partially so, and others were completely unharmed. It looked as though they were spread out because someone was inspecting and cataloguing the damage. She twisted her mouth to the side, determined, and stepped up to a pile of papers. The right corners of this specific pile were burned away, and one of the pages disintegrated in her hand. They appeared to be information on land—the land the asylum sat on, she discovered, reading further. She saw the name Perry Hannah and then a few notes about the hospitals in Pontiac and Kalamazoo and Celia realized it was probably simply bureaucratic information about the building of the hospital. Both hospitals were closer to the Green home in Detroit, and Celia had a sudden flicker of shame at her own ignorance. She'd been tricked into being sent all the way up north here, hidden away. But she could have been just as easily hidden closer to home. She should have known, should have suspected...

But she was glad of it. Overjoyed, really, that if she had to be locked away that it was far, far away from Simon and his family. She was tired of their awkward dinners, and the painful outings and all the pretending. She was sick of the life Simon made her live, the lie he demanded from her.

She sighed and ran her fingers along the tops of the files, keeping an anxious ear out for any sounds from the hallway. Her finger skimmed over one page, and with a tiny sliver of pain on her fingertip, she knew she had found it. Celia hadn't even known precisely what the ghost had her searching for, but the moment her finger caught the corner, it sliced in, and she pulled her hand to her mouth and tasted blood from the paper cut. It stung and the finger throbbed like a heartbeat. Extending her uninjured hand, she plucked the guilty file from the stack.

Celia Green

It was her.

She bent over it, finger still in her mouth and bleeding. Cautiously, she flipped it open, not knowing what she would find, unsure if she would like what she saw.

But, instead, she saw almost nothing. Just three slips of paper. The first was an official intake form, signed by both Drs. Norbert and Munson. A small piece of paper was clipped onto it, which was a note from Dr. Munson. It read:

John,
I understand that this patient has been admitted to your direct care as specified by her family. Please keep me apprised of her progress. I confess, I am puzzled. In our brief meetings, I can find nothing seriously amiss with her faculties, and am persuaded it can only be a melancholia that some fresh air and northern sunshine should soon remedy.
I hope I am wrong in my fear that perhaps she was admitted for reasons unrelated to her health.
—J. D. Munson

Narrowing her eyes a bit, she smiled. She could almost see the kindly Dr. Munson writing this note, perhaps as a hazy warning to Dr. Norbert that he did not see madness. This calmed her. Perhaps she was not what she imagined she must be. What Simon had told her she most certainly was. Carefully she placed this first intake form and note back into the folder, and took up the other papers within. They were both letters, and she recognized the handwriting. Both from Simon. She felt her stomach begin to sour. How was it that even the words his hand wrote filled her with such revulsion?

The first was dated the end of February, right when the illness had been its worst. Even before he had been sure, he already had been planning to be rid of her. Of them. She grit her teeth and read.

John,

You told me once that an asylum is the perfect place to vanish someone whom one wishes well rid of. I have need of a disappearance now. I know you will not refuse me, as there is between us a debt unpaid. Consider this the day it has come due.

If you are thinking that I too am implicated in the debt I speak of, I would caution you to recall what a careful man I am. It would not do to cross me, John. You aren't half clever enough to play my game.

I will arrive with your new patient within a fortnight. I will not telegram.

S. G.

Celia found that she was shaking, and that her forehead had begun to sweat. She felt ill, desperately, and fought the urge to lay on the cool tile floor until the nausea passed. What more could there possibly be to read? She took a deep breath and swallowed bile and then pulled her gaze back to the remaining letter.

This missive was dated only a month before. Not too long before Simon's last visit.

John,

I received your latest letter, and I must say I was furious when I came to read its contents. <u>You</u> presume to question <u>me?</u> She is there because I wish it, and you must fabricate a reason for her to remain there. Do it, and do not concern me.

She was witness to the event, John, and even an imbecile like you must realize that after it happened, she had to disappear. For all that she playacts at innocence and sweetness, she is a loathsome, clever creature. You must watch her more carefully. Do not allow her to be made a pet, it was a mistake I almost made—and it is vital to remember who is in control. She is wicked! I still hold your secrets, John. Fool that you were to entrust them to me, fool that you were to involve yourself and not expect me to hold it over you.

S.G.

Her mouth had gone completely dry, and her hands shook violently. It was clear. She was *not* mad. Not mad. If anything, his letters showed him to be the lunatic. Threatening, suggesting, admitting to his own evil in his treatment of her. She had been committed for convenience to a pleasant prison for diseased minds and made to believe she was unsound as well.

Simon *was* clever. An asylum was the perfect place to vanish someone—for who would ever believe a madwoman?

She tucked the letter back into the file and closed it, returning it to the pile she had taken it from. Then, thinking better of it, she pulled the two letters from Simon and the note from Dr. Munson out, folded them, and stuffed them discreetly and quickly into her bodice.

It had been quite a while since she had left the common room, and so far, she had not been missed, nor had anyone chanced into the hallway. She walked out, timidly, into the corridor, but the ghost was still nowhere to be found, and neither were any staff or other patients. She exhaled a great breath of relief and gently closed the office door behind her, a finality of the experience sounding in the metallic click. Celia stood against the wall for a moment taking gulping breaths of air like water, waiting for her heart to slow, waiting to master herself once again. She would not cry, or grow angry, for neither emotion would aid her now. She wondered what the secrets were that Simon held over Dr. Norbert, and thinking of the ghost, she thought she might already know. In which case—Simon could be as afraid of what she knew as she was afraid of him. But, he'd locked her away. Making all of her truths mad ravings, all of her confessions the ramblings of a lunatic.

She could wait. She could listen and watch and plan. Celia knew now that she wasn't mad, or, perhaps, she was, for only someone a little insane would have ever trusted Simon Green. But she didn't need an asylum—she just needed to escape from him and his nefarious plans. She had been placed here, disappeared here, and she knew that by hook or by crook, she would need to ensure that she vanished back out.

Ground Laurel: Perseverance

2011

Eve was standing outside the theater, looking into the bookshop window next door. It was a proper book store, this one on Front Street. With a brightly colored children's section and bestsellers mixed in with classics and staff picks. Not a chain bookstore, or an elitist specialty shop like Folded Corners. She bit her lip and rolled her cardigan sleeve down to look at her watch. She was exactly on time, which almost never happened, and she felt a little chilly in the cool summer evening air. She also felt a little foolish, standing there, trying not to look too eager or excited, but also trying not to look alone and pitiful. It was hard balance to strike, and Eve had never been much for balancing.

She hadn't grown up here, but something about Traverse City felt like home. Maybe because it was a city that paraded as a small town, complete with a picturesque main street and Lake Michigan waiting just behind the sweet shopfronts. It really was a lovely place, and even in the winter, when the tourists fled and the locals were left with snow piled along the roadsides and the frigid lake and slick ice on the back roads, she thought it was the perfect town. There was always the promise of summer here, and beauty abounded through the seasons. It was home now, she thought, and it did really feel that way, most of the time.

She checked her watch again. Two minutes past. Well, parking could be difficult downtown, especially now, in the summer, so close to the weekend. She was tapping her foot, and then, catching herself, she stopped and set her face carefully, looking back into the window of the bookshop as though she wasn't waiting for anyone at all.

"Sorry." She heard the voice behind her, his voice already sounded familiar to her ears and she smiled in spite of how foolish she felt to have arrived first. She turned around to face him as he continued speaking.

"Miriam couldn't find the keys to the lost and found and a woman came in— very upset, swore she'd left her purse in the library. I told her, no purse was turned in, but she insisted, and then Miriam couldn't find the key, as I said." He exhaled, spreading his arms wide, his hands upward in a physical apology. "Sorry, again."

She waved him off, as though she couldn't have cared less. "What happened?"

"I just told you" He said, uncertainly, giving her a strange look, "Miriam couldn't find the key to…"

"Yes, yes, I know. What happened? Was the woman's purse there?"

He studied her for a moment, an indecipherable expression on his face, and then he laughed, full and throaty. "It was on her arm, actually. Apparently she hadn't checked there, and we thought it was a different purse she was looking for, because surely, it couldn't be the one she was wearing before our eyes."

He laughed again, and ran a hand through his mussed hair, and she smiled. She rolled her eyes in commiseration, and he motioned for her to walk, and they fell in step, side by side on the sidewalk.

Eric asked her about the rest of her day, and she told him about the few other customers she'd had, and about a Mary Stewart mystery she'd been reading during the slow hours. He talked to her about a group of middle schoolers whom he'd caught doing something inappropriate behind the shelves. It was a nothing conversation. One of those not quite small talk type discussions, but something about it felt good to Eve. It felt so *normal*. She talked like this with her parents, and on the phone with some of her friends, but she realized as they walked that she hadn't made a new friend in years. That's what Eric felt like. Someone worth trusting and laughing with, and as small as it was…it was huge for her.

Trust was a tricky thing. You had to give it to someone in order to have something worth trusting. And Eve hadn't been someone worth trust for a while.

They settled into a cute bistro that she'd walked past with her dad a few weeks ago, and they were silent as they perused the menu. Other than that brief silence, the rest of dinner was full of conversation, though by the time she'd cleaned her plate Eve couldn't say what it had been about.

And then he pulled a small notebook out of his pocket. It was the type that has a ring along the top, like police officers use in movies to take witness statements, or reporters use on tv dramas when interviewing someone. He licked his finger and flipped the pages. Still talking about the year he'd come in second place in the town's cherry pit spitting contest, but her attention was centered on the notebook.

He'd found something. She could feel it. Eve didn't know if it was women's intuition or something more...supernatural, but the shiver down her spine told her that dinner was about to take a startling turn. He cleared his throat, suddenly, and she knew her suspicions were about to be confirmed.

She couldn't help but smile when he said, "So, I dropped back down to the archives today, and I... found something."

"Hmm, I had a feeling."

He looked at her curiously and smiled a lazy half

smile. "You did, did you? Well, your feeling was spot on. I think I may have struck asylum gold. Though, I hope you were not too attached to your Celia Green, because I think I may have found some distressing news about her."

Eve's throat became dry, and she reached for her water glass, and gulped down a few mouthfuls, and then wiped water from her lip. Sloppy, she thought. She huddled a little closer into her cardigan, and tried to discard the stricken feeling that had settled over her, like a shadow on a sunny day. She didn't really care about Celia Green, she told herself. It wasn't as if she knew her.

But something about that thought felt false. She'd seen her writing, had looked at her drawings, and experienced a weird kind of kinship when she had drawn parallels between their...experiences. She didn't want to hear bad news about Celia.

"Is it...very troubling?"

Her question gave him pause. He closed the notebook and set it on the table, looking at her carefully. "I think it is," he answered, finally. Not taking his eyes from her, he motioned to the waitress for the check, paid quickly, and stood up. The whole experience, from his answer to his standing up was perhaps thirty seconds, but it had seemed both shorter and longer as he had studied her the whole time.

"Let's take a walk" He said, as he helped her up from her seat. Their arms were linked as they walked from Front Street across the highway to the beach. They did not discuss where they were walking, instead both sort of following the other, or their feet having some silent communication that pointed them both toward the lake's edge. Eve walked the beach often, with the dogs, and in the winter she came with her parents when no one else was around. The beach belonged to you alone in the winter, only the odd passerby, who never seemed to wave or offer "good morning" in the cold months. As if the cold air froze their friendliness. But Eve liked it that way, the loneliness of it. Perhaps Eric could see inside her thoughts, or was thinking along similar lines, for after a few moments he said, "I'll be heartbroken when summer ends. I always am. I think about the beach and the festivals and taking out the boat all winter long."

His voice was a little sad, and the admission seemed as though it had been ripped from him, instead of volunteered, though he'd said nothing strange or embarrassing as far as Eve could tell.

"You wouldn't like summer all the time," Eve replied, surprising herself. "It's something you need to look forward to in a way that only shivering and snow drift days can bring."

He nodded, seemingly satisfied. "You're right at that. I couldn't imagine living…where'd you say? In the south? Louisiana and Texas was it? That kind of heat could drive you crazy."

She nodded, smiling slightly to herself. He had no idea.

"So, the news?" She asked after another few moments of walking. It was fully cold now, and fully night as well. The stars were out, bright and clear and the moon winked above them in a way Eve would have thought romantic if the unreasonably heavy sadness of Celia Green's affairs weren't sitting on her chest. He started to reach for the notebook, but then realized he wouldn't be able to read it in the dark and stopped suddenly, hand in mid air. The hand hung there for a moment, awkwardly, before he brought it up and ran it over the top of his head as though he'd meant to all the time.

He paused, mid step, and sat down on the sand, hugging his knees to his chest. She sat down next to him, closer than she would have dared normally, but beneath the stars with the moon in her eyes and the chilly air she grew brave.

"Tell me" She pressed gently, her words almost a whisper in the lake wind night.

He sighed and tapped the pocket the notebook was in, and then began to speak.

"I'm afraid, as I said, that it's not good news. I didn't realize until dinner how wrapped up you… we…both are in her story. It's just sad, you know. A lady—young lady, younger than us probably—sent up here, probably for some silly reason, tucked away. You know, Traverse City wasn't even officially a town yet in those days. You'd have to feel like you were at the ends of the earth almost. Abandoned by the world. Division street was literally the demarcation between the town and the asylum. The divide between them. The townspeople were a little…leery of the patients and the doctors. All foreign to them, strange, I'm sure the idea of a bunch of insane people living nearby wasn't popular with regular folk…"

His words drifted off, and his gaze was forward on the murky black horizon line that she couldn't see but knew was there, somewhere. The moon glinted off the waves, and the cadence of them lapping the beach was steady and regular as a sleeper's heartbeat. She wanted to ask him questions, but her voice felt rusty in her throat, and Eve realized she simply wanted to listen, to wait for the story to come from him however he wanted to tell it.

"I used to hate living here. Hate is a strong word. But I didn't like it much. I was one of those kids at school with big plans, and big ideas. I was going to go far away, be someone important. Live in a beach house in Malibu and surf every day or something cliché like that. High school kid stuff, you know? I was going to make a lot of money, or be really important. I didn't know how, I just knew I was going to be famous. It was important that people knew who I was."

She placed a hand on his arm. He laughed a little, at himself.

"And then I grew up. I realized that sort of thing doesn't matter, not really. But I also realized I'd spent so much time thinking about how famous I was going to be, and how successful, that I'd never ever thought about *how* I was going to achieve all that. I went to University, and then came right back here. I never left at all. All my big plans and ideas, stuffed right back into this small place."

He didn't speak again for a few moments. Eve didn't think he was feeling sorry for himself, but instead reflecting on choices. It was an easy thing to do in the dark near the water. It always made her a little emotional. The quiet, the steady beat of the waves, the way that night stole away some of your inhibition.

"It's not that small of a place" she said, after a time. "and there are certainly worse places to end up."

He reached up and grabbed her hand. "Oh, definitely. I wouldn't trade places with anyone at the moment." He squeezed her hand a little and she felt the blood rush to her cheeks.

She bit her lip, and looked up, deciding. Eve opened her mouth, prepared to tell him everything, and then he spoke again.

"Anyway, I'm sorry if that sounded maudlin. I didn't mean it to be. It's just…it seems strange to find myself here sometimes. Not that it's a bad thing," he said squeezing her fingers gently again. "But anyway, I do have that gloomy news to share."

Her mouth closed, silently, and she inhaled, drawing her whole story back into herself, and waited for him to begin what he'd learned of Celia's.

"So, this afternoon, I spent some time in the archives. The bus from the retirement home came by, and Miriam really enjoys chatting with people her own age, so I made myself scarce. I wasn't exactly sure what to look for, you understand. I'd tried some online research, but women are notoriously difficult to trace—historically, society isn't very good about making note of women, I'm sorry to say. But, anyway, I made no headway there really. I did find the husband, one Simon Green, but he seems like kind of a nasty piece of work. Some court cases for fraud, a criminal case, and then a strange death—I didn't look too much into him once I was sure he was out of the picture."

Eve furrowed her brow, but realized he couldn't really see her expression in the darkness.

"What do you mean?" She asked, her voice coming out a little louder than she intended, breaking through the night sharply.

"I mean, well, she disappeared. You saw the article from downstate…and well, there was one in the local paper here too, with a little more detail.I thought there could have been a misprint, but it seems that it was true. And she wasn't found. I don't know how else to say it. That second article was only slightly more forthcoming than the one from Detroit. And then—it seems like the whole thing was hushed up, because there was no mention at all of her disappearance after the second day they ran the story. It was only mentioned in the Grand

Traverse Herald, which was what the paper was called before it was changed to the name it has now. It was just a small piece, perhaps to prevent people from freaking out about an escaped patient…I don't know."

"Could there still be a mistake?" Eve asked, her voice a little high, slightly more excited than she had meant to sound. "Could that be why the story was pulled so fast? Perhaps she was found, or had never escaped at all."

She felt rather than saw him shrug in the darkness. "I really don't know, but, I don't think so. Finding an escaped patient would be news, it would make them look good, you know. Like, 'nothing to see here folks, all under control'. It's definitely weird."

They were silent for a few moments, the sound of the waves crashing loudly in Eve's ears. Definitely weird. She almost felt like someone was tugging her sleeve there in the dark on the beach, urging her up. As comfortable and pleased as she was to be holding hands in a romantic place with Eric, she suddenly felt as though she must get up and *do something*. Eve couldn't simply leave Celia and her mystery to sit on a shelf.

Reluctantly, she let go of his hand, and began standing up.

"Do you have to go?" He asked, his voice quiet. "I'm sorry if it's late, I admit I wasn't watching the time."

"It's not that," she admitted. "I was just wondering….did anyone else happen to go missing around the time Celia did? Any other patients? Anything like that?"

He stood up, sighing. "If I didn't know better, I'd think you were using me for access to the archives, and before you ask, yes, I have the keys to the library."

He sighed again, dramatically, and Eve laughed as they held hands and headed back into town for their cars.

"Who says you *do* know better. Your access to the archives precisely explains my interest in you."

He squeezed her hand, lightly, and her stomach leapt. And then she quickened her pace, that strange ghostly tug still pulling on her sleeve.

Crocus: Abuse Not

1888

As she found her way back to the common room she blinked her eyes rapidly and yawned. She was so fatigued from working outside, so absolutely overwrought from the files, and the ghost that led her a merry chase and followed behind her footsteps. She felt her very flesh drag at her bones in exhaustion.

A ghost appeared before the door to the common room, but only fleetingly, paying Celia no mind, and she shook her head smiling. That disinterested ghost was just about the least unusual thing she'd experienced that evening. In fact, it was oddly comforting. The ghost vanished into the door, probably searching for a relative who was now an asylum resident. Or perhaps the ghost had been an area fisherman who'd been curious about this hidden forest hospital and had decided to peek in before crossing over to the Lord. For most of her life, this had been Celia's experience of ghosts. Just a specter waiting on a street corner, or following a beloved daughter home from school, making sure she was safe from beyond. Perhaps a spirit idly wandering the streets, or riding on a train car, disappearing at the same stop forever. They were spirits to wonder about, to puzzle and to inflame her curiosity. No longer. Celia had her very own haunt now, and she didn't have to be curious, she knew who the woman was. But did she mean Celia harm? She had thought so, at first. But now, it didn't seem likely, instead it seemed that she was trying to offer some type of protection or message that Celia just wasn't clever enough to decipher.

She put her hand to the doorknob of the door that the ghost had just disappeared into, but found she did not want to enter. Inside the common room there was no Annie. Instead, there was only the sad shadow woman that was Nelly Gromer, umbrella-less and despondent. Nurses and orderlies who watched and listened but probably wanted nothing more than their dinner and their bed. A broken Myrtle, having lost Blind Sarah, and Caroline the Queen of the Northern Michigan Asylum, if nothing else. If Celia wanted her spirits lightened, then the common room was clearly not the place for that. A room of shattered lives was all that was behind that door.

She turned and looked to the left. A long corridor that turned into a hallway that led to the ward that housed her room. She knew she couldn't get in, as her room would most certainly be locked,

176

but she'd rather sit in front of her door and act the confused, soft-headed innocent than endure the common room. The ward seemed to stretch on forever, and she yawned in earnest now. She couldn't think, couldn't plan, not until her head was clearer, her mind sharper. For the moment, she was safe here. A prisoner, yes, but away from Simon was away from harm. She wondered what he would think of the fact that she felt an asylum for lunatics preferable to his company? Perhaps one or two of his mistresses would understand if they'd been around Simon Green when he was in a temper. When the handsome angel's face slipped off like water running down a hill.

The ward was darker than usual, but she saw something as she came closer to her door. A movement. Very slight, just the tiniest twitch of something—so minute she almost dismissed it as imagination, but it was not. It was the faint last frost on a winter's window before spring kind of sight.

Her own room lay just beyond, beckoning at the end of the corridor, closer to the stair. Before her, clearer now, was Sarah's ghost. Blind Sarah, Celia thought, what a ridiculous moniker. She was a little ashamed of herself for even thinking it, but she didn't know the woman's last name. Sarah's ghost was alone this time, and less foreboding than she had seemed in Celia's fire dreams. She was standing outside a doorway, her hands pressed upon the wood. There was something in the stoop of her stance and the way her wrinkled face set against the door that moved Celia. She looked fragile and cold, and about as steady as a toddler's legs. She was dead, Celia knew, she could feel the cold death of her spread across the ward like fog, but she was no less pathetic for it.

In the last moment, her head came up, vacant milky eyes that saw nothing, even beyond death, but Celia knew that the ghost knew she was there all the same. Inside the room, Celia heard voices. One was calm, kind and somewhat familiar. The other was low, but growing louder, it was deep and unnatural and angry, but Celia had no doubt it was a woman's voice. After a moment, she realized it was Dr. Norbert's voice that was calm and gentle, and this so jarred with her conception of him, of the letters she'd read, that she pushed next to the ghost and put her ear to the door. But by this time, she did not need to. The woman's voice was shouting, angry, snarling and venomous, though for all its volume, there was no strength behind the voice.

Then, somehow, she recognized it.

Pushing open the door she ran in, and surveyed the scene before her. Dr. Norbert bent over Annie who was writhing on the bed, her face grey and ugly. She looked to Celia to be half dead or more and moving farther in that direction every moment. "What have you done to her?!" Celia cried, just as Nurse Bell came to restrain her.

Dr. Norbert looked up at the sound of her voice, confused, eyes wide. He did not answer Celia, but instead nodded to Nurse Bell, who pulled Celia back into the corridor with a strength Celia could hardly believe the small woman possessed. Once she was back into the hallway, Nurse Bell's grip loosened, but her hand still grasped Celia's arm, leading her to her own room at the end of the ward.

Celia was shaking, but determined to master herself. Swallowing, she slowed her steps deliberately, so that Nurse Bell was forced to slow too, and turn and look at her. Nurse Bell was young, and would be pretty with her cap off, but at the moment she look harried and more than a little frantic. "Come now, Mrs. Green, I'm sure you've need of some rest."

But Celia did not budge.

"What was Dr. Norbert doing to Miss Barnsley?" She asked, her voice intentionally calm, yet firm.

"Come now, Miss, isn't any of our business. Dr. Norbert knows what he's about, and the morphine patients can be wild, you know."

Celia started to repeat her question, but then stopped, the truth clicking into place. She knew about opium, of course. Her father had told stories about it from when he had traveled in the Orient, and most of her favorite novelists had someone or another who was an opium eater. But morphine was newer, stranger, stronger. Annie was an addict, then. It explained her odd manner, her disappearances, her hollow health and frequent glazed expression.

She cleared her throat, threw off Nurse Bell's hand, and continued walking toward her room. The nurse didn't say anything about Celia's sudden action and probably, Celia reasoned, didn't even realize her slip of Annie's illness, or perhaps the woman thought Celia already knew.

Once locked inside the room, Celia waited until she heard the retreating footsteps of the nurse before she sat down in her little wicker chair grateful for the familiar harsh sound of the protesting woven wicker, and placed her hand over her mouth. As though she were holding in a scream of a thousand feelings and the beginnings of a hundred thoughts. But there was no sound. She no longer knew what to think. Dr. Norbert was wrong and hateful for trapping her here in the asylum when he knew she did not belong. His manner to her was strange, but perhaps this could be accounted for by the circumstances of her commitment to the hospital, worried that Dr. Munson would find out, that his lie should be discovered. He did not know how to behave around her. It did not make him any less odious to her, but it put him and his actions into a slightly clearer focus. She closed her eyes firmly.

Annie.

She knew not if she had truly written to her brother to come and fetch her away from here, but if so, was where she was bound better than the care she received here? She had thought Annie was her friend, but did madness and addiction know true companionship? Was it even possible that one could befriend someone who was a stranger to their very selves? She chewed her lip, ruminating, but also ashamed at the bent of her thoughts. Every soul is in need of friendship, just as when she thought herself mad, she did not think to deny herself the balm of fellowship and trust. Annie had lied to her, just as Dr. Norbert lied, just as Simon lied. But Annie was different. Her lies were not to give pain to Celia, they were to ease her own anguish.

Still, Celia felt that she was surrounded by deceit, and only Owen—dear, lovely, perfect Mr. Flynn— was a last ray of sunshine against that enveloping dark.

She was so tired, and yet there was so much to think on. To plan. To prepare. But not now, nothing useful could be accomplished on so much exhaustion and so little rest.

She smiled once more to think of Owen's blue grey eyes that looked precisely like the silver lining she yearned so desperately for in the stormy rainclouds of her situation. And then her smile faltered, and she brought both hands to her face and wept, as a child might. Wildly and madly as if her heart had been pulled apart and left broken in her chest.

Bud of a Moss Rose:
Confession of Devotion
1888

The morning had dawned bright and cheerful, ignoring the raging emotions in Celia's chest. She had joined Owen outside as usual, his whole being seemed to thrum with the beauty of the day. He was like the forget-me-nots in her eyes, blue like the calm of her father's love and she felt as though she couldn't catch her breath when his hands were close to hers in the soil. She tried to convince herself that she was corseted too tightly, but she knew that wasn't the case. Silly, daft, absurd…the way her own mind and body betrayed her even amongst the dark revelations of the night before.

She was in love with him.

It wasn't so much as a sudden, cheek-smacking realization, but instead it had slipped over her like smoke. She had noticed the feeling as it began gathering, those moments when they first met, but it had been so inconsequential, so easily waved away that she hadn't paid it much mind. But now it surrounded her on all sides, enveloped her utterly, until it became the air she breathed.

He was whistling this morning, every moment of him was music. Every so often a lyric he sang or two of another one of his mysterious Gaelic songs she loved so well. They were working on the grounds outside her window today. Celia had thought to point out her window, but felt shame in it. The letters, Simon's letters were tucked into the pocket of the green dress she used now exclusively for gardening. They almost burned at her hip, and she looked down every so often to be sure if her pocket hadn't caught fire.

The desire to show Owen was overwhelming. Proof! Evidence that she was not mad, but was trapped here, that nefarious deeds had led to her imprisonment. The thoughts tumbling away in her head mingled with the sound of Owen's voice, his presence, the heady scent of the flowers and the wind in the trees—it overwhelmed her utterly. Celia rocked back onto her heels and drew the dirt covered gloves off her hands. She let her eyes trace the tops of the pine trees. How different it would be to be guarded only by the wood, the sloping hilly forest beyond, hemmed in by the lake. That glittering blue, the same as the forget me not flowers and the calm of the man she loved.

What purpose could she have in telling him the truth? He could do nothing. Even if he felt... something for her, she was still under Simon Green's power, odious as he was. Could she even prove herself? Her word against Simon's...how far could she really go?

At some point in the heat of her rapid thoughts she had begun to cry. Not out loud, but silent hopeless tears of frustration that slipped out despite not being called upon to do so. She heard Owen's merry tune die on his lips, and then she heard him shift to look at her, and she quickly drew her hands up to wipe away the treacherous tears, still stealing away across her cheeks like thieves in daylight.

"Celia, what is it? What's wrong?"

Was it abominable of her, the tiny thrill that traveled to her breast to hear the concern in his voice? She did not care.

She braved a weak smile, biting her lip. She wanted to tell him, to show him, to unburden herself and lay the truth before him and see his reaction. But what did she hope for? Would it even make a difference? She was desperate not to lose this small happiness that to her seemed all encompassing.

Before she even had a chance to decide her hand was already reaching for her pocket and drawing out the letters.

Words bubbled like boiling water on her lips but she did not have the voice to speak them, so instead she handed the letters over to him silently.

Owen looked at her, puzzled, and then pulled his gloves off, laying them gently on his knees. She watched his eyes as they moved across the pages. He finished one, holding it in his hand as though it were poison, and then the next. His face became stone, all traces of song and laughter removed.

"Where did you get these?" He demanded, his voice as much of a scowl as his expression.

"I…I found them in Dr. Norbert's office. I, well, it sounds like madness, I know, but I followed a ghost. She led me, you see, and his office, well, it wasn't locked. Because of the fire, I imagine, and, well, I had to know. Do you see?"

Her voice was quaking and desperate and she was ashamed of this as well. She was not used to feeling strong, or showing strength, having had it ground out of her for so long. But she swallowed and held her head up, willing to take on any doubts or questions he might have, or even a scolding for entering the doctor's office. She inhaled and waited.

Instead, he simply nodded. Grey blue eyes that should have been cold marble bored into her with fiery heat.

"And this is your husband's hand?"

She clenched her teeth, but nodded, feeling the tears gather again unbidden. A clean breast is what she had hoped to make, but it was too much. Too much for this moment.

"I'm sorry, Celia…" He began again softly, misunderstanding her tears. "I…I know it must hurt for someone you love…"

She faced him squarely, eyes wide, tears freezing in place. "Love?! I don't love Simon! As if anyone could even be fooled into such an emotion for him. There was excitement, attraction, briefly…even affection, but not for him. For the illusion he presented me with. For the man he claimed to be, convinced me he was, until he had me under his power completely. He created a life for me that I could not escape. He took advantage of a woman alone, after my parents died. Using a brief, disingenuous acquaintance to lure me into his web. That is not love. My life has been misery every day since then." It sounded melodramatic, even to her own ears, but by God—it was true! All of it!

Owen looked at her, dumbfounded. "I had no idea. He…he isn't violent?"

Celia stared at the trees, memories surfacing in the waves of her mind. She shuddered. "Yes. He is. There is nothing tender in him. Only the desire to tear others down, to make them weak. He is violent, but violence I can abide. He has hurt my body in ways I had not imagined one could hurt another. But it is what he did to my mind. The slow scraping away of myself. He primed me for madness, and then made me believe my mind was not my own."

Owen's stony face liquified into a torrent of sadness. At some point he reached for her, his hands on her arms as though he would pull her to him, but he held himself back. She had no such restraint. She closed the space between them and felt his body mold to fit hers. Safe. Celia drew away quickly though it was like a physical ache to do so. She looked around, searching for nurse's eyes or patients who could be watching. Alone.

She took a deep breath, relieved, and studied his face. Yes, there, perhaps...perhaps she had been right. She inhaled deeply, gathering herself together, decision made.

"Owen, I am not a free woman..."

"I know, I know...I'm sorry..." he began, but she held a hand up.

"Allow me to finish. I may not be free at present, but I have loved you from the moment I first heard your singing outside my window."

His eyes went wide and he stood up. She panicked. He was walking away. Probably over to find a nurse to have her taken back in. She felt bile rise in her throat. Madness. Insanity to think he felt...but he was heading back.

He held a forget-me-not. Just a small posy. He tucked it behind her ear, and then stepped back. Before she could say anything she saw Nurse Dockert heading their way from the asylum entrance. No! At this moment to be pulled away?

She smiled, desperately. "Oh, Owen. The flowers, the message of them. But, of course, I could not forget you, I've just told you how I feel."

He returned her smile with a larger one, and then his eyes turned sad, following the approach of the carrot-haired nurse. He met her eyes with his own, intensity flooding his next words.

"Forget-me-nots carry a different meaning than their name would suggest."

Panic again. "Oh?" Celia asked, biting her lip.

His voice was low, only for her ears. "Forget-me-nots signify true love."

She felt relief and happiness that gathered in her stomach and rushed upward like champagne from the bottle. It pulled the corners of her mouth and her eyes.

"And Celia…" he added, just as Nurse Dockert was upon them, "As I said before, I would see you vanished as well, just as the letter says. Let's think on it, you and I."

It felt like a promise.

Then the nurse was there, chattering away as she had begun to do more and more often with Celia, and she led her away. Celia glanced back one last time at Owen, as the nurse gestured at the flowers and commented on the weather and pointed out all manner of things on the grounds. But Celia saw only forget-me-not blue.

Sweet Peas Departure

1888

The next day dawned with a drizzling rain. Just a smattering of a mother's proud tears trickling down from the clouds above, so negligible that Celia could barely believe it had been adjudged too wet. But buckets of rain or teaspoons, she was kept indoors and on the day of all days that she desired most to be out of them.

She had dreamed again the night before of her ghost, and of Sarah, but this time there had been no licking flames surrounding them. Instead, the dream was filled with mist and the woman and Blind Sarah had grasped at her fingers with slippery palms, as though they were all underwater. For whatever reason, the experience within the dreamscape had not been frightening. Perhaps it was because Celia had ever found comfort in water. A warm bath, a night swim in the lake, cooling her feet in the river as it rushed by her paying her toes no mind at all. Water quenched fire, after all, and it was the same blue as the blue of the sky, the blue of calm and steady, and now, to her at least, the blue of love.

At the moment she was sitting in the dayroom frustrated and anxious. She had fallen asleep with Owen Flynn on her mind and awoken to find him still biding there. He loved her! That nothing could be done about it didn't matter, not in this moment. It was enough to love and be loved in return. She wanted only to see him again, to confirm the truth in those grey eyes, to bask in a little happiness, even if it was doomed to be fleeting.

Myrtle rocked back and forth beside her, the older woman's ample form moving in a swaying, troubling rhythm that intruded on Celia's thoughts.

She looked over and saw that Myrtle's lips were moving and her eyes were focused on nothing, or perhaps focused within, seeing something that was visible to her alone. Without thinking, Celia reached over and placed a hand on Myrtle's arm, soothingly, as one would a child. Myrtle's forearm was clammy with sweat, and looking closer Celia saw it beading and dripping off the woman's temple as well. She continued to pat the arm, wanting to remove her hand from the disturbed woman, repulsed, but feeling guilty for it.

A folding fan smacked into the hand that patted Myrtle's arm and Celia pulled it back rapidly in reaction to the sudden stinging pain. She looked up to see Caroline staring at her, seated on Myrtle's other side, eyes full of venom. The intensity and hatred she found there shocked Celia and she drew herself back against her seat.

"Don't touch her." Caro said sharply, stabbing the fan in Celia's direction. Celia nodded and fixed her eyes in the opposite direction. She remembered Annie's warning that Caroline could be violent, but the level of rage behind those big brown doll's eyes was terrifying. It reminded her of a man who'd once tried to rob her mother and father on a family trip through Austria. They didn't speak German, and the man's anger seemed to intensify when her family could not understand his demands. Murderous, her mother had said in a whisper after it was all over. And that was how it seemed, as though the fact that he could not make himself understood infuriated him. As if her family's ignorance of his language was a personal insult. In the end he had attacked her father with a stick, and then ripped his money from his pockets before spitting and running off, leaving Celia and her mother, hands covering their faces and wailing.

Caroline looked the same as that man. As though she knew Celia didn't understand, didn't belong. For the first time, Celia grew afraid that her sanity might actually put her in danger, she became aware that it separated her from the women around her in a fundamental way.

Just then, a small noise in the corridor and an anxious looking man walked into the day room. Tall, blonde hair like fresh buttermilk, and a long straight nose and bright eyes. He looked like...she wasn't certain. There was something achingly familiar about him. She felt she'd met him before, but knew she had not. And then the truth hit her. Andrew Barnsley. It had to be.

He was precisely like Annie, tall and lanky but with grace and the pink of health in his cheeks. He looked uncertain and she found herself standing up, moving toward him deliberately. He narrowed his eyes a moment, as if unsure if he should be afraid of a patient coming toward him. Then, what she expected was his natural affability won out, and he smiled. Easily and large, as though the smile was always waiting at the corners of his mouth.

"Andrew Barnsley?" She asked quietly, stepping quite close and putting out a hand. To her delight he blushed and nodded. She suspected he was given to blushing.

"Yes, ma'am. You have me at a disadvantage." He gave her a little mock bow and she inclined her head. "I'm Celia Thorne—I'm a friend of Annie's. She told me about you, and you looked so much like her, I just knew..." She didn't finish the thought, drawing her hands widely apart as though to express something, but as she did it, she wasn't sure what it was she was hoping to say to Mr. Andrew Barnsley.

He nodded, obviously uncomfortable, and she wondered if this too, was a habit. Just as his smiles came so easily to his mouth, perhaps talk of his sister made him uncomfortable. But if she had given him any discomfort, he was wonderfully polite about it.

"You're taking her home then?" She asked, after the moment had dragged a beat too long.

He nodded again, cheeks pinking. "Yes, ma'am.

Not home, per say, but there's another hospital, closer to our house. Now that our father is dead, you see…" He made the same expansive sweep of his arms that she had, and she took it to mean that it had been his choice to bring her home now that his father couldn't gainsay his decision. She smiled, which elicited a further blushing to pass across his cheeks.

"Well, I will certainly miss her, but I know how dearly she has been looking forward to being reunited with you."

He nodded, catching a nurse's eye, who beckoned him. Celia realized that Annie, her only friend, was leaving, and she wouldn't be saying goodbye. In fact, her last real memory of her would be Annie, moaning pitifully for the drugs her body had become a slave to. She felt a little sick, and wished they'd had a proper farewell, as friends would, outside of an institution's walls. A real farewell, with embraces and kisses and promises to maintain correspondence. But this was an asylum, not a garden party or two friends parting at the train station.

She had to leave here. Celia began to panic, and grabbed Andrew's arm as he nodded his head and mumbled how pleasant it was to make her acquaintance. He seemed to be pulling away from her and the day room and everything about the asylum that disturbed him, and toward his sister. His whole being seemingly set on keeping a promise to deliver her nearer to home.

He tensed when she grabbed his arm and whirled back around, fear of the hunted in his eyes. Celia marveled at how different he was from his intrepid, friendly, bold sister. What a pity it was that Annie's mind and body rebelled against her. What a tragedy that she had been born a woman, in a world where her personality would have made her a powerful man. Before he could become overly alarmed at her touch, she spoke, keeping her voice calm and steady. Her father would have called it her 'drawing room voice', practiced and polished, it betrayed none of her inner turmoil. She'd been trained well.

"Please" she said, "It would be lovely if you could have Annie write to me when she gets settled. It would...mean a great deal to me."

She raised her eyes to his, so like Annie's, and yet lacking the engagement and fire. He nodded, and mumbled some appropriate, polite response and then followed the nurse out the door. He'd been in the day room for no longer than ninety seconds, and yet her sky had fallen again.

Not mad.

Trapped here.

In love with Owen, loved in return.

Haunted by a ghost.

Ruled by Simon.

And now losing her only friend. Even if she was an addict and mostly a stranger. Celia felt terribly alone.

Nurse Dockert approached her. Her red hair was fighting a war with her nurse's cap, and it looked as though the riot of frizzy red curls was winning. She seemed awkward to Celia, as if she'd lost some of the sharp angles of herself, and had somehow rounded smooth in a way that should have made Celia more comfortable, but served only to make Celia confused and a little suspicious.

Nurse Dockert offered a small smile, just a minute softening of her nurse-face into something that for the merest moment resembled friendship. She handed Celia a letter surreptitiously, drawing it out from between the pages of what Celia recognized as the nurse's logbook.

"Wanted to be certain this got into your hands." She said, quietly, and then floated over casually to Caroline's side, catching her clenched fist in mid-air, though Celia was uncertain who Caroline's intended target had been. Perhaps some invading foe into Caro's kingdom that only she could see.

Celia tucked the letter into her dress pocket, understanding from Nurse Dockert's manner that there was some element of the clandestine about it. She stole a quick glance at the door Andrew Barnsley had exited out of, wondered for the briefest moment if she could convince him to remove her from the asylum too. Could he help? Would he be willing? If he had half of Annie's gumption he would. Perhaps, if she offered him her ring as payment? She stared down at the tiny golden and emerald shackle on her second finger and rolled her eyes, turning away from the door.

No. It was clear that for all his affable manner and easy smiles, he had only a sliver of Annie's courage, and he'd clearly used it all in coming here .

Waiting until after his father's funeral to dare and bring home his 'shameful' addict sister.

Clenching her teeth, angry somehow at Andrew Barnsley who owed her nothing, and at men in general for deciding so much of women's lives—and doing a rotten job of it—if she said so herself. She retreated to the window seat of the dayroom, hand clutching the thin letter in her pocket and she looked out onto the green expanse of the lawn. The flowerbeds she'd helped to plant were there, every bud of every flower holding a sunlit memory of Owen, or a single searing moment of happiness and freedom for herself. Suddenly, it occurred to her that Dr. Munson was marvelous, for if she were mad she knew those moments of soil-covered gloves and sunbeams in her hair would have been a soothing balm to a broken mind. In fact, she could admit freely that even without being mad the gardening and purpose the work provided her had healed something vital within her.

And of course, Owen.

His voice, and those sturdy shoulders, the way his mouth turned to the side when he was about to say something silly. His stories, the ones he made up to amuse her and those she knew he'd heard from his mother. His gentleness with the most fragile of flower petals, and his sheer physical strength when digging up a bed or hauling soil on his back.

She sighed aloud, startling herself, and then reacher into her pocket and drew out the letter, angling her body toward the window. It wasn't unusual to receive mail in the asylum, but one could always count on every missive being read first, by a nurse or a doctor to ensure the contents would not be too distressing for the intended recipient. But this letter was sealed fast, her eyes would be the first to read it since it arrived. Celia felt the furrow in her brow as she examined the unbroken seal, and then carefully, soundlessly, she ran her finger under the enclosure and gingerly slipped it open. She pulled a single sheet of paper out from the small envelope and instantly recognized the cramped and craggy script used by the Green family lawyer. She drew the letter closer to her face and read, each sentence evoking a different, troubling feeling, setting her heart to racing.

Dear Celia,

My dear, my dear. This is my fourth letter to you, all others having gone unanswered. Simon says this is irrefutable proof of your rapid mental decline, but I cannot believe it to be true. I believe I did remark on our last meeting that you seemed—different, but I would never have believed you to be mentally deficient or disturbed. Because of this, I ask you to please trust that I have already set in motion every cog in the legal machine within my power to obtain your release from the asylum. However, Simon Green has powerful friends, I fear. I have kept him from the inheritance left to you by your parents, and have no fear of being unable to retain that fortune for you. Fret not, my dear, I will endeavor to remove you! In the interim, I am at your disposal, and desire nothing more than to hear from you, however I can.

Yours faithfully,
Harold Q. Montague

Celia's hands were shaking as she finished reading the letter, and she quickly folded it back up and placed it in her pocket, then looked around to see if anyone had been watching. Her eyes met Nurse Dockert's and the nurse nodded, and then looked away. Obviously the nurse had felt something was amiss, and had, in her way, tried to make it right. But what did she suspect? What did she know? Could she be trusted? Celia shook her head at her own thoughts. Nurse Dockert had done her a kind turn, but she was not her friend or her ally. She was simply an honest, caring woman who was looking out for Celia in a small way. The woman had a family no doubt, and Celia would not ask her to put her position at the asylum in jeopardy. Still, her assistance gave Celia a little strength, a little hope.

The letter itself was a revelation. She felt a sudden twinge of guilt that she hushed away, and resolved to deal with it later. Obviously Mr. Montague had been trying to write to Celia for a long time. These letters had been blocked, or taken, or thrown out, no doubt by Dr. Norbert or Nurse Brattle in their strange allegiance to Simon. Which made her consider again, what was Simon's relationship to the doctor? Why was the man so afraid of Simon? She exhaled, bewildered. It seemed that all she had now were questions without answers. At least the fortune was safe, even though Simon would pursue it with more force as time went on.

Outside, it had ceased raining. Celia looked out over the front lawn of the hospital once again. The sun caught Owen Flynn's copper hair and she smiled, as an idea bloomed in her mind like one of his flowers.

She looked over at Nurse Bell, drawing the woman's attention and then nodded her head toward outside. The nurse peered outside the window herself, and seeing it was clear again, stepped forward and nodded in permission. She was perfectly willing to have one less patient to watch and instead hand her over to gardening duty. Celia followed behind Nurse Bell's white uniform, the clicking of her shoes on the tiled floors keeping time to the rhythm of Celia's runaway plans.

Lavender: Distrust

2011

They had walked to the library. At first it had seemed mad to do so, late at night, with a man she hardly knew. But after a few steps she'd begun to shake off some of the tension, noticing that there were still kids out riding bikes and families leaving the restaurants in downtown Traverse City.

Eve wasn't often out so late. Not anymore. She thought about the times briefly when this would have seemed early, when she would still be at home, preparing for a night out partying, waiting to feel abandon, freedom, nothing. Her mouth was dry. There had been a time in her life, a long time, that she had craved nothingness.

Exhaling, she turned her head a little bit toward Eric. He was telling her something about growing up here, and she all at once felt guilty for being lost in her own thoughts. "I'm sorry, what were you

200

saying? I was building castles in Spain."

"Ah, woolgathering, were we? Instead of listening to the triumphant tale of the time I skateboarded from one end of Front Street to the other doing kick flips on every other block with a group of other rapscallions?"

"Riveting, how terrible to have missed the tale."

He laughed, a dreamy kind of warm sound that instantly made Eve smile.

"Well, yes, I concede that it may not *sound* impressive, but to a 13 year old boy who was very late into puberty, it was epic."

"Epic, huh? Doesn't take much up here, I suppose."

He laughed again, and Eve was almost embarrassed by how hot her cheeks felt. She wanted to keep making him laugh, which sounded strange, even in her own head.

"No, it doesn't take much. So imagine the scale of adventure it is to have met you, Eve Parish."

He said the last just as they approached the doors of the library. He let go of her hand to unlock the doors, and then reaching back he grasped her fingers and pulled her in through the door of the library with him.

Something about the stacks and myriad shelves of books in the darkness felt magical to Eve. Reading had been her first and truest addiction, the pastime she craved most. Reading to her was both curse and cure. Like a wine she could not stop drinking, and yet it never seemed to make her drunk.

(Though she had awoken many mornings after a long night of reading until 3am or later to discover she had an awful headache and not nearly enough sleep.)

He moved to turn on the lights, but with the streetlight outside and the moonlight through the windows, she stopped him.

"Leave it just like this. There's something lovely and wonderful about it, isn't there?"

He swung her hand back and forth, as a child might, and squeezed her fingers. "There is, indeed. Ok, I will leave it like this upstairs, but we will definitely need all the light we can get in order to work downstairs."

"Deal" she said, and they walked toward the door that led to the basement archives. He paused suddenly, and handed her the ring of keys, taking a moment to pick out the correct one.

"On second thought, let yourself down. I think in addition to light, we are going to need coffee."

Eve nodded and approached the door, twisting the key in the lock and flicking on the light before descending into the basement, leaving the marvelous darkness and books behind.

She paused on the step and texted her Dad where she was. He replied with an emoji of a ghost, which, knowing her Dad, could really mean anything. She smiled to herself as she carefully walked down the stairs, and then headed over to one of the piles of papers Eric had indicated the first time she'd been there, and started looking.

Mainly, she looked for the name, *Celia*, the date of the disappearance he'd located, August 17th 1888, or initials. A few minutes later Eric joined her, sitting on an uncomfortable looking wooden stool with a ripped leather top that had padding straining to come out of it. He turned on a little radio in the corner she hadn't noticed before, but she never really heard the music, so focused was she on Celia.

Why did it matter so much to her that they found her? She couldn't say, and so she was glad that Eric didn't ask. Every so often one or the other of them would take a sip of their rapidly cooling coffee, or sneeze from the dust, but other than that, there was no sound but the radio.

It was pleasant, the stillness and silence. There weren't many people Celia felt comfortable spending silence with. It was a rare thing, really. It's simple to be around people in a crowded room, or to make meaningless conversation in a group, or in a busy restaurant. But to simply *be* with another person the way that one is with oneself, that is a tall order indeed.

After about twenty minutes, Eric pulled out a newspaper dated from the week after Celia went missing, and they both pored over the pages, but there was nothing, not even a follow up story about her disappearance. Eve asked to see the article he'd found originally that *did* report on her vanishing, and he produced it quickly and she scrutinized every word, every sentence for a hidden meaning, until, blinking rather rapidly, she enthusiastically stuck the paper right under Eric's nose.

"Here! Look at this! How stupid are we? Idiots!"

"What, what? I don't see it."

"Look, at the beginning of the article, they call her Celia Green, but what do they call her in the middle?

"Where... I don't see....Oh. Celia Thorne. That *is* odd. Why use both names?"

Eve shrugged, but her eyes were wide and excited, and they both approached the stacks with renewed vigor. But after another hour of searching, they'd found nothing more at all, at least not in the newspapers.

"Should we go over the patient files now that we have exhausted the newspapers?" Eric asked, halfheartedly.

"Yes, I suppose so." Eve replied, feeling slightly lukewarm herself about the prospect. The old patient records would be written in ink that was faintly brown or tan with age, and the letters would be small and cramped and difficult to read. They could be here for hours yet, and still miss something in the cramped writing used at the time.

"All right, let's get started then." Eve said, donning a lackluster smile that made Eric laugh again.

"Don't get too excited now. This *is* all part of my incredibly effective seduction plan, after all. Nice dinner, romantic walk on the beach, hold hands, then take a lady to my basement library lair where I force her to get dusty and sleepy and regret coming out with me at all."

"That does sound effective. I'm sure you've held many ladies in the palm of your hand after a night like that."

He shook his head, sighing, as he located the correct files. "Ah, too many to count, Eve, too many to count."

She laughed in spite of herself, and then yawned. Due to the contagious nature of yawns, Eric answered hers with his own, his mouth opening large, and his eyes, when he finished, were watering.

"I'm not certain coffee is going to cut it, Parish."

Eve shrugged, only half listening, and blinked her eyes a few times as she went over the tiny, cramped writing that was so beautifully executed as to be almost art, that old-fashioned swooping, flourished writing that one only sees on cards that one has paid to be hand lettered. But for all its beauty, it was incredibly difficult to decipher. They both pored over the sheafs of patient records, some bound in dusty leather books with rickety spines and others obviously torn out of books that had not been strong enough to preserve them within. She'd moved her head forward and back, as though adjusting her distance from the page aided in translating the minuscule scrawl.

Eric wasn't having much luck either, and sometimes he would finish a page so forcefully that Eve was afraid he'd harm the paper. She still sipped her now cold coffee, though it wasn't cold in a pleasant way, how it often is when iced during the summer, but instead it tasted bitter and artificial and caused her face to screw up in disgust when she drank it. The mood had shifted, no more lighthearted banter or flirting, they had both settled into a less friendly silence than they had happily inhabited before. She wondered why, what had changed? And she couldn't help but feel that it was the names on the lists in front of them. Pieces of someone's life distilled into their name and intake date, the city they were from and their age. Occasionally there would be a note about why they were being committed, but not always. It was sad in the way that gravestones were sad. The whole of one's life and experiences being contained in the dash between one's date of birth and date of death. And now, a patient's entire existence within the walls of the asylum condensed to the bare facts. No note on if their family ever visited, or if they missed home. No indication if living in the asylum had been the greatest freedom of their life, or the most terrible imprisonment. How did they spend their days within? How did they keep occupied?

Eve supposed this was why she was so entranced with Celia. She had a clue about her feelings. She had some brief, subtle hints as to her mental state, how she occupied herself, who she was as a woman. And she was someone who could not be contained within an asylum. She had broken out, after all.

More than anything, Eve needed to know what Celia did when she broke free from the asylum. If she ended up dead in a ditch or in jail or in a loveless marriage to someone who took pity on a madwoman. Or did she, maybe, perhaps, find some greater purpose? Could she have risen above her troubles, her greatest follies, her unhappiness and made a life for herself somewhere else?

Eve knew precisely why she needed to know what happened to Celia, and it was because she thought perhaps the end of this woman's story might give her a hint of her own.

She realized she was no longer looking at the names on the page, and instead her eyes were filled with tears. She blinked them away, embarrassed, dragged her cardigan's sleeve across her eyes to clear away any remaining proof. This action caught Eric's attention, but he mistook it for another sign she was fighting sleep.

"I told you, Parish. Coffee is just not cutting it."

She shook her head, "Tough. Get back to work, mister."

"What we need is crack cocaine."

He said it in an undertone, almost to himself. He was already back to examining the list before him for a date that would match up with Celia's disappearance.

She watched him for a moment, face frozen. Her heart was pounding, suddenly, and her palms began to sweat. She pulled them down, away from the precious pages, and wiped them on her dress. Her stomach had dropped and she felt ill. Eve clenched her teeth, and looked down at the list before her, eyes swimming. She was embarrassed, and she was angry. Tired, maudlin, frustrated and *angry*.

Irrational, she knew, but she couldn't help it.

"What's wrong, Evie?" Eric had paused in his inspection and his eyes were fixed on her face. She didn't answer. "What's the matter? Did you...find something? Are you okay?"

She clenched her hands in her lap. This was stupid. So unbelievably stupid. She had no reason or right to be upset with him, and yet, here she was, having a full scale attack. She tried to calm herself, to rationalize, but she couldn't. She should have said something earlier, should have been truthful from the start. This was exactly what happened when she wasn't up front. Situations like this. One wrong word, and suddenly, she wasn't herself anymore. Or, rather, she was that Eve. The Eve she'd run from.

"It's not funny." She said, her voice a whisper, the cadence of it unrecognizable.

"What's not? Or, what? I'm sorry, did I say something?"

"Drugs...they're not funny."

"What are you, a D.A.R.E counselor?" He quipped, attempting levity. She wasn't looking at his expression, but she could feel the tension in the air, feel his discomfort. She was ashamed, and wished she hadn't said anything at all, but somehow she was still set on explaining herself. She was powerless to the feeling, and this scared her most of all. Out of control. That's the scariest feeling there is. No control over yourself, watching through a lens of panic, screaming inside to change things, but unable to stop. Like watching yourself get drunk, the voice in your brain finally whispering, "oh no, you've had too much. Please stop acting so foolish," but it's too late, and now you have to ride out the night.

"No, I'm not." She finally said. "I'm a recovering addict. I spent a year in one of these kind of institutions, you know. Just like these patients. I'm just like them."

He waited a beat, and she looked up, desperate to observe his reaction. He half smiled, one corner of his mouth jerking upward, and his brows came together with an unvoiced question that she was certain, if given voice, would sound like, "Are you serious?"

And then he laughed.

She didn't wait another moment. She grabbed her purse and ran up the stairs of the basement and burst out into the darkness of the library, noticing briefly that it had lost its magic. It now seemed like there were too many shadows and the sheer number of books was oppressive. She ran out the front door, sprinted down the steps and didn't break her stride until she was at her car. She was sobbing, uncontrollably. He had called after her, words she hadn't heard, and followed her until she left the front door of the library. She'd heard his feet pounding behind her, but she'd had to get away.

He'd laughed.

She'd told him the most raw and painful thing about her. Her biggest secret, her most bloody wound. And he'd laughed.

Heartbroken, she realized there was very little chance she'd ever find out what happened to Celia Thorne. But if it was anything like the feeling she had right now, she figured she was better off not knowing.

Rosemary: Remembrance
1888

For the first few minutes after the nurse left they had carried on gardening as usual. She'd drawn on the gardening gloves and grabbed a spade, carefully pulling up soil and tucking pansies under a summer weight blanket of earth.

They didn't speak, but she felt the change between them, nevertheless. Had there always been so much longing betwixt them? The feeling was as thick as it it could be without slicing. When all the world around them became quiet and settled again, and all that could be heard was wind and bees, she spoke.

"Owen, did you mean what you said yesterday?" She was proud of how casual her voice sounded, how confident the question had seemed. He stood up and brushed off his hands, fixing her in place with his stare.

"I'm not one to tell tales, Celia." He replied, simply.

She swallowed, and her next question was like a stone in her throat, his sincerity had unnerved her, and the question became almost impossible.

"I never thought for a moment that you were. But, would you…would you help me escape?"

Before she even had a moment to exhale he had nodded yes, not even pausing to consider it, as if he had long decided his answer and had only waited for her to ask. He moved over to the wheelbarrow for a flat of sweet peas, and drew her attention.

"These signify 'a departure'." He said, putting the lot of them on the ground near where they had been planting.

"And these?" She asked, motioning to the pansies. She was still in disbelief that he'd agreed. And so easily. He had agreed, hadn't he? She hadn't imagined it? There were a hundred questions on her lips about her escape, but instead he spoke of flowers and something told her she should listen.

"You occupy my thoughts." He said, without taking his eyes from the sweet peas.

"And you, mine," she answered, a little dazed. "But how could we accomplish it? The escape?"

He met her gaze and laughed, out loud. "First, I was answering your question. Pansies mean 'you occupy my thoughts', though, in truth, I thought I had made it plain that you are constantly on my mind. And as for the escape, you only have to tell me when, and I'll bundle you out of here and send you wherever you'd like to go. Don't worry a moment abut that."

His face was troubled though, and her stomach plummeted at the meaning of his speech.

"You…you wouldn't want to come with me then? I suppose not, of course. I had only thought that…well, it doesn't matter. You still think of me as a married woman. You have a life and work here of course, it was a…a silly thing."

He'd kneeled down near her and extended a hand to pluck dead petals from a bloom, but then suddenly stopped. He moved his face strangely and then looked at her as though she was speaking French.

"I don't give a good goddamn if you're married, especially to a man who'd commit his wife for naught, from what I can see. And I don't give a damn about my job here at the asylum. Jobs there are a plenty for a man like me, but you…Celia… you. I never assumed, never dreamed…that'd you, Celia, do you want me?"

She cried out. A strange inarticulate sound that released all of her worry and contained all of her disbelief.

"Of course! I think I would go a little mad if I was made to go without you!"

They stared at one another. "Damn nurses. Damn hospital! If I was able, Celia, I'd pick you up and carry you all the way to my little house where I'd kiss you proper." He said, voice low, almost a purr.

"I'd like that, I think."

"I reckon you would." He said, a gleam in his eye.

Owen and Celia worked side by side in the soil, his hand coming to touch her glove when working together to dig or to pat down the earth, and it should not have been a thrill when they did, but somehow it was. His touch made her shiver, his hand on her hand. She ached to clasp his rough, calloused hand with her own naked palm, to feel something real and true and honest. She pushed these thoughts from her mind and returned to their earlier conversation.

"So we have an escape to plan" She said as she settled back to her task, as though her heart wasn't about to pump out of her chest.

"That we do."

They were silent a few moments, lost in their thoughts, when Celia remembered the letter.

"Oh!" She gasped, throwing her gloves off and pulling it quickly from her dress pocket."Oh! Owen! I've a letter! It's to do with all the money!"

Her words knocked his head upwards and a confused expression lit his face. "A letter from whom? And what money? Your husband's?"

She cringed at his use of the word. "No, it's

mine. Well, I mean, it's mine to deal with. Here, take a look at the letter." She handed it over eagerly, and Owen brought it close to his face, using his body to shield the words from the glare of the sunlight.

When he was finished, he flopped back to sitting on the grass and scratched his head. He looked so much like a young boy in that moment that she rather regretted bringing him into her troubles. It occurred to her that not only would he be leaving his position, but, recalling Dr. Munson's words about how he had met Owen, she realized he would be leaving friends behind as well.

He hadn't spoken since reading the letter, and had not noticed the shift in her attitude that his thoughtful mood had brought on.

"Have you many friends in town, Owen?" She asked quietly.

"Yes, of course." He replied absently. "Been here most of my life haven't I? The good doctor didn't just bring me along for my gardening skills. Helps to have a local man you can trust." His voice was still as far away as his thoughts and he didn't see the pained look on her face.

"Oh, Owen. You cannot come with me. You built your whole life here. I can't...I won't take that away."

Coming back to himself, he frowned and folded the letter back up. "Don't be daft, woman. What kind of life would it be, mooning over you? Making a fool of myself? No, thank you. No, I only admitted to friends here because they'll help us in a pinch—don't you see? But there's the matter of the money. That's what I'm thinking on. What did you mean it was 'yours to deal with'?"

She looked away, and sighed. "Exactly that. It's not money for spending. That's what I meant. It's….complicated. But I won't touch a cent of that money."

It was his turn to sigh, but this time in exasperation, and then he looked around, furtively, the pair of them paranoid to the point of distraction.

"I'm not interested in your money, Celia, but I'd like to know what's wrong with it that you disdain it so much." He spoke as if he were not speaking to her at all, as if he were asking the flowers they'd just planted or the wind. As if he didn't expect an answer to the question. But she knew better.

"I…I can't say. It's complicated, as I said. I just… I can't leave the asylum until I've written back to Mr. Montague and figured out what to do with the money. And…I know this won't make sense, but I've got to do it in a way that will keep me safe. From Simon, I mean."

"I'll keep you safe from Simon." Owen replied gruffly.

She laughed and then reached out to touch his hand, drawing it back as she realized her error. She could not touch him here. Not yet. Patience.

"I know, Owen. I know you would. But, there is unfinished business that I must conclude. I'm sorry."

She could feel the gold and emerald band on her finger beneath the glove, and for a moment she imagined it grew painfully tighter about her finger. A moment later, and the feeling was gone.

Celia patted the spade about in the dirt, smoothing out the surface of the soil as if setting an idea in stone. Yes, it could easily be wrapped up. She would just need to write to the lawyer. Did she dare tell him the truth? Was she certain she even knew it herself? There could be no other answer, and she was dullard enough that it had taken her so long to discover. Perhaps it was because she could not imagine that anyone, even Simon, could do something so dastardly…

"Don't do that." His voice broke into her thoughts. She had been chewing her lips as she thought, and at some point she had drawn blood. She tasted the blood on her tongue and recoiled, it was made more upsetting by the train of thought she had just been a passenger upon.

"At some point, I'll need those lips for kissing and I'll ask you not to ruin them to bits beforehand."

She returned the smile he gave her, but from behind a glove, and gave him a little embarrassed laugh.

"Write your letter then" he said, "and I'll make sure your Mr. Montague receives it. And if he takes too long in his reply or if you come to grief here, I say damn whatever the complications are with the money. I like you for yourself, you know." He paused, and his face changed. "Now, Miss Thorne, do be careful with the soil there, it needs to be dug properly, not patted. Take the blooms—not two in one hole mind you!"

His brisk, husky voice had grown louder at the end, and Celia looked about, befuddled, before Nurse Bell's white hatted figure came into view.

"Afternoon, Mr. Flynn." She greeted him, smiling brightly. "The flowers are lovely as ever, though I can't say I'd expect any less from a man with your talents" Celia realized with a start that Nurse Bell was flirting with him. A wave of molten jealousy pulsed through her, to be replaced with something else. Was she so ruthless as to see the woman's obvious interest as a potential opportunity?

Owen grunted his thanks in Nurse Bell's direction, and then, as if realizing his rudeness, smiled and tipped his cap to her.

Celia stood up. "Is it time, nurse?" She asked weakly. Nurse Bell nodded, barely looking at her.

"Have a wonderful afternoon, Mr. Flynn" Nurse Bell called back cheerfully as she led Celia away, with only a moment for Celia and Owen to exchange a look that communicated none of what either of them wished it to, and was altogether unsatisfactory.

Nurse Bell was young and pretty, but still, as they walked, Celia felt as though the woman was looking her over, appraising her. She thought of her slightly dampened brow, the curling golden and brown hair.

She was small in stature, standing a head shorter than Nurse Bell, but she was not overly slim. She didn't run to fat either, but was strong in a solid way that she was proud of. "No shrinking violets here," her father would say, gathering her and her mother close, and when he said it, it was as a great compliment, and still was to Celia. No shrinking violet, indeed, Celia thought. She would need to be a more brazen kind of flower to emerge from her current fix.

Nurse Bell's appraisal ended, and surprisingly, she spoke, though her voice was tinged with something that Celia found ugly.

"It must be pleasant to spend your days with Mr. Flynn." She said the words casually, but then looked askance at Celia as if expecting her to sputter and faint.

"If you mean that it is pleasant to spend my days useful and amongst a heaven of flowers, then yes, it is tremendously pleasant. Although, Mr. Flynn is the overseer only of the appointed activities Dr. Munson has assigned." Celia did not meet the nurse's eyes, but she was certain the woman pinked at her reply.

"Yes, of course. I didn't mean to imply…that is to say, that's precisely what I had meant."

Celia nodded as though she had known it all along. She walked with Nurse Bell to the lavatory where she bathed and dressed and from there back to her room. The nurse helped her to arrange her hair, which she had no need of assistance with and felt that the woman must be sticking close for another reason.

The nurse had gasped to see her scars, as all the nurses did the first time they helped her with her bath. When she'd lifted her eyes to Celia's she had only shook her head, an inscrutable look on her face. It did not trouble Celia to discuss the scars—not really. Anyone who saw them couldn't help but be curious. Excepting the one on her forearm given her by a frightened dog she'd gotten too close to, the rest were from Simon. He was clever, of course. They all looked as if they could have been self-inflicted. Small cuts, and places where the skin had not been allowed to heal, the scabs having been torn off again and again until the flesh was mottled and raised when it had finally healed over. But she didn't bother to tell the stories—for who would believe her? Especially after they had met Simon. He was careful and slippery as a snake's belly. He'd pulled a master stroke in stowing her away in an asylum.

It looked as though Nurse Bell would linger, and Celia was desperate to write her letter to Mr. Montague. Feigning a headache she asked to be retrieved in time for supper in the dining hall, and Nurse Bell's eyes went wide at the Lady of the House style dismissal. Celia took a deep breath in and sighed as the woman left. Well, she had acted as lady of the house for a time, hadn't she? In another life?

Another life, she thought. That was precisely what her goal was now. A life away from this asylum. A life with Owen Flynn, she cared not where, and thinking of Nurse Bell's infatuation and how it might be used, she realized she cared not *how* it was accomplished either.

Celia retrieved the little sketchbook Dr. Munson had given her from the place she'd wedged it in the little writing desk and tore out a sheet of paper. Remembering that Owen had retained the letter from Mr. Montague, which was just as well, she made a note to tell him he'd find the lawyer's correct address on it. She paused and wrote out some of her feelings on the next page in the book, ignoring the sheet she'd torn out, needing to clear her mind before she began. She did not like to indulge in self-pity, but it was cleansing to pin down some of those runaway thoughts and worries.

It has become clear to me that I must get out. I might be called mad, but I think only in the way we all are. The ghosts come less now, or perhaps there are simply fewer ghosts in this lonely, lovely woods. The woman is the key to all of this, I know it, I think I've always known it, in a dark place I didn't want to look. I will find her out.

She set down her pen and flexed her finger, snatching up the torn out sheet and beginning the letter with a clearer head.

Mr. Montague,

I have received your latest letter—though only through a confederate at the asylum that I think cannot be trusted again. However, I do have a friend here, who will be the sender of this letter. Please write to his direction so that he might be the message bearer forthwith. Mr. Montague, you were ever a friend to the family, might I be correct in thinking so? Might I trust you in something strange, that I think if accomplished rightly will achieve both of our aims? I am enclosing to you a letter from Dr. Munson to Dr. Norbert, but pray do not ask how this letter came to be in my possession. There is too much to explain. But I wanted you to have some token of proof for your files that I am as sane as I claim to be.

To the point: the funds. I deeply regret that I cannot elucidate further at this time, but I do not want them, and I do not lay claim to them. All that is important to me is that Simon Green does not come into possession of them. Please draw up whatever needs to be done in order to bequeath these funds to the Hutzel Women's Hospital in Detroit. I believe you know the reason that I should wish them to have it, and I believe the prior version of my will grants this bequest as well.

Do not ask why I have decided this. If you have further questions, please, feel free to have Simon investigated thoroughly. I believe if you begin opening closets, so to speak, you'd be amazed at the skeletons you will discover.

I will send again when I have more to say, and do make all necessary arrangements in haste.

Until then, I await your reply.
C.

She replaced the pen and tucked the sketchbook back into its hiding place, testing to see it was secure. She then folded Dr. Munson's note to Dr. Norbert into her own letter, blotting her initial with one final flourish before tucking it into the concealed pocket of her lavender dress. It was old now, and a few years out of style, but it had been from the last batch of gowns her mother had commissioned for her. Brilliant Mama! With practical pockets she'd thought made her look wider, but now were saving her life.

A knock on the door, and Celia was certain it was Nurse Bell again, overly solicitous suddenly. It surely wasn't time for supper?

The door opened before she could say a word, and Nurse Bell grinned strangely. And in walked Simon.

Yellow Chrysanthemum:
Slighted Love

1888

All the breath left her body like a ship suddenly becalmed at sea. He was staring at her, a familiar expression on his face. It was a smile that wasn't. It didn't touch his eyes and it barely grazed his mouth. He licked his teeth under his lips in a vulgar manner, but it appeared that only she noticed it.

The nurse blushed and nodded at him and somehow Celia was being ushered into an empty room—Annie's empty room. Here the nurse deposited them, and Simon whispered something to Nurse Bell before she left them alone together. She thought she'd heard a giggle but was uncertain if this was truth or her own paranoia. After all, if there *was* madness in her, it was planted there by Simon Green.

They were alone. This was against hospital policy, but she'd guessed he'd paid Nurse Bell in some form or fashion, perhaps even with the money Celia had authorized to him on his last visit. Dr. Norbert was probably well aware of Simon's comings and goings, but was too frightened to interfere.

Knowing all this hardly mattered. It was his very presence that filled her with dread. She felt sick as his eyes slipped down her body, could feel the memories like ghosts of his hands on her like tormenting demons. The letter to Mr. Montague was suddenly heavy within her pocket and she was certain somehow that Simon would know it was there. That he would find it—rip it up in front of her—and have Celia locked in chains in the basement of the asylum somewhere deep in that golden sandy stone where no one would hear her.

A cry escaped her mouth, but it sounded like a wounded animal, and it shamed her to hear her own fear, especially as she saw the reaction it had on him. Simon stepped closer, his hands grasping onto her forearms like shackles. Those golden sunlight curls and hard green eyes the color of something reptilian and cold.

"My darling Celia! Aren't you pleased I've arranged for us to have time alone? I remember a time when you practically bounced into my arms to have a moment just us two—and now I can hardly remember the last time I held you in my arms at all!"

Celia's stomach heaved at the memories. Shame washed over her, though she knew not why. He had hidden himself so well, she could hardly go on blaming herself for his own viciousness. Marshaling her strength she pushed him away from her bodily.

"I'm certain that you've had no shortage of replacements." She spit the words at him, and then regretted it. She didn't care how many other women there were, and she knew better, truly, than to antagonize him.

He appeared amused. "I've always said you were a kind of witch. Seeing into my thoughts, perhaps? Or has a ghost whispered my conquests to you?"

She merely looked away, staring at the wall, and wondering why Annie's room had remained unoccupied in a hospital splitting at the seams to fit more patients and a waiting list to boot.

"Or, perhaps there's nothing special about you at all, and you're just a very clever liar. That *was* your main use to me, after all. Looking the part. Playing it well. Though you…foolishly thought there was something noble about it, no doubt." He picked at some imaginary speck on his coat and sniffed. "But perhaps you are more intelligent than I gave you credit for, hmm?"

He looked at his nails as if there was something more interesting happening on his fingers. Celia knew this tactic, and her whole body tensed, and then—he struck.

Simon grabbed her by the arm and whirled her around until her back was to him. His mouth was right at her ear. She shivered, involuntarily, and waited. That was all one could do with Simon.

"So…you've been behaving? Sticking to…" He began, and out of the corner of her eye the ghost appeared in the room. Celia could not see the expression on the spirit's face, but the apparition seemed more solid. Her presence made Celia bold and before Simon could finish his thought, she asked.

"No. I have not been 'behaving' and I do not intend to. Before you say another word, Simon, tell me, what is it that you hold over Dr. Norbert?"

Celia felt his body tense then relax behind hers, and an airy laugh sprang from his chest.

"There's some vigor for you! Bravo, Sweet Celie, I do believe this is the most interesting you've been in some time." He exhaled, and then licked her ear, making her shiver again, and her stomach heaved. He repulsed her. She wondered if he knew, and that was why he did it? Or did he still believe there were feelings between them somewhere? She swallowed bile and he continued on, punctuating his lazy words with chuckles.

"Clever girl for noticing about Norbert though. You've noticed the odd reverence the weasel seems to hold for me then?" He chuckled again, enjoying some private joke that Celia doubted was in the least bit humorous, except to a monster like Simon. He swung Celia around to face him and studied her face a moment.

"Why not? Why not, indeed? It's not as though you could tell anyone. No one believes the insane wretch, do they?" He guffawed.

The ghost stepped closer, grabbing Celia's hand, leaving little, cold, tingling sensations on her palm and along her fingers. Whether the intention was to give comfort or take it, Celia did not know.

Simon circled her, then opened the door and leaned out, briefly, looking about, satisfying himself that no one else was listening.

He stepped back in and regarded Celia, at first warily, and then, he smiled and waggled his eyebrows as if the whole thing was absurd.

"Well, my dear, I am going to tell you, though mother would say I shouldn't give you anything you could use, especially after, well, no, we won't speak of that. But, mother is wrong, wrong, wrong, isn't she? There's not a damned thing you can use in here, can you? Letters are even...difficult to receive, no?"

He offered her a baited look that she did not rise to. She'd already known, after all, who'd stopped her letters. She blessed Nurse Dockert silently, but nodded for him to continue.

"Well, our Dr. Norbert and I knew each other when we were young. We were...neighbors, he and I. Always been interested in the medical arts was Norbert. Nasty habits really. Dissecting and surgery and cutting things open. A very dirty, bloody business. A strange boy, you understand. You couldn't stumble upon a dead cat without him slicing it up and seeing what was inside. He wasn't very popular with the other boys, I don't have to tell you."

Simon was smiling and between that and the story Celia really was repulsed to the point of nausea. She swallowed the feeling down as best as she could and tried not to look too closely at his expression as he spoke.

"And Norbert grew up, a lonely boy. But you know me, don't you Sweet Celie? I can't help but collect lonely things. They are so useful. So glad to be of help. So happy to be noticed and thought of."

He grinned that alligator smile, and she couldn't believe she hadn't seen how cold-blooded he was from the first. She must have been truly blind to have missed such evil.

"So, I kept him around. I invited him to the house, and if we weren't precisely, 'friends', well, Norbert certainly believed so. And so when I began to have a problem with a certain…lady, who was, ah, how shall we say it so that we do not offend your delicate femininity? A lady who was not quite right. A lady who needed, shall we say, special medicine to make her, well, more obedient and…pliable. And whenever this lady had her problems, medical or, emotional, say, or when she was acting, how shall I put it? Mad? That seems an appropriate term to use in this place. Well, the good doctor came then. Don't you remember, Celia? Don't tell me you didn't remember Dr. Norbert?"

The question was not really a question, as he was not even looking at her. It was said only to humiliate her. To remind her of what she had done. The ghost gripped her hand still tighter, but her face, her face was only a vague mist. As if she could not show her face here. Celia did not know why the ghost would stand with her against Simon, but she was glad of her presence, even if she was the only one who could see her.

"I still don't understand," she said finally. "So he helped you before as he helps you now. He does your bidding because you offer prestige through your friendship? Is that what you would have me believe?"

He laughed, low and hollow. "No, you unbelievable idiot. He does what I say because I know what he has done. I know his mistakes. And so do you. So quit playing as though you do not. Deception doesn't suit you, Sweet Cee."

She furrowed her brow in confusion. Perhaps Simon had gone a little mad. She could easily see how. This game he was playing was enough to put anyone over the edge. But she wondered…did she know more than she realized? How much had she buried?

"And before you ask, yes, I am implicated too, of course. Though thankfully this does not occur to Norbert. He cannot see beyond the end of his own reputation, and he has sufficient enough other skeletons lurking from our youth to be afraid of me. The tongue is mightier, my dear, for those of us with the power to wield it."

He smiled, as if he had performed a trick, and Celia wished she could throw her arms around the ghost woman beside her and take comfort from a being that wasn't completely made of darkness, as the man before her surely was. Had there really been a time when she thought him handsome? Amusing? Kind, caring and thoughtful? She almost felt bad for Dr. Norbert, no matter his sins, he was even now being used by Simon as he used everyone around him. All pieces on a gaming board that only he could see. She detested him.

"Now…" He began, but he appeared smaller to Celia, inconsequential. The figure of Owen Flynn towering above him in every way.

"Now what?" She asked, gathering her anger. The ghost, a woman she knew, for certain now, if she hadn't admitted it before, let go of her arm and pressed a finger to her lips before passing out of the threshold of the doorway.

For a moment Simon seemed nonplussed, but then recovered, rolling his eyes dramatically. "Celia, my dear, you haven't been talking having you? Blabbing about nonsense? None would believe you, my heart. In case you had some type of notion of revenge, or justice, or some other such thing. You are a woman, and adjudged mentally unsound, and so…I hope for your sake you are not making life in the asylum more…difficult for yourself."

He closed the distance between them as if to strike. His lazy careless expression was gone, replaced by hot fury, how he managed to call that look to his face so quickly she could not guess.

"So help me, woman! You'll keep it shut. Or you'll rot in here! Or…"

But she cut him off, though she did not know where the courage to do so came from.

"Or what? Will you vanish me somewhere more remote? You'll never get your hands on the money then!"

He brought his hand down hard then, and it crashed into her face. She felt the blood begin flowing from her nose, and the sting on her cheek that would be red within moments and bruise soon enough.

"You'll keep that mouth firmly sealed, as I have told you to do so, and you will gain nothing by opening it. And as for the money, as the spouse I stand to inherit should anything…occur."

He raised his hand again, and Celia tensed, though his words pricked more than any physical pain he could inflict. Could he kill her? Simon Green was odious violent and cruel—but kill? She didn't think so. Or perhaps it was that she hoped not.

And then she realized, just before his second blow landed. Dr. Norbert could kill. He was a doctor, he had seen death before. And Simon was right. It didn't matter if she told the truth or not, they'd never believe her. Never.

Simon grabbed her shoulders, face red and gold curls coiled like devil's horns. She steeled herself for whatever was coming next, and then Dr. Munson appeared in the door, followed by the ghost.

Celia collapsed as Dr. Munson shouted, her last thought before the blackness took her was that she'd never heard the kind doctor raise his voice before.

Rhubarb: Advice

2011

Eve spent the next week feeling a prize idiot. She had arrived home late, to her father fussing around with water in the kitchen, pretending to not be waiting up for her. He had shuffled around a minute, stealing looks at her face, and then had decided against asking her any questions, and said a brief goodnight before heading back into his room. He'd had a bag of oyster crackers sticking out of his robe pocket, and a tall glass of ice water in his hand. On any other night it would have made her grin all the way upstairs to her bed. Her mother endlessly complained about crumbs in the bed and missing groceries, and it was her father's odd nocturnal feeding habits that caused this, though her mother was never awake to catch him.

It hadn't been enough to cheer Eve that first night, or any of the nights following. She felt a fool.

She had been tired, on edge, so desperate for things to go well between them, and walking on eggshells about her past. She supposed she had been waiting the entire time for him to find out, or for something to come up and she'd be revealed bare before him, and he'd lose interest in her, and in her silly asylum project.

What rankled the most is that she felt that she was right. He had lost interest in her. But, how much of that was her own fault? Maybe it was her reaction? Perhaps it was the level of over-reaction. She couldn't stop thinking about it. It was the first thought she had in the morning and it took up space in her mind on her walks with the dogs, usually her favorite time of day, where her head cleared and the world was its most marvelous to her. She pondered the thunderous exchange all through her work day, and ruminated over his terrible laugh while she tried to read in bed at night. He'd even ruined reading for her. Reading, her safe, or, perhaps *safer* addiction. For reading was never really a harmless pastime, was it? It introduced her to different worlds, realities, perspectives, loves, horrors, jealousy, treachery, sorrow, loss. There was no safety in reading, but it didn't leave trails and scars down her arms. It didn't transform her into a person that she not only didn't recognize, but didn't want to. But even that haven was gone. Instead Eric Chapel and that terrible, ugly laugh. But also...all of the pleasant pieces of their evening. The feeling of his hand in hers. The comfort of their silence together. The outline of his face in the moonlight and his voice in the darkness. The way the library had felt—almost like a place of worship—when they had come into it without lights. Their banter, their shared passion for her project…it had all seemed…perfect. No, not perfect. Perfect was not a word, not even something Eve hoped to attain. It was…lovely. Even in just the brief time she'd known him, he'd made her life brighter, more vibrant and open to possibilities. And now, she felt, paler. Darker. Cut off from opportunities she hadn't imagined before him.

She sat at work on Friday morning and sighed. It had been a full week since she'd seen him. And it wasn't only Eric that she missed, but Celia Thorne too. Eve had tried to tell herself she didn't care what had happened to a woman who'd lived 130 years ago, but she did. She still felt a connection to her, however tenuous. What had happened to Celia? What had her life become? Where in the world had she gone?

It had been a busy week at Folded Corners, orders coming in from all over the state and from a few foreign countries as well. Her boss had made a few acquisitions on his travels, a few of them quite rare, and Eve had spent time sleuthing through old records and difficult-to-navigate databases to establish provenance and worth. A few of the items she had almost immediately sold, before she'd even had time to properly list them. This had occupied her time and kept her more than usually busy, but it had unfortunately not managed to crowd out her anxious thoughts.

She was finally getting through the flood of e-mails that had come in while she had been otherwise engaged, when a figure walked into the shop. As a general rule, Celia was friendly to customers, and glad to do so, but she was so focused on responding to the message before her she had only uttered a half-hearted hello and welcome before re-focusing all attention on the screen before her.

After a few moments, however, it became clear that the person in the shop was not browsing. Instead, it seemed that she had come to stand a few yards away from her desk, and was waiting for her to look up. Which, after a moment, she did.

Miriam.

She wasn't certain why it should surprise her so completely. After all, Miriam was a librarian and so books were obviously of keen interest to her. But it did surprise her, because Miriam was clearly there to speak to her, though doing a very poor job of pretending she wasn't. Her eyes squinted through her tortoiseshell glasses, dashing over the spines of the books on the shelves before her. But Eve could tell the older woman wasn't really reading them, in fact, she doubted if she saw them at all.

"Miriam, can I help you?" Eve felt herself flush a little as she uttered the words, realizing half a breath too late that she didn't know her last name, and wasn't certain if calling her by her first name was a breach of etiquette.

She needn't have worried. Miriam merely gave a hint of a smile as if she hadn't realized it was Eve at all, and it was quite a surprise to her to find herself in Folded Corners. "Evelyn, how nice to see you again." She said in a brighter voice than Eve had expected. Her large grey eyes were watery, and they looked so much like a rainy day that Eve was moved to peer outside to inspect the weather, but there were no windows in the basement of Building 50, and so she nodded at her instead, and cleared her throat, stumbling over words.

"It's...it's just, Eve, actually..."

"Nonsense. It's Evelyn. And if it isn't then it is now." She smiled a little, one corner of her mouth quirking upward in a fashion that gave Eve the impression that the woman was either being friendly or mocking her, and she leaned toward the latter.

"Well, can I...help you find something?"

Miriam sniffed and looked around, seemingly disapproving of a place that charged for books, and despite herself Eve felt a tiny ripple of shame that the shop did so, though, if they did not, she would not have a paycheck.

"No, no. *I* am here to help *you*. I understand there was a quarrel? I'm sure it's not my business, but, when one is grey and one's skin has creased and rumpled, it is simple to make, well, really anything one's business. It is expected for older ladies to meddle. I have attained my majority in meddling, and so meddle I must." She smiled now, a toothy grin that showed off a row of surprisingly white and straight teeth. "Veneers," she indicated, tapping her front right tooth with a long, glossy, fuchsia fingernail.

Eve nodded, though whether she was nodding in acknowledgement of the veneers, or in agreement for Miriam's permission to meddle, she wasn't sure. She thought it was probably both as no other alternative seemed immediately apparent.

"As I said" Miriam began again, her voice a trifle louder, "I understand there has been a row?"

Eve cleared her throat and opened her mouth, and then coughed. Her eyes watered and she felt very, very silly. "Yes, well, sort of." She finally rasped out when the coughing fit had passed. "Is that what he told you?"

Miriam chuckled, and tightened her rayon polka-dotted scarf's knot a little tighter. "Told me? Eric has *told* me nothing. Nothing at all. We work all day, his eyes are stuck in the computer. His answers are clipped, his eyes are downcast, but he says *nothing.* Simply waves me off when I ask a question. And I may be his great aunt, but I *will not* be waved off by a moody young man."

Eve nodded and made a face that she thought communicated effectively that she understood that Eric's mood was her fault entirely, but Miriam wasn't having it.

"So, there has been some kind of disagreement. Whose fault?" She asked the question sharply, as if trying to catch Eve unawares.

"Well, his, or, really, it was mine. It was...a kind of misunderstanding, you see..."

"No, no, no." She said, cutting Eve short. "It's no business of mine, as I said. I mean to *meddle*—not step on anyone's shoes. Or toes. Whatever the saying is. In either case, I will step on no shoes or toes. So, I take it there has been a quarrel, wherein both of you were pigheaded in some way, and now both of you are miserable to the point of distraction, but neither one is confident enough to apologize and cancel the whole thing out."

Eve considered for a moment, and tilted her head. If only it were that easy. Was it that simple? Could she simply explain herself and say sorry? She could...she would, truly...but. But that laugh. She couldn't forget it. It rang in her ears, mocking. He had heard her truth and laughed at her. At the very least he thought her addiction and confession was silly, at the very worst his first impulse had been that she was worthy of derision. Just because his great aunt thought he felt badly about it now didn't take away that reaction.

"I don't think it's that simple," she replied finally, unable to meet Miriam's eyes.

Neither one of them spoke. Miriam made a noise in her throat and set her mouth in a line that Eve couldn't read. She then proceeded to walk around the shop. If Eve's mother were there she would have described it, fairly accurately, as 'puttering'. She'd lean in close to a certain spine, seemingly smell it, and then twist her mouth up as though the book was no longer ripe. She'd amble over to a different shelf and *almost* touch a book or two, fingers hovering over the top, before snatching those fingers away as if some strange miasma was reacting with her skin. She puttered and wandered and drew close to a shelf and then backed away, as though making sense of a seeing eye poster that demanded she move her vision back and forth to clearly make out the hidden picture. Eve eventually glanced back at the e-mail she had been writing and sighed, silently, and began to type again. Obviously Miriam had said what she had come to say and she had nothing else to impart to Eve. It made her a little sad, as if she had failed a test. Perhaps she had.

Miriam stepped near the door, and sniffed the air again, as though trying to detect some odor that was a portent of things to come in the air. She squared her shoulders and stared at Eve, the kind of stare that brings one's eyes up immediately and one is forced to take notice.

"I say, most of life really *is* that simple, Evelyn. It is we who strive to make it more complex than it ought. Think on that."

She adjusted her scarf, sniffed the air again, and was gone, but the air of her disapproval hung around the covers of the books the rest of the day.

Hemlock: You Will Be my Death

1888

The rest of the evening was hazy, and Celia found that when she tried to recall just what had happened, she was unable. Whether it was from the shock of Simon's presence, or the blessed intervention of Dr. Munson, she also couldn't say. But he had left, and she was escorted back to her room, where she had soon fallen into an easier sleep than she could have conceived, without the nuisance of racing thoughts or plaguing anxieties.

In the morning, upon waking, Celia brought her hands to her temples, and wondered if it was possible that she had imagined it all. Then she moved her palm from her temple to her cheek, and knew that she had done no such thing. Her touch also brought fresh sensations of pain, as though before she had felt for the wound her brain had denied it was there. Her cheek felt rough, mottled, and swollen. She wondered if it had bled, and briefly, what it now looked like, before moving to get out of bed to discover for herself.

The face that stared back from the mirror was her own, but it was also a stranger to her. It was, indeed, swollen, and the skin was broken in a few places along her cheekbone probably from Simon's many and garish rings. She stared down at the band he had given her to wear, the way it ensnared her finger. Why hadn't she seen it at the time for what it was?

A trap.

But one she yet could pull herself out of, even if she could not do so unscathed. It was still worth the freedom, no matter the cost.

Celia wondered what had happened to Simon. It was clear he had been made to leave, but she could not imagine he did so without protest. A moment later and Nurse Dockert rapped at the door and then entered without waiting for Celia's reply. Her eyes told Celia how she appeared to others without a word uttered. Nurse Dockert's face filled with pity, and then her mouth quirked, and opened a fraction, words she meant to say, wanted to say, but somehow couldn't. What do women say to one another at such a time?

Celia stood up and allowed herself to be led to the bath in the lavatory. She undressed, carefully, her whole body sore, from the tenseness, fear or the blows themselves, she could not say for certain, but it was most probably a mixture of the lot of them. Celia allowed Nurse Dockert to bathe her, though both of them knew she would only become dirt-covered and sweat-laden out of doors in the garden soon enough. She needed to clean the dried blood from her, and the memories of his hands on her arms, her face, her body. She needed to cleanse him from her, and it seemed that Nurse Dockert understood this, and Celia was grateful.

While she poured water over Celia's head, everything about her now soap and bubbles and wet, Nurse Dockert explained in a low, soothing voice one usually reserves for the very young or very aged.

"...and then Dr. Munson, he said, well, it doesn't make a lick of sense, I'm sure. But he said that he felt as if something—someone, like, had a hold of him, pulling him to that room. Thought it was a kind of spasm maybe, or nerves or something like. Whatever it was, he got there in time to get that Mr. Green away."

Celia had looked at her then, needing to know the rest, and Nurse Dockert poured a little more water over her head and then stood up, reaching for a scratchy but sturdy hospital towel.

"Mr. Green claimed you had attacked him and he was naught but defending himself, but I don't think that would have fooled even poor Caroline here in the asylum...that is, I meant...well, begging your pardon, Miss...Celia."

Celia shook her head in disbelief as she was efficiently dried off, and then dressed.

"Well, Dr. Munson, he wasn't having any of that nonsense. He asked Mr. Green to leave, forthwith—I might add—and your Mr. Green became awfully sore. Raised his voice, demanded to see Norbert—as if that would make a bit of difference! Munson is Norbert's superior here, after all! Anyhow, he made his demands, but Dr. Munson stuck true. Told him he's the hospital administrator, and that for the foreseeable future it was better for your healing if Mr. Green did not deign to visit. He caused a right ruckus then, of course. Said he'd be having the documents drawn up to have you transferred somewhere else. It would be difficult to do though, so don't worry your head about it. Dr. Munson is well respected. But I've never seen the doctor so troubled as after Mr. Green left, Miss Celia. You could hear him pacing the office half the night. Well, at least I could, because I was on shift last night."

They were both quiet, lost in their separate thoughts, while Nurse Dockert braided Celia's long honey hair and twisted it about her head so that it would be "out of the mud".

As they stood, Celia turned and thanked her, squeezing her hand, trying to impart some of her feeling into the gesture. Kindness—oh! She would never take it for granted again. Nurse Dockert with her feisty red hair and freckled cheeks looked like an angel to Celia and she realized with a lump in her throat (that she hastily swallowed) that the woman might, in fact, be as close to one as she was like to see.

From her pocket, Nurse Dockert drew out Celia's folded letter to Mr. Montague, and pressed it into her palm.

"This...this was beneath your dress when the orderlies came to fetch you to your bed after the excitement of yesterday. I thought that maybe you needed it kept safe."

They stopped in Celia's room to collect her gardening boots and then headed down the corridor and the stair, out into the sunshine of the day. They had taken an unfamiliar path, past the telephone room and Matron Gillman's office. Past the reception room and down a strange stair that patients were not usually taken down. They went through the lower level—basement level really— and passed by a a series of storage rooms, a vault, the pantry and then a short stair that led up a few steps—and then outside.

Outside, where Owen, wide-eyed and desperate looking waited for her. Her eyes had instinctively gone to Nurse Dockert's face to see her reaction to Owen's expression, but she'd already begun walking back, turning the other direction, toward their usual path. Celia didn't know if she'd been led down this clandestine way to keep others from spying her bruised face, or if it was to allow Owen a private moment. She did not care which it was.

Celia flung herself into his sturdy chest, and his arms encircled her, sealing her in more soundly than the phony wedding ring on her finger. They stayed thus, her head on his beating heart, her tears on his coat, and his on her head for some moments, until Celia finally gathered the courage to break away.

"I think they are going to kill me." She said, stepping back. Celia felt hopelessly dramatic uttering such words, but it was true, wasn't it? That was what she had come to understand he would do —was planning to do, if she signed the papers. Did that make it any less sensational?

His mouth opened in an expression that was a mix of horror and confusion, and his face grew more stricken as he took in her injuries. He raised a hand, as if he would lay it gently on her face and heal it, but then quickly pulled away, and looked around before gesturing for her to walk with him toward the gardening shed.

"We must do all we can to appear normal" he said in a low voice. She nodded. The gardening shed was near to the shop building and as they passed by she heard men hard at work in the carpenter shop and women in the soap room. She shivered to think of all the danger lurking in this place. Celia had imagined that being locked away against one's will was the greatest terror—but it was far and away the least. There were saws in the carpenter's shop and the smithy ran on fire and metal. Places to be secreted like the boiler room or coal shed, or a simple adjustment to her medicine or something added to her morning jam. She thought of those lonely, dark, cold storage rooms she'd walked by with Nurse Dockert. How long would it take someone to find her if she was trapped down there? Would they find her body at all if it was hidden there? She shivered again, knowing that her mind was a runaway wild horse this morning—but when she thought of the poor, dead, ghost woman, murder did not seem so fantastic.

He led her to the shed and picked up a few items, it seemed at random, but then brought her to the asylum's vegetable and herb garden, where she'd met him the first day. He handed over her gloves, which she put on mechanically, and then they began picking and weeding, carefully filling out a basket for the asylum's kitchens.

"I'll kill them," Owen said, clearly and calmly they settled into the task.

"You'll do no such thing," she replied, without looking up. She told him then. About Simon's visit, and what Simon had said, and about the ghost woman and about Dr. Norbert. She told him the whole scene without emotion or hysterics, and yet, when she looked at his face, she saw his darling angel's kiss freckles had disappeared in the angry boiling red expression. His eyes were hard, his mouth rigid. He made no pretext at weeding any longer, instead flexing and relaxing his fingers. His whole body was that of a pointer dog on a hunt. Immovable stone, resolute. She gasped, suddenly afraid of him, and the effect was lost, for his whole face cleared, and his hands came to rest at his sides like a helpless child.

"I'm…I'm sorry, my girl. I…I didn't mean to…"

She put a hand to her mouth and shook her head. "No. Enough. Anger and control and coldness was what landed me here. We cannot think like them. We *must* be different, can't you see?"

He nodded, and she exhaled. Reaching into her pocket, she handed over the letter for Montague and he promised to post it when they broke for breakfast. They planned then, and in words it couldn't have been simpler. One day, when she came out to work with him in the gardens, she'd steal away. He would pay a few people in town to look the other way and then they'd rendezvous and escape to somewhere else. Boston, New York, maybe even out west. Somewhere else, where no one knew them at all, and the only madness anyone would accuse them of was for each other.

In words, it couldn't have been easier. Like planning a picnic or choosing the rail times and schedule to Chicago. But, they both knew despite their excited whispers that the execution of the plan would be a different thing entirely.

Celia was afraid. Even as the sunlight caressed her hair and her gloves reached into the cool earth. His voice was close and singing and again she thought she'd never heard a more beautiful sound in the world.

She was crying then, gasping sobs as if she were flailing in her own tears. He was crouching near her, but not too close, as the male patients had been led out earlier for their nature walk and could pass back by at any time.

"Celia what is it? If it's your husband that's troubling you, I swear…" And the suddenness of his anger turned her head to see those flint grey and lake blue eyes and she calmed, though she could still taste the sorrow in her throat when she asked,

"Would you really love me without any money at all?"

And he was nodding, his face filled with something she couldn't quite understand, and she went on, "And with my ghosts?" He nodded again, and she inhaled sharply. So sharply she almost felt the blade of that breath cut into the words in her throat.

"Even if…"

And then the men emerged out from the woods, walking mechanically, some of them, and others so regular and normal in appearance that they seemed embarrassed to be out walking with such a group.

The moment was broken though, and Celia swallowed the secrets back down to where they sat in her stomach. Mad, mad, she had thought she was mad. Had believed she was—truly. Well, she was mad. Had to have been to have agreed—and then, the ghosts. It was all madness, and none of it was. Simon really could have talked her into anything.

She opened her mouth, willing the words to come out and set her free, one more gate open, one step closer to that new life she dreamed of. The male patients were gone now, having filed back into the asylum as docile as lambs. It would be a half hour or more until the women came out for their constitutional. It would have to be now.

Celia squared her shoulders and exhaled the breath she hadn't realized she held. She felt the blade in her throat sever whatever had been holding the truth back.

Owen was already listening, waiting. She liked that about him. The waiting. She'd bet he could wait her truths out forever.

"It was the name, you see. 'Celia'. I never noticed it much before, but...well, you see, I'll need to start closer to the beginning, I suppose. When I first met Simon Green I was on a train with my parents. He had flirted with me, of course, and shown interest—wild interest even. And he said my name over and over, 'Celia, darling Celia, sweet Celie...' it was like a love spell or an incantation. That's what I'd thought anyway, at the time. I had no reason to think anything else, of course. I was smitten, he *is* devilishly handsome before one knows him, and once I knew him...well, it was too late. But it wasn't just the name, you understand. There were many similarities, which is why I suspect I was chosen. The name was just the bow on top. The ashy blonde hair, our parents dying around the same time, not too long after I'd met Simon. Mine in a train accident, they were musicians, you see. Did I ever tell you that? I don't remember. It was what they did, but such a small part of who they were, it hardly seems important. But we traveled around a lot because of it. We always had a garden wherever we were though—that was true when I told you that. Nothing like your flowers and plants, just easy to grow, local things or exotics my father found Lord knows where. Sometimes we didn't even stick around long enough to see them bloom. But anyway, that's not what I was telling you. There were similarities, as I said. Her parents died in a carriage accident. I found out later her mother had shot her father and then herself in that carriage. Not really an accident if you think about it, which I have done quite a lot. But they called it so, though, I don't know why. Sounds better, I suppose. Madness ran in her family, Simon told me."

"Simon…your husband?" Owen asked, one eyebrow pushing down so that his eye squinted. She hoped with all the twists and weavings of her rambling confession he was keeping up, she didn't know if she was up to repeating it.

"Yes. Well, no. Celia's husband."

He looked even more confused and she couldn't fault him, and so continued on as smoothly as she was able with her tale. But like a river, truth turns and jags and sometimes runs rapidly, she inhaled and let out the next words like a wave.

"So, as I said, the hair, the name, both orphans. But, I was rather poor, and she was rich. Rich as

Croseus as they say, though I must admit my education wasn't thorough enough to ever cover precisely who Croseus was. But, the other Celia was always at home. I haven't the faintest idea how they first met, but they were married, you see? She was content to haunt the halls and rooms of their house, didn't like leaving or being around strangers. When Simon first told me about her, why, I felt *sorry* for him, if you can credit it! Trapped with his mad wife. I never considered he might be the very thing that had driven her so. Madness is always driven, isn't it? It never simply appears, or arrives, or floats along, one is always propelled toward it, like an arrow at a target. But, at any rate, yes, she never went out, from what I could gather."

"Celia...I don't...I don't understand." Owen looked almost ill. His expression told her that he did, indeed, understand, but didn't want to. Worry creased his face and Celia looked around before extending out one gloved hand and patting his knee in a motion of comfort. This, however, only seemed to concern him more.

"I'm afraid it's true. You've seen Simon. To someone like me, orphaned, working as an assistant to a school teacher, with no one—well! He re-appeared in my life after seeing him on that train those years before, and he looked like an angel from heaven. All that gold hair and those gleaming green eyes, and I did pity him. In the beginning, I did. He convinced me that I was really doing no wrong. And there was nothing...nothing shameful about our relationship. He needed me, or, I was made to think he did, and I suppose he did need me—to use me. He was always one for convincing. We went to the theater, and to dinner, and I don't know if he planned the whole thing, or if it really did start off innocently, though I can hardly say Simon and innocent in the same sentence, but I *was* Celia. And she was Celia. And so I was his Celia, and everyone believed it because no one knew much of what she looked like. She wouldn't leave home, remember? What a nice little trick, wasn't it? We had the same hair, and she was only a few inches taller, which can be easily fixed with the right shoes, and her figure was a trifle fuller than my own, but who was to know that? He even had me visit her lawyer—our Mr. Montague. I didn't understand precisely why at the time, but of course, I wasn't meant to! And he said, well, he claimed I was helping them both. That if I didn't come out he'd find someone else, someone that everyone knew wasn't his wife, and would I want to be responsible for Celia looking like a fool? But of course, *I* was the fool. I suppose I wanted to believe it. Who ever wants to believe they are doing something wrong, when there is an option to believe they are not?"

Celia thought she heard a door open, and looked around, eyes wide. They were still alone. She avoided the glimmer of understanding and fear on Owen's face.

"I know. It *is* insane. I believe he made me a little mad. And even if it wasn't already in her family. I believe he did the same to her too. Every time she miscarried, which was happening far too often ever for a woman of sound mind, she sank a little deeper into the madness. Crying, howling like an animal. My heart broke for her, truly. I was practically living in the house by that time, you see. Simon's mother too, horrible woman. She went to work on me as well. I swear I wasn't certain who I was half the time. And the ghosts were everywhere then."

She was quiet a moment, chewing her lip. Celia was a little sad to realize he wasn't reminding her not to. But she sighed, set on finishing, knowing she had to, if not for him, then for herself.

"The last miscarriage killed her—the other Celia. Poor soul. I was the first to know it, I think. I had remained with her, I don't know why. I suppose because I hated thinking of her alone in that house with all that sorrow and only Simon's horrible mother as company. Simon was out, with another woman, of course, though I pretended I didn't know, and I must say, I really didn't care. I was glad, if anything. When he was with someone else he wasn't bullying me. But that night, I saw her spirit for the first time. She looked...better. I'd only seen her a handful of times in the flesh, you see, and it was always when she was her most ill and mad. But the night she died, her spirit looked serene and at peace, just as a spirit should. Simon of course, when he found out, was terrified to lose her money."

Her voice broke and her eyes filled, but she pushed the next reluctant words out.

"I don't know how he did it, but he convinced me that I was wrong. That Celia wasn't dead. That there was no other Celia, that I was the mad one. He told me that the last few months really seemed to have done me in and he'd feel better if I rested somewhere. I needed to go to a spa, he said. Somewhere exclusive and private to regain my health. I protested! I fought him on it! I told him I knew about the death and the guilt of it weighed on me, and it was true! Eventually he gave in. Admitted that Celia was dead, but said I really wasn't well. Just look at my hysteria! Look at how I was behaving! I was unhinged, he told me, going insane, more so every day. Then he'd coo, and comfort me and said it would be better if I went away, just for a bit, while news of the death became known and people asked questions. I knew him for the vile thing he is then, of course I did, but I had no one else, did I? I knew no other life but the happiness of my life with my parents and the terrible thing that he offered me. I did want to get away. Away from him! I even began to think that her death was my fault for a time, that somehow, I had killed her. And he... he let me think it. And... I believed it. I really did think I had gone mad. Nothing made sense, I barely knew who I was anymore. And so when I arrived here...I didn't know"

"But it wasn't a spa." Owen said, voice hard.

"No, of course it wasn't. It was here. And...and I felt I was mad. I really believed it. Why else would they have accepted me at an asylum? Perhaps everything Simon had told me was true, and my own life was imagination and madness. Maybe I truly was his insane wife. Why else? I couldn't trust myself, couldn't be sure, until I saw those intake papers. I'm Celia Thorne, and the only mad thing I ever did was trust that Simon Green had a decent bone in him. He's rotten. And he made me worse than a harlot. He made me ashamed to be myself. I'm sure Celia Green's body is buried behind the big house her own money paid for in Detroit, and he's hidden me away here until he can get his hands on the rest of the fortune, which only my signature can now provide."

"The whole thing is…incredible." Owen put a hand over his mouth and looked at the sky, eyes wide. "It's something out of a novel, surely."

"Yes, I know. And all because of a name. When you've never been anybody it's easy for someone to make you believe you're someone else. Or that you could be—even that I was somehow doing her a favor by becoming her. And hang it! I admit, I enjoyed it at first. Being mistaken for a rich and important Celia with a handsome husband and the world at my feet. Of course I did…until I saw it was a real life that I was taking over. A real woman… who was sad and hurt and going mad. And she haunts me still. It is her spirit I see, her phantom hand that brushes mine and she that appears to me. I thought at first she was an angry, vengeful spirit. But she comes only to comfort me. As women must, you know? Against the cruelty of men. I am glad for her haunting, though I do not deserve the kindness of it."

He nodded, considering her words. He ran his hands over the soil and sniffed the air. "Celia… there is one thing I must say."

"Only one?"

"At this very moment, yes. Celia, we can't take that money." He met her eyes with his own, and his expression wasn't unkind, but instead determined.

"You said 'we'" she replied in a hopeful whisper.

"I did. But we really cannot. It is wrong, you know that. We don't need it, my darling…"

She smiled. "Oh, Owen! I'm so glad. I've already authorized Mr. Montague to give it away. In the letter you're set to post this morning, I've instructed him to revert back to the previous version of her will, which gives the money to the women's hospital. I never could have kept it, Owen, never. I couldn't do that to Celia! You'll still take me away? Even after all of…this?"

Owen leaned in and grabbed her gloved hand, "Celia, the day we met you gave me your real name, do you remember?"

She nodded, "I did. You're right, and it was odd, because I couldn't think why I'd done so. God, but I was afraid of Simon. I still am."

Owen looked around again, the women were now beginning to come out. "I don't blame you," he said simply, and something in his tone made her look up and study his face.

"You know Myrtle?" he asked from seemingly nowhere, eyes back on the mint he was picking. "She's from town here. Her son grew up here, too. He's a few years older than me, but we used to fish together on a sunny day. Well, old Jack locked her up here tight, on account of him owing her a pile of money after she helped pay for his shop in town. He strolled in the asylum after it was built and said, 'my ma's mad', and told a few tales and soon enough she was admitted. It's terrifying how simple it is for a man to put a woman he finds difficult into an asylum."

Celia thought a moment, and frowned. She would have liked to feel a little pity for herself, but so much of her misery sprang from her own choices. She was paying for them now, but did she deserve Owen's forgiveness? Or the other Celia's? Perhaps not. But she'd take it. Celia Green was dead, and the old Celia Thorne was too. A new life. That's what she'd said. And now he knew all. He knew what she was, what she'd done, and he still looked at her with love in his eyes.

The women were passing now, and they went back to their gardening. He sang a little under his breath and she smiled to herself and hummed along. This. This is what she dreamed of. A bright garden with him beside her. She looked up, momentarily, and her idyll was broken.

Caroline was staring at her strangely, eyes hard and cold and full of hate.

Primrose: I Can't Live Without You

1888

Days passed, and nothing was done. Sometimes Celia feared that she had imagined her confession to Owen, had dreamed it all up one night. But then she would be delivered, as always, out of doors to assist him in the garden again. Every day for a week, he shook his head, even though she knew it was too early to expect a reply back from Mr. Montague. Owen checked the mail, daily, he assured her, as they had agreed to put their plans for her escape off until they'd heard back from the man.

It wasn't an easy task, waiting. Some days Celia would awaken and curse herself. There was no real reason to put off her going until she received a reply from Montague. He had her instructions, all would be amended to precisely how Celia, the other Celia, had desired it. Any evil that Simon had worked through her, any deeds he had committed by using her as his faux wife would be reversed. She would only wait until she was safe to send a letter explaining where she thought they might find the poor woman's body. She knew that Simon Green wouldn't have let it be buried too far from where he could keep an eye on it. His wife was worth more to him dead than she had been alive, as terrible as it was to admit. But only if he could get her money—which Celia was determined that he would not. If not for her own sake, for the sake of the ghost that had been the woman she sympathized with so strongly.

But two weeks passed, then three and the letter still did not come. Gardening by Owen's side held the same sweetness, but was also imbued with a desperate tension. Both of them holding back words unsaid, both of them straining to maintain a calm neither of them possessed. The high sun of August was bright and hot, and the wind off the lake couldn't blow in cool enough. But even in the midst of the heat and the sheen of sweat on her forehead, she knew that September and Autumn lay around the corner. If they were forced to tarry at the asylum much longer, what possible pretense could they invent that would enable them to continue to see each other? Men would be brought out for harvesting whatever yields there were from the fields and gardens. The flowers would cease to bloom, and soon the cold winds would blow down from the north, and she would be back inside, staring out a frosted windowpane, trapped. Not only trapped as she was now, as a patient at the asylum, but trapped inside, stuck, closed in and without Owen.

Then one Tuesday night, three weeks after they'd sent the letter, she was seated in the common room, reading. She had been asked by one of the nurse's to play the piano, but had declined, claiming a headache. The truth was that she now couldn't think of music or song at all without hearing Owen's voice, and to hear it in her mind made her heart ache, and she would lose her resolve entirely. And so she sat, reading quietly. She was reading Wilkie Collins, "The Woman in White" and she could hardly believe it was kept in the asylum at all. Whomever had placed it in the library was either absentminded, hadn't bothered to read it, or extraordinarily cruel. A woman, placed against her will in an asylum wearing a dead woman's name…it was…diabolical. And so close to her own story that she reddened as she finished the novel, wondering if anyone could guess her secret from her book choice.

And then Nurse Dockert came in, holding a letter for her. The carrot-headed nurse's usually red and rosy face was drained of color, and her lips were taut and flat as she handed the letter over. Her eyes bored into Celia's, communicating a message that she couldn't understand. She narrowed her eyes and tilted her head, hoping to invite a confidence, but the woman looked around, eyes darting around skittishly and then shook her head. She dropped the letter to Celia's lap and skittered away.

The whole experience left Celia confused. What had that been about? It was obvious that Nurse Dockert had something to tell her, something distressing. But what it could be, she had no idea.

Her mind began leaping from one worry to the next. Something had happened to Owen. No, she had just seen him an hour ago and he had been on his way back to his cottage. Perhaps her letter to Mr. Montague had been intercepted and she was in trouble. Perhaps they had found the little diary she had made in her sketchbook! How embarrassing that would be! How would she explain it? She sat there, thinking, thinking, worrying and fretting, and tapped her foot on the floor as she did so. Suddenly, she heard an unusual, frightening sound. Caroline.

Nearby, Queen Caro sat on a balloon-backed chair, spine rod-straight, and one could almost imagine a crown perched upon her head. She was glaring at Celia. Caroline's face was filled with rage, and she stuck out her arm, pointing her finger imperiously at Celia's foot. "Stop that tapping! Now! Stop that!" She snapped the words. She didn't shout, but her voice was filled with venom. Celia silenced her errant foot, and dipped her chin in Caro's direction. Caroline turned her face away from Celia, giving her the cut, and Celia couldn't help but be bewildered. Annie had warned her about Caroline, but circumstances in the common room had grown more and more uncomfortable since Annie had left. It was as if Annie's bright sunniness had kept everyone in balance. Myrtle was a shadow of herself, Caroline was always looking daggers at Celia, as if it were her fault Annie had gone. The rest of the women, Agatha and Nelly and a dozen others she hadn't met properly but smiled at when she saw them, all seemed down as well. There was less mirth in their gaze, more exhaustion on their features. She tried to convince herself it was the turning of the season, but the season hadn't turned yet.

She exhaled and closed her finished book, snatching up the letter that the Nurse had delivered. How stupid of her! She had almost forgotten the damned letter. She couldn't believe that Mr. Montague would have written her at the asylum, not after she had specifically instructed him to write to her by way of Owen. It was with this doubt in the identity of the author in mind that she discreetly tore open the envelope and ran her eyes over the contents.

It was from Andrew Barnsley, and the contents broke her heart completely. He had written as a friend, and she was pleased that he should do so. But Annie was dead, her own life taken. At first she could not believe such a thing possible. Annie was too kind! She burned too brightly! How could the light of her be snuffed out so absolutely? She felt the tears come and she welcomed them, allowing them to fall like rain onto the page. She wondered if perhaps it had been too much, taking her away from the Northern Michigan Asylum and transplanting her into an unknown hospital in Chicago. Perhaps the doctors were not so kind as Dr. Munson, and perhaps the world surrounding her new home had been less lovely and green. She couldn't imagine what had provoked her to take her life. But Andrew Barnsley wrote,

"I pray that your trouble, whatever it is, may soon be put

right so that you may live yourself, and for her."

She would live for the both of them. She promised herself, and looking upward at the ceiling in the common room, and wishing it was sky, she promised Annie too. "Oh, Annie!" she said aloud, perhaps a little louder than she had meant to.

Before she had even a moment to register what was happening, Caroline stood and rushed at her, arms out and a cruel snarl coming from her mouth. To see the change so quickly wrought in her was overwhelming, and Celia, small as she was, shrank back into her own chair, as if to hide and knowing how foolish it was to try. Caroline leapt on her and scratched and yelled and screamed. Once when Celia was a child she had seen two cats fighting, and that was what she was put in mind of. Except she had no claws of her own. Instead she covered her face as best as she could and huddled into the chair too surprised to move or call out. Caroline's nails tore at her cheek and the bodice of her dress, her hair and arms. Her hands were everywhere and her hot breath. Strange, disturbing animal-like noises came from her mouth and Celia cowered, and tried to stand up. But Caroline was much larger than her, and had the fury of madness adding to her strength. Finally, orderlies rushed in and pulled Caroline off, who was still flailing, trying to scratch at Celia. Celia chanced a glance at her, and the expression on her contorted red face was terrifying. It was as though a monster lived inside what was normally Caroline's lovely face. A creature of hate and terror and insanity. Looking into Queen Caro's eyes, Celia realized that she, herself, had never been mad. Not like that. And if poor, deceased Celia Green had been mad, it had been a quieter, sadder kind. Not a madness to be locked away, but the type that needed care and love and kindness.

She reached her hand up and felt where Caroline had succeeded in injuring her face. A little hair had been yanked out, which suddenly hurt awfully, and pulling her hand away from her cheek, she saw bright blood on her palm, and then felt the sting. How strange that it hardly hurt at all until she had seen proof of the wound. As though if she had never inspected it, she would have never felt the pain. A nurse she did not know rushed over and helped her up, leading her to her room. Celia still clutched the letter from Andrew Barnsley in her hand, as if it were a talisman, and soundlessly she followed the nurse first to the lavatory, so that her injury might be cleaned and then across the hall to the infirmary so that her cuts could be treated. The entire time the kind nurse cooed, and dabbed, washed and patted, Celia did not speak. It was her only reaction. She had not seen it coming, after all, and was so surprised that it had happened at all that she was struck dumb. She had seen real madness. Firsthand. It seemed strange, she had been in this asylum for more than six months, and tonight was the first night she felt she had seen true insanity. When the nurse she did not know pressed her hand and asked if she would like to return to her room, Celia nodded yes, and smiled as if to reassure the woman that she wasn't going to go into hysterics at any moment.

But when they returned to her room, Nurse Dockert was waiting, her face still pale, her red corkscrew curls looking slightly less frenzied than usual, which somehow worried Celia. Everything about the woman drooped.

"Thank you, Nurse Tellner. I'll take charge of her from here. Come along, Miss Celia."

Celia smiled again at the other nurse and approached Nurse Dockert, who opened the door to her room to reveal a terrible surprise. She was all packed up. All of her things. Her belongings, her writing box, her clothing, her books and toiletries. All snapped up tight in cases and waiting silently, to be carried out. There wasn't much. Just three small cases that Celia could pick up herself if she was allowed to, which of course she was not.

On a night full of surprises, first the letter, then the attack and now this, Celia was still silent. She could hardly believe it, and she couldn't begin to understand it. She opened her mouth to speak, but no sound came out, so instead it hung open, dumbly, until Nurse Dockert spoke.

"Caroline got you good then, huh? I've been telling them, over and over, 'you have to move her farther down the ward with the disturbed folks' I told them. 'I don't care who her father is' I said, 'that girl is a right danger' and so she is, apparently. Hate that she had to hurt you, Miss Celia, for them to take notice of how violent Miss Caroline can't help but be. Sad case, that."

Celia nodded, noncommittally, and gestured

silently at her things.

"Oh, Miss. I thought maybe you didn't know. I suppose then that it's a rare blessing that Caroline hurt you so. For now you are in your room early, and you will have more time to...prepare. I'm so sorry, Miss, honest. Telegram came in last night, it did. Said you were to be moved to a different asylum, out east somewheres. Your husband, that is, Mr. Green, stated that you were to be placed on the 7:18 train back to Grand Rapids, and he'd have someone meet you there."

Celia let out a little gasp, and then collapsed onto the floor. She hadn't intended to behave like one of the silly, spineless females from the type of novels she abhorred, but it was....so unexpected. Even for Simon, it was...unprecedented cruelty. He truly hoped to hide her and torment her into submission. She pictured in her mind, her future. Simon, shuffling her from one asylum to the next until she truly became as mad he claimed she was. She gasped again, but did not cry out. No.

"You are to be escorted to the train station by Dr. Norbert himself in a half hour's time. He will retrieve you from your room, and an orderly will bring your things. Though, they are very light. And don't think of escaping down the stairs I showed you the other day, don't even think of it, Miss Celia. No one will be in this hallway for the next twenty minutes at least, but this door will be locked tight, very tight, and that is how Dr. Norbert will find it, when he comes. But don't think of trying to get away."

Before Celia could respond, or react to the woman's words, Nurse Dockert stepped toward her and squeezed her hand. She whispered something, that Celia couldn't quite catch in the moment, and then was out the door. If Celia hadn't been so bewildered, she would have seen tears on ruddy cheeks, and she would have thought for all her bluff and bluster, that Nurse Dockert was the most beautiful woman in the world.

Celia sat on the floor a moment longer, looking around. She then stood up, gingerly, and walked to the door. She tried the handle. Unlocked. Of course. But that didn't mean she could believe it. Why? Why had the nurse decided to help her? Celia grabbed her traveling cases and opened them up, re-arranging some of the contents so that all of her most important items fit into just one. She set the other two back upright, and kissed her writing desk goodbye. It felt like saying goodbye to her father all over again, so many memories she had from that desk, but she kissed it and said a prayer in her heart. She took the little sketchbook out of the hidden drawer and concealed it within the pocket of her skirts, and stowed the letter from Andrew Barnsley and from Mr. Montague in there as well. She wasn't certain what she would do with them, but she couldn't leave them in the desk to be found, no matter how hidden that drawer was.

She smoothed her skirts, and took a deep, calming breath, and stepped to the door. She put her ear to the wood, and listened. Never had silence sounded so irresistibly lovely. Trembling, she put a gloved hand on the door and opened it, and stole out into the hallway. She paused, and listened again, and encouraged by the silence she moved on, farther down the ward, toward the steps that Nurse Dockert had showed her, so many weeks ago. She had no time to think of getting a message to Owen, or of finding his cottage. Her mind was on getting away from the asylum, as far away as possible. She didn't care if she wandered the town all night afterward to find him, she only had to get down those steps.

Celia easily found the steps, and tip-toed stealthily down the stairs, alarmed on the first step at how loud her little boots had clacked on the stair. She paused every few seconds and listened, but heard nothing but her own breath. She was breathless with fear until she arrived at the doorway that led outside, and put her hand to the knob, filled with happiness. She was almost out.

The door began to move inward though, and Celia was forced to flee backward, quickly, as two voices could be heard in the crack of the opening door. Celia panicked, needing to move swiftly, but also as quietly as possible. She ducked into one of the store rooms that she had passed by with Nurse Dockert on that day three weeks ago. She stole to the back of it and sat on the stone floor, waiting, trying not to breathe.

The two voices that came in were vague. She could not tell if they were male or female at the first, and she hoped they would simply disappear up the steps and away from her. But they did not.

Instead the voices came closer, a man and a woman's, and both familiar to Celia, though she couldn't yet place them. The woman giggled coquettishly, and Celia frowned in the complete darkness of the storeroom. She wasn't sure what was being stored in here, but she thought maybe it was bed rolls, or some type of linens, and she hoped this wasn't exactly the type of room these lovers were looking for.

For it seemed to Celia that 'lovers' was precisely what this man and woman were. She heard a few whispered snatches of conversations, nothing articulate to her as she hugged her little case to her chest like a life preserver. She heard what sounded like wet mouth noises, which made Celia cringe. Who in the world was down here committing such acts? It couldn't be patients, so it must be staff.

And then she heard it. They had come into the room, the same uncomfortable noises emitting from the two of them, and some light moaning from the woman. At any moment, they would realize she was there, and she'd be doomed. And if she claimed they had been up to something inappropriate, it would be attributed to her madness. She was being sent away tonight anyway, no one cared for her anymore. The kissing stopped, and Celia strained to listen for how close they were, while at the same time trying not to listen at all, an impossible task, and her nerves were already ragged. She had been so close to escaping. And now....now she was so close to being found out.

The man spoke, and Celia had to hold in a gasp.

"Later, later, Mary, my dear. I have an errand to run."

The voice was Dr. Norbert's. Celia sat, stunned. There was no one she would rather have been trapped in the room with less, no one she would less want to hear kissing. She felt sick to her stomach. This was the man tasked with depositing her at the train station like a discarded package. She swallowed bile.

"Where are you going?" The woman's voice whispered, and then Dr. Norbert moaned in a way that made Celia extremely uncomfortable.

"Mary...Oh, Mary. Don't do that. I'm to take one of the patients to the station. She's being sent away."

"Oh, that Celia Green. Going to an asylum in the east or something."

He groaned again. "Mary, you must stop. I have to take the damn girl now. And I don't know about an asylum out east. If that's what old Simon Green put out then I'd be very surprised if it were true."

The woman, who Celia realized was Nurse Bell laughed breathlessly. "I can't think of what you mean...Simon Green seems like a lovely, ooh, lovely, marvelous kind of man."

"You don't know him very well, my darling Mary. And I think it's better that you don't."

They were kissing again, and Celia felt even

more ill. She needed to get out. They were too close. They knew too much about her, and now she knew too much about them. Nurse Bell broke away from the kiss and walked toward where Celia was hiding. Celia pressed herself against the stone wall, and felt a piece of the stone shift behind her back. Nurse Bell must have heard it too, because she paused.

"Did you hear something?" She asked, taking a step closer to Celia. Celia held her breath. The rock behind her was slipping, and at any moment it would make a noise as it hit the ground. The storeroom was in complete cool darkness, but even now her eyes were adjusting to the very small amount of light let in by a window at the very top of the subterranean room. The window was covered with a screen, but a little light filtered down. She could just make out the outlines of the nurse's white uniform, and her cap. The figure of Dr. Norbert stepped forward, his hand coming to Nurse Bell's body, and Celia pressed herself into the wall, almost hoping to merge with the stone itself and disappear inside of it. Anything better than being caught alone with Dr. Norbert.

"It's probably just rats" He said, and she gave a little shriek, pushing him away.

"Rats! How could you even…!" she began, when another voice sounded from the hallway outside the storeroom

"Begging your pardon, Doctor, I hope I am not…interrupting, but I *believe* you are needed to transport the patient."

It was Nurse Brattle, all energy drained from her voice. Celia almost felt bad for the woman, finding the doctor she adored in the arms of another woman, so grossly clandestine as this. There was no battle-ax left in Nurse Brattle, but Celia was glad she'd had the gumption to interrupt the lovers at all.

"Ah, yes, indeed, Nurse Brattle. We were…we heard rats here in the storeroom and came to chase them out."

"Yes, Doctor, of course. But, they are waiting."

Celia continued to hold her breath as first Nurse Bell, then Dr. Norbert left the storeroom. She listened in the dark as their footsteps echoed up the stairs. Any moment and they would discover she was gone and escape would be almost impossible. Nurse Brattle hadn't yet moved, however, and Celia waited, hoping the woman would disappear up the steps as well.

"Rats, indeed." Nurse Brattle said quietly in the doorway to the storeroom. "As if there weren't traps in every corner." She let out a ragged breath that Celia was certain contained a sob, and slowly walked away. Celia listened for her steps to echo up the stairs as well, and then when all was silent, she turned slowly, and reached behind her as the stone dropped. She grabbed it before it hit the floor and then felt along the wall for the place it had fallen from. It was very near the floor, just a few inches, but if it had fallen down in the darkness it would have been enough to break the silence and alert the doctor and nurse. She breathed out in relief. The spot it had fallen from revealed a hole beneath her hand, which gave her an idea. Quickly, she reached into her skirt's pocket and drew out the little book, and the letters and stashed them within. She started to stand up, but the small amount of light caught the emerald on her hand. Her false ring. The emerald the terrible green of Simon's eyes. It was the loveliest gift she'd ever been given, and the ugliest thing she'd ever been made to wear. It was a ring made of a lie, made of death and treachery and torture. She pulled it off and stuffed it into the hole with the papers, and then fit the rock snugly back in place.

She dusted her skirt off, and felt immediately, lighter. As though she had already cast her burdens away. She picked up her case and stepped to the doorway, and then listened. Silence, again.

Celia walked up the steps and carefully, so carefully, she opened the door and stole away onto the grounds of the asylum. It was too light out. She couldn't hope to search for Owen yet. He was back in his snug cottage, completely oblivious to what had happened to her. To the fate Simon had tried to assign to her. Perhaps it would be better if she left him out of her plans, after all. As much as she loved him, as much as she couldn't imagine her life without him—could she really condemn him to a life on the run? Could she expect him to do that for her? Would she even want to ask that from him? If this day had taught her anything, it was that she would never be safe. Never truly. Not from Simon. She would have to make a decision. She squared her shoulders and headed away from the town and toward the trees that led to the bay.

But she would have to wait for nightfall before she could emerge at the lake's edge. She quietly, quietly, silently, silently, crept into the edge of the forest, and disappeared into the trees, a sober despair and longing lodged in her throat.

Lily of the Valley:
Return of Happiness
2011

Folded Corners wasn't open on Mondays. It was an odd kind of weekend to have, being off from work on a day that everyone else was heading back to the grind. Eve's boss, the owner of the bookshop, was inordinately flexible about closing the shop on other days as well. The majority of their business was conducted online, and Eve could track orders and inquiries from her computer at home just as easily as she could in the shop. That said, excepting the trip she had taken with her parents to Charlevoix the year before and the time she had flu, she hadn't taken off a day besides Monday the entire time she'd worked at Folded Corners.

Until now.

Today was Tuesday, and she had spent the entire weekend feeling mostly sorry for herself, and then being angry with herself for being so emotional. Her mother had given her a speech about feminism, which she agreed with wholeheartedly, but didn't feel helped her in this situation. Her father awkwardly tried to console her, but she pushed them both away, kindly. They'd already worried enough about her, she didn't want to be a source of anxiety to them any longer, especially regarding a problem with a man that was probably half her fault.

For some reason she couldn't shake her sorrow. She didn't even exactly understand where it was coming from. Maybe it was the giving up on Celia. She felt she had been tracking down a missing person, as if she was going to save Celia, somehow, and then she'd just walked away from the search. Dropped the flashlight, left the trail and left Celia alone, lost in the woods somewhere, wondering if Eve was still coming for her.

Which was ridiculous. Celia was long dead. And didn't care if Eve found out her story or not.

But it was still important to Eve. Yet, she had given up. And she didn't like giving up. She didn't like the feeling of leaving things…unresolved. Her divorce, her abandonment of herself, her addiction, her therapy, her slow redemption and now… the missing Celia Thorne.

She had worked Saturday and Sunday, slogging through late summer tourists who weren't interested in purchasing, and then had gratefully taken Monday off to recharge. But then Tuesday rolled around, much too quickly, and she wasn't quite ready to go back.

So she hadn't. Eve had emailed the owner of Folded Corners that she was ill, which was at least true mentally, and then slept in. Her parents pretended they weren't surprised and her father had brought her tea at 9am, her mother had carried eggs to her room at 10am, and they both peaked in at 11 to ask if she needed anything.

If nothing else, it was embarrassing. Not the relaxing day at home she'd envisioned to finally banish grief she didn't really deserve to feel. She barely knew Eric. But it hadn't felt that way. It had felt...electric. And...nice. Nice was such a weak word. But there was something true about it. Being with him was nice. Working alongside him was nice. Talking with him, laughing with him, holding his hand, all nice.

And now she'd ruined it. Or he had. Or they both had. Who knew? She had thought when she left rehab that she was done with drugs. But that was what addiction was. You were never really done with it. It was never really done with you. Looking behind her shoulder, checking in on herself for the rest of her life. And that was fine. She'd made peace with that, and herself. But she'd never considered, until recently, what it would be like to put that on someone else's shoulders.

She had gone for a run, showered, read five chapters of a new novel, and then sighed. Her Dad had headed into work and her mom was in the garden. Eve was bored. Bored of her own mood and her self pity. Enough. She leashed the dogs and took them out to the woods across the street from her parent's house. The same woods that held the asylum, and Building 50 and work. She laughed at herself as the dogs plunged ahead, practically dashing to sniff every tree in the forest. Even when she took the day off work she couldn't help but hover around it. Maybe she missed the books. They were easy to miss. Every one of them a trip somewhere new, a different life, a different opportunity, a different set of eyes to see the world through. That was what books were, a ticket to anywhere and anyone.

But no. Eve had spent enough time escaping into the lives of other characters. She needed these trees and these woods and to see life through her own two eyes today. She walked for hours. It was easy to do in the woods in Traverse City. She avoided the trails that tourists preferred and instead scaled up and down the hills and ran with the dogs until all of them were out of breath. She headed back as the day folded into twilight.

Eve would go back into work tomorrow, set her smile and stop all this nonsense. She inhaled that late summer air, just a hint of lake water contained within it, and looked both ways before crossing the street to head back home.

Except...there was a strange car in the driveway. The dogs had regained their energy, impossibly, and barked happily as they approached the front door. She opened the door to hear the voices of her father and Eric talking at the dinner table.

"Hey, Evie! You've got a visitor."

Her dad's voice was overly happy and his face was flushed. She couldn't tell if it was because he'd had a beer or because he was a little embarrassed at being caught at the table with what he'd obviously figured out was her beau.

"Well, I'll...uh, leave you two to it. Your mom and I are going to...watch a movie down the basement."

And just like that, her parents skedaddled, taking the suddenly sleepy dogs with them.

They were quiet for a moment, both of them. And then suddenly, they were both talking.

"I'm..."

"Why..."

"Did you..."

"Listen..."

They both closed their mouths. Eve bit her lip and Eric inhaled, and then sighed. He put up a hand, and then spoke.

"Listen, please. I'm really, really sorry. I have to tell you that, first and foremost. I've spent the past week and change trying to figure out what in the world provoked my reaction, and then planning to come and apologize, and then losing my nerve because I felt like such an ass. But, I apologize. I wasn't...laughing at you. Or at your past."

"What were you laughing at then?" Eve asked quietly before sitting down carefully at the table.

He inhaled, and touched a finger to his mouth. "I guess because it seemed so…silly. Not that you had the problem, that's not what I mean. I mean… well, it seemed so ridiculous that you thought it was something to be ashamed of. I mean, we all have a past. We all make…mistakes." She started to interrupt, but he held a hand up again. "No, you don't know all my deep, darks, Eve. But, I'd like you to. At some point, you know. I'd like if we both… knew about each other. I'm sorry I laughed, honestly, but it had nothing to do with you."

"I believe you," she said. And she did. "I'm sorry for running away that night. I was overwhelmed. But I've regretted it since, and…wanted to talk to you too. Your aunt came to see me, you know."

He laughed. "I know, I know. Imagine what she has been like with me this past week."
Eve shook her head and laughed too.

They were both quiet again, but it was that nice quiet. That comfortable, pleasant quiet that filled her up. She'd put the kettle on for tea, and they talked about the novel she was reading and the paths she'd taken in the woods that day, and the large family that had visited the library that day, ripping books off the shelves. Normal conversation. Pleasant. Nice. Warm.

And then he gasped, and slapped his hand to his forehead. "Oh my God! I completely forgot! I was so happy that you forgave me… and I had been talking to your Dad…but Eve!"

"What is it?!" she practically yelled. His excitement had infected her immediately.

He pulled some printed pages out from his pocket, and spread them flat on the table, smoothing out the creases made by being kept folded in his pocket.

"What is it?!" she asked again, leaning over toward him, practically touching, close enough to kiss him.

"After our…tiff, I was obsessed with finding out what happened to Celia. I had to know, you see. I can't explain it… it was like, like…if I found Celia then I could earn your forgiveness. It was a weird goal I set for myself. And, well, I found something."

"What is it!" She asked again, with no patience whatsoever.She grabbed his shirtsleeve and shook it

He grinned. "Ok, ok, I'm telling you. I found someone else who left, a week after our Celia disappeared."

"Who?" Eve's voice was breathless.

"The head gardener at the Northern Michigan Asylum. Man by the name of Owen Flynn, originally from the Traverse City area, had worked with Munson downstate, apparently. He left the asylum though. Young guy. Strange, I thought, that a young local guy would leave a plum head gardening job at the asylum."

"And?" she demanded, face close to his.

"And, it was because he was offered another plum job at the newly opened Grand Hotel on Mackinac Island. A very swanky new position, one he probably couldn't turn down."

She sighed. "Well, I'm glad for him, but I guess he hasn't anything to do with Celia, then." She felt her face fall, and she felt silly, but she almost could have cried.

He grinned even wider. "Oh, but it had everything to do with Celia. He was in love with her, I think."

"Why's that?" Eve asked, a little hope creeping back into her voice, though she couldn't think why she dared.

"Because…" He began, and then uncovered the printed article he'd brought.

It was from a newspaper, and it was old. The picture was poor quality and fuzzy, but if you looked close you could just make out a man and a woman in turn of the century dress, staring into the camera, the Grand Hotel behind them.

"Because he married her," Eric replied and began reading from the article.

"…Mr. Flynn, and his wife, Mrs. Celia Flynn are local favorites on the island. Mr. Owen Flynn for his undeniable prowess as our resident green thumb and his wife for her talents in teaching the young ladies of the island the piano. The couple has settled into the life on the island since their arrival five years ago, and say they cannot imagine living anywhere else on Earth."

Eve smiled. A real smile, and blinked at some tears in her eyes. "You found her. And she did have a happily ever after."

"Looks like it," Eric said. "And *WE* found her. Both of us. I would never have even known to look for her if it weren't for you. We found her."

He leaned in then, still grinning, and kissed her lightly. Just a butterfly wing kiss on her lips, and she drew her breath in.

"It all ended up okay."

"Things generally do. If you see it through until the end."

She leaned in this time, and kissed him. A real kiss. Long and slow and warm.

And nice.

Epilogue

Forget-Me-Not: True Love

1893

She would never tire of life on the island. Some felt that it was isolated or lonely, or even a kind of cage. She'd been in a cage before. Locked up. This was just the opposite to Celia. The winters were cold, it was true. But the balsam and pine mixed with the scents of the water of the straits surrounding them all year long and the summers were heaven on Earth. She didn't think there could be forests more lovely than the woods around the asylum. But, the woods here were magical, and the town was a fairytale dream.

Dreamiest of all was that this was her life. Her new life. Owen had found her that night when she had escaped the asylum. It was deep, dark night, and she was standing in the moonlight on the shore of the bay. She wasn't certain what she would do, or where she would go, but she hadn't intended to drag Owen along with her into the muck she'd made of her life. But he'd found her anyway. She didn't know how, and neither did he. But he said he had felt restless in bed, and so he had taken a walk and the walk had pulled him to her. Her ghost had winked in and out then in the moonlight. And Celia knew. It was the spirit's doing. Bless you, Celia Green, Celia had thought then, and never stopped thinking, actually. She'd never seen her ghost again.

He'd accepted the position on Mackinac and they moved the next week. They'd settled into the northern island, and she could hardly remember any other life. Only when memories crept in late at night, ghosts of Simon's hands, ghosts of her parents and of those fearful moments of the life... before. When those memories skulked in, unwanted, she'd pull her husband closer to her chest and cling to him until the memories left her. They came less and less now.

But the ghosts. They were with her always on the island. But they were like the spirits of old. Just passing by her, tipping their hats, or barely noticing her at all, going about their ghostly paths, only visible to her eyes. There was comfort in that. And comfort in the life that they had built on the island. And a comfort in their sleeping daughter in her cradle and the flowers her husband planted at the hotel.

And the Grand Hotel itself was a kind of comfort. The guests, the elegance of those visiting the island. The fashions they wore, the family they brought, the leisure they enjoyed. All of them, coming to her island home for a break from the world outside.

How lucky was she? To live in a place that other people waited all year to visit. To have a life filled with the music she taught the village girls to play on the piano and her husband's songs to sing her to sleep. To be loved by a man she adored. To have a child with her golden hair and his grey-blue eyes.

To be free, finally.

Celia was quite mad with happiness. Why shouldn't she be?

Historical Note

Historical Fiction is just that, Historical *and* Fictional. There are many aspects of this story that were lifted directly from old railroad maps, or archival information about the old asylum, articles on Dr. Munson, and from the interesting, (if very long-winded) tour of the Traverse City State Hospital that I attended on a visit back home. I gathered a lot from this tour and took copious notes: aspects of what the asylum looked like, felt like, was filled with, and stories of individuals who spent their time, or their life, there.

For the modern day layout of the city, very little has been changed. The library is precisely where I placed it in the novel, (though the interior and the archives in the basement are straight from my imagination). The basement and other renovated floors and outbuildings of the asylum, now called, The Village at Grand Traverse Commons, or "Building 50", appears as I have described it, complete with bookstores and knick-knack shops and bakeries and bistros. Alas, the wine bar is no longer there, but it was at the time of this story. And there is indeed a fabulous bookstore on Front St, and lovely restaurants for a romantic evening.

The flowers, plants and their various meaning were taken from the same book Celia references, *The Language of Flowers*. Floriography was a very popular cryptological means of communication during the 19th and early 20th century. Sometimes it is simpler to allow a posey to say what we cannot, eh?

Finally, with the exception of the great Dr. James Decker Munson himself, the entirety of the characters in the novel are fiction. That is to say, you won't find them in an archive or a record book, but they are very real, indeed, to me.

The Author

ALEXANDRIA NOLAN was born and raised in Michigan's second motor city, Flint. She attended the University of Michigan, earning a Bachelor of Arts in English. In 2008, Alexandria moved to Texas to teach History, English and Writing. In the spring of 2013, she left teaching to write.

In addition to several other novels set in Michigan, Alexandria has written two collections of short stories and maintains a lifestyle blog, AlexandriaNolan.com. She also is a frequent travel contributor to various online and print publications. She loves to read, travel and read about traveling.

She reluctantly resides in Houston, Texas. But the southern locale is made mildly bearable by her incredibly dapper husband, small dog and two very lovely lady cats.

For full list of published works visit:
amazon.com/author/alexandrianolan

Acknowledgments

Traverse City is a special place. In fact, calling it such is so paltry a description for it that I find myself almost immediately apologizing. It is the kind of fresh northern place that is not only uncommonly beautiful, but seems to be filled with wonderful secrets. Secrets beneath the waves and in the branches of the pine forests and beneath the concrete of the city streets. Lives lived within the city long ago, and those being lived now, in the present moment. I must acknowledge the inspiration I get from the asylum itself and from the forests surrounding it. One almost could believe they hear audible whispers from the past. But I must also acknowledge the present sources of inspiration. Building 50 itself in its most recent incarnation, my Dad, for tracking down stories and books for me on the Traverse region. The community at large that always makes me feel so welcome. And most especially, the folks at Horizon books, who inspire me to continue writing about Michigan and Traverse City and all of the magic that exists in the Great Lakes State. Jill, thank you for your comments and criticisms. You make me better.

A firm and heartfelt *thank you.*

And of course, I must acknowledge my first set of eyes, my brilliant mother. I love you more than kittens and frosting.

Other Works:

Shears of Fate: A Novella of Memory and Madness
(2013)

Wide, Wild, Everywhere: Short Stories for Wanderers
(2014)

Starlight Symphonies of Oak & Glass
(Starlight Symphonies No. 1)
(2014)

The Library of Panopticon
(2015)

Moonlight Melodies of Copper & Pine
(Starlight Symphonies No.2)
(2015)

The Word Collector
(2016)

**Scattered the Night:
A transcript from a gathering of the Tale Teller's Guild**
(2017)

Forget Me Not Blue
(2018)

Coming Later 2018:
Sunlight Serenades of Wind & Iron
(Starlight Symphonies No. 3)